RETROTOPIA

Novels by John Michael Greer

The Weird of Hali:

I – Innsmouth

II – Kingsport

III – Chorazin

IV – Dreamlands

V – Providence

VI – Red Hook

VII – Arkham

Others:

The Fires of Shalsha

Star's Reach

Twilight's Last Gleaming

Retrotopia

The Shoggoth Concerto

The Nyogtha Variations

A Voyage to Hyperborea

The Seal of Yueh Lao

Journey Star

The Witch of Criswell

The Book of Haatan

The Hall of Homeless Gods

RETROTOPIA

A Novel by
John Michael Greer

Published in 2024 by
Sphinx Books
London

British Library Cataloguing in Publication Data

A C.I.P. for this book is available from the British Library

ISBN-13: 978-1-91595-215-8

Typeset by Medlar Publishing Solutions Pvt Ltd, India

www.aeonbooks.co.uk/sphinx

CHAPTER 1

I got to the Pittsburgh station early. It was a shabby remnant
of what must once have been one of those grand old stations you see on history vids, nothing but a bleak little
waiting room below and a stair rising alongside a long-defunct
escalator to the platforms up top. The waiting room had fresh
paint on the walls and the vending machines were the sort of
thing you'd find anywhere. Other than that, the whole place
looked as though it had been locked up around the time the
Second Civil War broke out and the last Amtrak trains stopped
running, and sat there unused for forty years until the border
opened up again.

The seats were fiberglass, and must have been something like
three quarters of a century old. I found one that didn't look too
likely to break when I sat on it, settled down, got out my veepad
and checked the schedule for the umpteenth time. The train I
would be riding was listed as on time, arrival 5:10 am Pittsburgh
station, departure 5:35 am, scheduled arrival in Toledo Central
Station 11:12 am. I tapped the veepad again, checked the news.
The election was still all over the place—President Barfield's
concession speech, not to mention a flurry of op-ed pieces from
various talking heads affiliated with the Dem-Reps about how
bad Ellen Montrose would be for the country. I snorted, paged
on. Other stories competed for attention: updates on the wars

1

in California and the Balkans, recaps on the *Progresso IV* satellite disaster, bad news from the commodity markets about the ongoing copper shortage, and worse news from Antarctica, where yet another big ice sheet had just popped loose and was drifting north toward the shipping lanes.

While the news scrolled past, other passengers filed into the waiting room a few at a time. I could just make them out past the image field the veepad projected into my visual cortex. Two men and a woman in ordinary bioplastic businesswear came in and sat together, talking earnestly about some investment or other. An elderly couple whose clothes made them look like they came straight out of a history vid sat down close to the stair and sat quietly. A little later, a family of four in clothing that looked even more old-fashioned—Mom had a bonnet on her head, and I swear I'm not making that up—came in with carpetbag luggage, and plopped down not far from me. I wasn't too happy about that, kids being what they are these days, but these two sat down and, after a little bit of squirming, got out a book each and started reading quietly. I wondered if they'd been drugged.

A little later, another family of four came in, wearing the kind of cheap shabby clothes that might as well have the words "urban poor" stamped all over them, and hauling big plastic bags that looked as though everything they owned was stuffed inside. They looked tense, scared, excited. They sat by themselves in a corner, the parents talking to each other in low voices, the kids watching everything with wide eyes and saying nothing. I wondered about them, shrugged mentally, went back to the news.

I'd finished the news and was starting through the day's textmail, when the loudspeaker on the wall cleared its electronic throat with a hiss of static and said, "Train Twenty-One, service to Toledo via Steubenville, Canton and Sandusky, arriving at Platform One. Please have your tickets and passports ready. Train Twenty-One to Toledo, Platform One."

2

I tapped the veepad to sleep, stuffed it in my pocket, got out of my seat with the others, climbed the stairs to the platform. The sky was just turning gray with the first hint of morning, and a sharp wind hissed through the roof supports; the whistle of the train sounded long and lonely in the middle distance. I turned to look. I'd never been on a train before, and most of what I knew about them came from history vids and the research I'd done for this trip. Based on what I'd heard about my destination, I wondered if the locomotive would be a rattletrap antique with a big smokestack pumping coal smoke into the air.

What came around the bend into view wasn't much like my momentary fantasy, though. It was the sort of locomotive you'd have found on any American railroad around 1950, a big diesel-electric machine with a blunt nose and a single big headlight shining down on the track. It whistled again, and then the roar of the engines rose to drown out everything else. The locomotive roared past the platform, and the only thing that surprised me was the smell of french fries that came rushing past with it. Behind it was a long string of boxcars, and behind those, a baggage car and three passenger cars.

The train slowed to a walking pace and then stopped as the passenger cars came up to the platform. A conductor in a blue uniform and hat swung down from the last car. "Tickets and passports, please," he said, and I got out my veepad, woke it, activated the flat screen and got both documents on it.

"Physical passport, please," the conductor said when he got to me.

"Sorry." I fumbled in my pocket, handed it to him. He checked it, smiled, said, "Thank you, Mr. Carr. You probably know this already, but you'll need a paper ticket for the return trip."

"I've got it, thanks."

"Great." He moved on to the family with the plastic bag luggage. The mother said something in a low voice, handed over tickets and something that didn't look like a passport.

3

"That's fine," said the conductor. "You'll need to have your immigration papers out when we get to the border."

The woman murmured something else, and the conductor went onto the elderly couple, leaving me to wonder about what I'd just heard. Immigration? That implied, first, that these people actually wanted to live in the Lakeland Republic, and second, that they were being allowed in. Neither of those seemed likely to me. I made a note on my veepad to ask about immigration once I got to Toledo, and to compare what they told me to what I could find out once I got back to Philadelphia.

The conductor finished taking tickets and checking passports, and called out, "All aboard!"

I went with the others to the first of the three passenger cars, climbed the stair, turned left. The interior was about what I'd expected, row after row of double seats facing forward, but everything looked clean and bright and there was a lot more leg room than you'll ever see on an airplane, even in first class seating. I went about halfway up, slung my suitcase in the overhead rack and settled in the window seat. We sat for a while, and then the car jolted once and began to roll forward.

We went through the western end of Pittsburgh first of all, past the big dark windowless skyscrapers of the Golden Triangle, and then across the river and into the western suburbs. Those were shantytowns built out of the scraps of old housing developments and strip malls, the sort of thing you find around most cities these days when you don't find worse, mixed in with old rundown housing developments that probably hadn't seen a bucket of paint or a new roof since the United States came apart. Then the suburbs ended, and things got uglier.

The country west of Pittsburgh got hammered during the Second Civil War, I knew, and the closing of the border after Partition hadn't helped. I'd wondered, while planning the trip, how much it had recovered in the three years since the Treaty of Richmond. Looking out of the window as the sky turned gray behind us, I got my answer: not much. There were some

4

corporate farms that showed signs of life, but the small towns the train rolled through were bombed-out shells, and there were uncomfortable stretches where every house and barn I could see was a tumbledown ruin and young trees were rising in what had to have been fields and pastures a few decades back. After a while it was too depressing to keep looking out the window, and I pulled out my veepad again and spent a good long while answering textmails and noting down some questions I'd want to ask in Toledo.

I'd gotten caught up on mail when the door at the back end of the car slid open. "Ladies and gentlemen," the conductor said, "we'll be arriving at the Lakeland border in about five minutes. You'll need to have your passports ready, and immigrants should have their papers out as well. Thank you."

We rolled on through a dense stand of trees, and then into open ground. Up ahead, a pair of roads cut straight north and south across country. Until three years ago, there'd been a tall razor-wire fence between them, soldiers patrolling our side, the other side pretty much a complete mystery. The fence was ordinary chainlink now, and there were two buildings for border guards, one on each side of the line. The one on the eastern side was a modern concrete-and-steel item that looked like a skyscraper had stopped there, squatted, and laid an egg. As we got closer to it, I could see the border guards in digital-fleck camo, helmets, and flak vests, standing around with assault rifles.

Then we passed over into the Lakeland Republic, and I got a good look at the building on the other side. It was a pleasant-looking brick structure that could have been a Carnegie-era public library or the old city hall of some midsized town, and the people who came out of the big arched doorways to meet the train as it slowed to a halt didn't look like soldiers at all.

The door slid open again, and I turned around. One of the border guards, a middle-aged woman with coffee-colored skin, came into the car. She was wearing a white uniform blouse and blue pants, and the only heat she was carrying was a revolver tucked unobtrusively in a holster at her hip. She had a clipboard with her, and went up the aisle, checking everybody's passports against a list.

I handed her mine when she reached me. "Mr. Carr," she said with a broad smile. "We heard you'd be coming through this morning. Welcome to the Lakeland Republic."

"Thank you," I said. She handed me back the passport, and went on to the family with the plastic bag luggage. They handed her a sheaf of papers, and she went through them quickly, signed something halfway through, and then handed them back. "Okay, you're good," she said. "Welcome to the Lakeland Republic."

"We're in?" the mother of the family asked, as though she didn't believe it.

"You're in," the border guard told her. "Legal as legal can be."

"Oh my God. Thank you." She burst into tears, and her husband hugged her and patted her on the back. The border guard gave him a grin and went on to the family in the old-fashioned clothing.

I thought about that while the border guard finished checking passports and left the car. Outside, two more guards with a dog finished going along the train, and gave a thumbs up to the conductor. A minute later, the train started rolling again. That's it? I wondered. No metal detectors, no x-rays, nothing? Either they were very naive or very confident.

We passed the border zone and a screen of trees beyond it, and suddenly the train was rolling through a landscape that couldn't have been more different from the one on the other side of the line. It was full of farms, but they weren't the big corporate acreages I was used to. I counted houses and barns as we passed, and guesstimated the farms were one to two hundred acres each; all of them were in mixed crops, not efficient monocropping. The harvest was mostly in, but I'd grown up in

6

farm country and knew what a field looked like after it was put into corn, wheat, cabbages, turnips, industrial hemp, or what have you. Every farm seemed to have all of those and more, not to mention cattle in the pasture, pigs in a pen, a garden and an orchard, and a farmhouse somewhere in the middle of it all with lights on in the windows and a windmill spinning itself into a blur up above.

I shook my head, baffled. It was a hopelessly inefficient way to run agribusiness, I knew that from my time in business school, and yet the briefing papers I'd read while getting ready for this trip said that the Lakeland Republic exported plenty of agricultural products and imported almost none. I wondered whether the train would pass some real farms further in.

We passed more of the little mixed farms, and a couple of little towns that were about as far from being bombed-out shells as you care to imagine. There were homes with lights on and businesses that were pretty obviously getting ready to open for the day. All of the towns had little brick train stations, though we didn't stop at any of those—I wondered if they had light rail or something. Watching the farms and towns move past, I thought about the contrast with the landscape on the other side of the border, and winced, then stopped and reminded myself that the farms and towns had to be subsidized. Small towns weren't any more economically viable than small farms, after all. Was all this some kind of Potemkin village setup, for the purpose of impressing visitors?

The door at the back of the car slid open, and the conductor came in. "Next stop, Steubenville," he said. "Folks, we've got a bunch of people coming on in Steubenville, so please don't take up any more seats than you have to."

Steubenville had been part of the state of Ohio before Partition, I remembered. The name of the town stirred something else in my memory, though. I couldn't quite get the recollection to surface, and decided to look it up. I pulled out my vee-pad, tapped it, and got a dark field and the words: *no signal*.

7

I tapped it again, got the same thing, opened the connectivity window and found out that the thing wasn't kidding. There was no metanet signal anywhere within range. I stared at it, wondered how I was going to check the news or keep up with textmail, and then wondered: how am I going to buy anything, or pay my hotel bill?

The dark field didn't have any answers. I decided I'd have to sort that out when I got to Toledo; I'd been invited, after all. Maybe they had connectivity in the big cities, or something. The story was that there wasn't metanet anywhere in the Lakeland Republic, but I had my doubts about that—how can you manage anything this side of a bunch of mud huts without net connections? No doubt, I decided, they had some kind of secure net or something. We'd talked about doing something of the same kind back in Philadelphia more than once, just for government use, so the next round of netwars didn't trash our infrastructure the way the infrastructure of the old US got trashed by the Chinese in '21.

Still, the dark field and those two words upset me more than I wanted to admit. It had been more years than I wanted to think about since I'd been more than a click away from the metanet, and being cut off from it left me feeling adrift.

The sun cleared low clouds behind us, and the train rolled into what I guessed was East Steubenville. I'd expected the kind of suburbs I'd seen on the way out of Pittsburgh, dreary rundown housing interspersed with the shantytowns of the poor. What I saw instead left me shaken. The train passed tree-lined streets full of houses that had bright paint on the walls and shingles on the roofs, little local business districts with shops and restaurants open for business, a school that didn't look like a medium-security prison, and a baseball field with bleachers on the two sides and a sign proclaiming it as the home field of the East Steubenville Badgers.

The thing that puzzled me most was that there were no cars visible, just tracks down some of the streets and once, improbably, an old-fashioned streetcar that paced the train for a while and then veered off in a different direction. Most of the houses seemed to have gardens out back, and the train passed one big empty lot that was divided into garden plots and had signs around it saying "community garden." I wondered if that meant food was scarce here.

A rattle and a bump, and the train was crossing the Ohio River on a big new railroad bridge. Ahead was Steubenville proper. That's when I remembered the thing that tried to surface earlier: there was a battle at Steubenville, a big one, toward the end of the Second Civil War. I remembered details from headlines I'd seen when I was a kid, and a history vid I'd watched a couple of years ago; a Federal army held the Ohio crossings against Alliance forces for most of two months before Anderson's army punched straight through the West Virginia front and made the whole thing moot. I remembered photos of what Steubenville looked like after the fighting: a blackened landcape of ruins where every wall high enough to hide a soldier behind it had gotten hit by its own personal artillery shell.

That wasn't what I saw spreading out ahead as the train crossed the Ohio, though. The Steubenville I saw was a pleasant-looking city with a downtown full of three- and four-story buildings, surrounded by neighborhoods of houses, some row houses and some detached. There were streetcars on the west side of the river, too—I spotted two of them as we got close to the shore—and also a few cars, though not many of the latter. The trees that lined the streets were small enough that you could tell they'd been planted after the fighting was over. Other than that, Steubenville looked like a comfortable, established community.

I stared out the window as the train rolled off the bridge and into Steubenville, trying to make sense of what I was seeing. Back on the other side of the border, and everywhere else I'd been in what used to be the United States, you still saw wreckage from the war years all over the place. Between the

9

debt crisis and the state of the world economy, the money that would have been needed to rebuild or even demolish the ruins was just too hard to come by. Things should have been much worse here, since the Lakeland Republic had been shut out of world credit markets for thirty years after the default of '32—but they weren't worse. They looked considerably better. I reached for my veepad, remembered that I couldn't get a signal, and frowned. If they couldn't even afford the infrastructure for the metanet, how could they afford to rebuild their housing stock?

The cheerful brick buildings of Steubenville's downtown didn't offer me any answers. I sat back, frowning, as the train rattled through a switch and rolled into the Steubenville station. "Steubenville," the conductor called out from the door behind me, and the train began to slow.

From the window beside me, the Steubenville station looked like a scene out of an old Bogart vid. The platform closest to the train I was riding was full of people in outdated clothes. Most of them wore long raincoats that didn't look a bit like bioplastic, and all of the men and most of the women had hats on. Up above was a roof of glass and ironwork that reminded me irresistibly of the Victorian era, and let daylight down onto everything. The oddest thing about it all, though, is that I didn't see security troops anywhere. On the other side of the border, anywhere you saw this many people together there'd be at least a squad in digital camo and flak jackets, pointing assault guns ostentatiously at the sidewalk. I remembered the guards at the border, with their clipboards, holstered revolvers, and old-fashioned uniforms, and wondered how on earth the Lakeland Republic got away with that kind of carelessness.

The train finally rolled to a stop, and doors opened. The conductor had warned us that plenty of people would be coming aboard, and he wasn't kidding: it took better than five minutes for everyone to file onto the car where I was sitting, and by the time they'd finished coming aboard, nearly every seat was taken. The aisle seat next to me wasn't one of the empty ones; a family with three children settled in behind me, one child next to the mother, the second next to the father, and then Mom came up to me and asked if I minded having the oldest child sit next to me. I gestured and said, "Sure," and a boy of ten plopped into the seat. "Now you mind your manners," the woman told him, and he rolled his eyes, sighed loudly, and said, "Yeah, Mom."

That wasn't too promising, but he had a book with him, and as soon as he was settled in his seat, he opened it and didn't make another sound. I was curious enough to give the book a sidelong glance; it was called *Treasure Island*, and it was by somebody I'd never heard of named Robert Louis Stevenson. I made a mental note to look up the name and see if he was somebody new I should check out.

He wasn't the only kid in the car who was doing something quiet, either. Up three rows there was a girl in a blue checked dress and a bonnet who was reading something, too, and behind me, the two kids in the immigrant family were watching everything and not saying a word, though they didn't look quite as scared as when they boarded.

A couple of solid jolts shook the car. A moment later, I heard the voice of the conductor outside calling out, "Last call for Train Twenty-One to Toledo via Canton and Sandusky. All aboard!" Doors clattered, the locomotive up ahead sounded its whistle, and with another jolt the train started on its way again.

The station slid away, and I got a street-level view of half a dozen blocks of downtown Steubenville. The sense of having landed on the set of an old Bogart vid was just as strong. To judge by the couple of clocks the train passed—my veepad was still giving me a dark field and the words *no signal*—it was right around time for the morning commute, but there wasn't a car to be seen anywhere; the sidewalks bustled with people, and a couple of streetcars rolled past with bells clanging and standing room only on board. The train picked up speed and left the downtown behind, but further out was more of the same: streets full of comfortable-looking houses and apartment buildings, with people walking to work or waiting at streetcar stops.

Further on the houses spread out, and big gardens sprouted all over the place, with the last fall crops visible in patches separated by stubble and brown earth. A little further, and Steubenville blended smoothly into the same sort of farm country I'd seen since shortly after the train crossed into the Lakeland Republic. The farmhouses and barns looked well-tended, windmills spun and solar water heaters on the roofs soaked up what sunlight came through the broken clouds, and the roads I saw were unpaved but had fresh gravel on them.

A little further, and the train passed a work gang out in one of the fields. That wasn't surprising—back on the other side of the border, you saw prison work gangs doing labor on corporate farms all the time—but these didn't have the slouch and the least-possible-effort sort of movement you see in convicts. They were working their way across a field, digging up turnips as energetically as if they wanted to be there, and others came behind them just as methodically and carried the turnips away in bushel baskets. It was when I noticed where they were taking the turnips that my mouth dropped open.

Just past the field was a wagon with two draft horses hitched up to it. I wondered for a moment if this was an Amish farm—we've got Amish in our country, quite a few of them in what used to be the state of Pennsylvania before Partition, and they're among the few people who've done well in the postwar era—but the wagon had been painted in colors that, though they'd faded, had obviously once been bright. The people in the work gang weren't dressed in any sort of Amish kit I'd ever seen, either. I shook my head as the work gang and the wagon slipped out of sight behind the train, wondering what kind of weird place I was visiting. This was the twenty-first century, after all, not the nineteenth!

And yet it was like that all the way to Canton. To be more precise, it was some variation on the same theme of outdated technology and inefficient land use. All the farms were small, one to two hundred acres at most, and all of it was divided up into the sort of mixed farming that modern agriculture discarded most of a century ago. I didn't see any trace of modern agricultural tech: no harvesting robots, no nitrogen injection systems, no quadruple-wide megacombines, nothing. What I did see left me baffled, not least because there didn't seem to be any rhyme or reason to it. In one place I'd see trucks driving down paved roads and tractors in the fields, and twenty or thirty miles later it would be draft horses and wagons doing the same jobs.

The train passed through I don't know how many little towns, and those were the same way: in one I'd see paved streets and a few cars and trucks, in the next the streets were paved with brick and streetcars shared space with horsedrawn carriages, and then there were a few that had brick streets and no streetcars at all. The thing that puzzled me most, though, was that all of the towns, like nearly all the farms, seemed to be thriving. Every scrap of economic theory I'd learned in business school argued that small towns, like small farms, were hopelessly inefficient and couldn't possibly support themselves in a modern economy. I'd guessed earlier in the trip that there must be subsidies involved, but this far into Lakeland Republic territory, that explanation wouldn't wash. I reached for my veepad reflexively to make a note, remembered as I got it out of my pocket that it wouldn't get a signal, and put it away, feeling a rush of annoyance at the metanet's absence.

We got to Canton a little ahead of schedule, or so the conductor announced cheerfully, and stopped in the switching yard east of town to lose some freight cars, gain others, and add three more passenger cars and a dining car to the back end of the train. That went quickly, though it involved a lot of jolts and thumps, and before long we were rolling ahead into the city.

13

Canton was a fairly big town; according to what I'd read while researching this trip, it had plenty of factories until the crazy offshoring fad of the late twentieth century scrapped the United States' manufacturing plant and left the nation at the mercy of rival powers. I'd seen the gutted hulks of old factories outside Pittsburgh and a dozen other cities on our side of the border, and assumed that I'd see the same thing here.

I didn't. What I saw instead, as the train rolled through the outlying districts of Canton, were what looked very much like warehouses and factories open for business. There were no smokestacks to be seen, but the buildings had recent coats of paint on them, boxcars were being pushed down sidings by switching engines, and a mix of trucks and big horsedrawn wagons were lumbering past on the streets. Further in, the train passed the same mix of of office buildings, apartment blocks, and stores I'd seen in Steubenville, and then we slowed and stopped at the Canton station.

That had me remembering Bogart vids again. From my window I could see at least eight platforms to one side of the train I was riding, and through the windows on the other side of the car I was pretty sure I could make out two more. Signs on the platforms noted destinations all over the Lakeland Republic—Morgantown, Bowling Green, Cairo, Madison, Sault Ste. Marie—and the place fairly bustled with passengers heading for this or that train. Some of the passengers from the car I was sitting in got their luggage and headed out into the crowds, and some others came on board, stowed their luggage, and sat down; and the weirdest thing of all was that everyone seemed perfectly comfortable doing without security troops to protect them or modern technology to take care of their needs.

The train finally got under way again, and I got more views of Canton as the track headed northwest through town. About the time the houses started to spread out and the gardens got bigger, the conductor came through the door behind me and said, "Ladies and gentlemen, breakfast service is now open in

14

the dining car, and since so many of the people in this car have been with us since Pittsburgh, you're first. If you'd like to head back four cars, the dining car staff will be happy to serve you."

Just about everyone in the car got up and filed back through the door. I didn't. I'm one of those people who doesn't do breakfast; if I eat anything before lunch I end up with stomach trouble. The kid next to me went with his family, and the mother of the immigrant family took her two kids back to the dining car right after them. The father of the immigrant family, though, didn't join them. After a few minutes he and I were practically alone in the car.

I half turned in my seat, gave him what I hoped would come across as a friendly smile. "Not into breakfast?"

"Too keyed up," he said, smiling in response. "If I ate now I'd get sick to my stomach."

I nodded. "I couldn't help hearing the border guard say that you're immigrating. That sounds pretty drastic. If you don't mind my asking, what made you do that?"

His smile vanished, replaced by a wary look. "The wife has family in Ann Arbor," he said. "They're sponsoring us, and I got a job offer when we visited this summer. It seems like a good move."

"Even though you have to give up modern technology?"

The wary look gave way to something that looked uncomfortably like contempt. "Technology? Like what?"

"Well, veepads and the metanet, to start with."

By this point it was definitely contempt. "Big loss. I'll never be able to afford any of that stuff anyway."

"Why not? You've got as much chance as anyone. Work hard, and—"

His expression said "whatever" more clearly than words, and he turned toward the window and away from me.

"No," I said. "Seriously. I want to understand."

He turned back to face me. "Yeah? Did you hear my wife start crying there at the border, once they checked our papers?"

15

I nodded, and he went on. "You know why she started crying? Because she's been working three different jobs, sixty hours a week plus, to keep a roof over our heads and food on the table—and before you start thinking something stupid, mister, I've been working more hours than her since before we got married. This is the first time she's had anything to look forward to but that kind of schedule or worse for the rest of her life, until one of us gets too sick to work and we get chucked onto the street or into the burbs."

"And you think you'll be that much better off here?"

He looked baffled, then let out a short hard laugh. "You haven't been here before."

"No, I haven't."

"Then open your eyes and take a good look around." He turned back to the window, and I knew better than to try to continue the conversation.

The landscape rolled by. We were in farm country again, the same patchwork landscape of little farms and little towns, with the same weird incongruities between one place and another. I was paying more attention this time, so I noticed some of the other differences: paved roads, gravel roads, and dirt roads; in some places, streetcars and local rail service, and none of these things in others; towns that had streetlights and others that didn't. At one point west of Canton, as the train rattled across a bridge, I looked down and honest to Pete, there were canal boats going both ways on a canal, each one with a mule pulling the towrope as though it was two hundred years ago.

With my veepad useless, I didn't have anything to do but watch the landscape roll by. The people who'd gone to breakfast trickled back a few at a time, and the conversation I'd just had with the immigrant replayed over and over again in my mind. Of course I knew perfectly well that things were pretty hard for the poor back home, and the statistics that got churned out quarter after quarter showing steady economic improvement were strictly public relations maneuvers—there had been a modest upturn after the Treaty of Richmond was signed and the last closed borders between the North American republics opened up, but the consequences of the Second Civil War and the debt crisis that followed it still weighed down hard on everybody.

It's one thing to have some more or less abstract idea that times are tough, though, and something else to hear it in the voice of someone who'd been on the losing end of the economy all his life. I started to reach for my veepad to look up honest stats on the job market back home—those weren't easy to find without connections, but that wasn't a problem for me—and caught the motion just before my hand reached my pocket. What did people do in the Lakeland Republic, I wondered irritably, when they wanted to make a note of something or look up a fact?

I stared out the window, and after a while—the train was most of the way to Sandusky by then—noticed something that made the crazy quilt pattern of old technologies on the landscape a little clearer and a lot more puzzling. The train had slowed a little, and crossed a road at an angle. The road was paved on one side and dirt on the other; I could see tractors in the middle distance off to the left, where the paved road started, and draft horses closer by on the right. Just where the pavement began was a sign that read *Welcome to Huron County*.

That got me thinking back over the landscape the train had crossed since the border, and yes, the breaks between one set of technology and another worked out to something like county-line distances. That made me shake my head. Had the Lakeland Republic somehow divvied up the available technology by county, so that some counties got the equivalent of twentieth century infrastructure and others got stuck with the nineteenth-century equivalent? That sounded like political suicide, unless the Republic was a lot more autocratic than the briefing papers I'd read made it sound. Then, of course, there was the fact that the farmhouses and farm towns in the nineteenth-century counties looked just as prosperous, all things considered, as their equivalents in the twentieth-century counties, and that made no sense at all. The farmers with more technology should have outproduced the others, undercut them in price, and driven them out of business in no time.

Huron County slid past the window. Farmland dotted with little towns gave way to another pleasant-looking midsized town, which I guessed was the county seat, and then to farmland and little towns again. After a while, the conductor stepped through the door behind me and called out, "Next stop, Sandusky." A few minutes later, the train swung around a wide curve to the left, and ran just back of the shores of Lake Erie. Off in the distance, at a steep angle ahead, Sandusky's buildings could be seen rising up above the flat line of the landscape, but that wasn't what caught my gaze and held it.

Out maybe a quarter mile from shore was a big schooner with three masts, and big white sails bellying out ahead of the wind. It wasn't anybody's luxury yacht, that was for sure; from stem to stern, it looked every inch a working boat. From the direction it was headed, I guessed it must have left Sandusky harbor not long before, and was headed east toward the locks around Niagara Falls, or just possibly toward Erie or Buffalo—since the Treaty of Richmond, I knew, we'd been importing agricultural products from the Lakeland Republic, though I'd never bothered to find out how they got to us. I sat there and watched the ship as it swept past, wondering why they hadn't done the obvious thing and entrusted their shipping to modern freighters instead. What kind of strange things had been going on here during the years when the Lakeland Republic was locked away behind closed borders?

CHAPTER 2

The train pulled into the Toledo station something like ten minutes late—we'd had to wait for another train to clear the bridge over Sandusky Harbor, and then rolled along the Lake Erie shoreline for half an hour, past little lakeside towns and open country dotted with shore pines, before finally veering inland toward the Lakeland Republic's capital. All the way along the shore, I watched big two- and three-masted schooners catching a ride from the wind, some obviously heading out from the Toledo lakefront, some just as obviously heading toward it. The sailing ship I'd spotted outside Sandusky was clearly nothing unusual here.

Once the train swung due west toward downtown Toledo, it was more farm country—the twentieth century kind with tractors and pickups rather than the nineteenth century kind with draft horses and wagons. Then the same sequence I'd watched around other Lakeland cities followed: houses became more frequent, fields gave way to truck gardens, and not too long after that the train was rolling past residential neighborhoods dotted with schools, parks, and little clusters of shops, striped at intervals with the omnipresent streetcar tracks and, here and there, crossed by the streetcars themselves. The houses gave way eventually to the warehouses and factories of an industrial district, and then to the dark waters of the Maumee River, swirling and rushing past the feet of half a dozen bridges.

"Toledo," the conductor called out from behind me. "Our last stop, ladies and gentlemen. Please make sure you have all your luggage and belongings before you leave, and thank you for riding with us today."

As the car I was in reached the far shore, I got a brief glimpse of tree-lined streetscapes, and then brick walls blotted out the view. Some of the other passengers got their luggage down from the overhead racks. Me, I had other things on my mind; it had finally occurred to me that unless I could get a veepad signal, I had no way to call the people who were supposed to meet me and make sure we didn't miss each other, and I'd checked my veepad one last time and gotten the same dark field as before. I shrugged mentally, decided to wait and see what happened.

The train slowed to a crawl as we got into the station. The immigrant family across from me had apparently spotted somebody waiting for them on the platform, and were waving at the window. They already had their plastic-bag luggage in hand, and the moment the train stopped they hefted the bags and headed for the exit. I got my suitcase down from the rack; the boy who'd been sitting next to me went back to help his parents with their luggage, and I stepped into the aisle and followed the people in front of me up to the front of the car and out onto the platform.

A brightly painted sign said THIS WAY TO THE STATION. I followed that and the flow of people. Partway along I passed the immigrant family standing there with half a dozen other people in what looked like Victorian clothing out of a history vid—the wife's family from Ann Arbor, I guessed—all talking a mile a minute. The wife was teary-eyed and beaming, and the two kids looked for the first time since I'd seen them as though they might get around to smiling one of these days. I thought about the conversation I'd had with the husband, wondered if things really were that much better at the bottom end of the income scale here.

I went through a big double door of glass and metal into what had to be the main room of the station, a huge open space under a vaulted ceiling, with benches in long rows on one side, ticket counters on the other, and what looked like half a dozen restaurants and a bar ahead in the middle distance. Okay, I said to myself, here's where I try to find someone who has a clue about how to locate people and get around in this bizarre country.

I'd almost finished thinking that when a woman and a man in what I'd come to think of as Bogart clothing got up off one of the nearby benches and came over toward me. "Mr. Carr?"

Well, that was easy, I thought, and turned toward them. She was tall for a woman, with red-brown curls spilling out from under a broad-brimmed hat; he was a couple of inches shorter than she was, with the kind of forgettable face you look for when you're hiring spies or administrative assistants.

"I'm Melanie Berger," the woman said, shaking my hand, "and this is Fred Vanich." I shook his hand as well. "I hope your trip this morning wasn't too disconcerting," she went on.

That last word was unexpected enough that I laughed. "Not quite," I said. "Though there were a few surprises."

"I can imagine. If you'll come this way?"

"Can I take that for you?" Vanich said, and I handed over my suitcase and followed them.

"I'm afraid we've had to do some rescheduling," Berger said as we headed for the doors. "The President was hoping to meet with you this afternoon, after you have time to get settled in at the hotel, but he's got a minor crisis on his hands. One of the Restorationist parties is breathing fire and brimstone over a line item in an appropriations bill. It'll blow over in a day or so, but—well, I'm sure you know how it goes."

"Yeah," I said. "Ellen's been having to deal with squabbles between people in our camp every other day or so since the election."

21

"That was quite an upset," she said.

I nodded. "We were pretty happy with the way it turned out."

Outside the air was blustery and crisp, with the first taste of approaching winter on it. The trees lining the street still clung to a few brown and crumpled leaves. Just past the trees, where I'd expected to see cabs waiting for passengers in a cloud of exhaust, horses stood placidly in front of brightly colored—buggies? Carriages? Whatever they were called, they looked like boxes with big windows, some with four wheels supporting them and some with two, and a seat up top for the driver.

I blinked, and almost stopped. Berger gave me an amused look. "I know," she said. "We do a lot of things differently here."

"I've noticed that," I replied.

She led the way to one of the four-wheeled buggies, or whatever they were. Obviously things had been arranged in advance; she said "Good morning, Earl," to the driver, he said "Good morning, ma'am" in response, and without another word being said my suitcase found its way into the trunk in back and the three of us were settling into place in comfortable leather seats inside, Berger and I facing forward and Vanich across from us facing backward.

The buggy swung out into traffic and headed down the street. "Is this standard here?" I asked, indicating the vehicle with a gesture.

"The cab? More or less," said Berger. "There are a few towns with electric cabs and a fair number with pedal cabs, but you'll find horse cabs everywhere there's taxi service at all. The others don't produce methane feedstock."

I considered that. "But no gasoline or diesel cabs."

"Not since Partition, no."

That made sense to me. "I'm guessing the embargo had a lot to do with that."

"Well, to some extent. There was smuggling, of course—Chicago being right next to us."

22

I snorted. "And Chicago being Chicago." The Free City of Chicago was the smallest of the independent nations that came out of Partition, and made up for that by being far and away the most gaudily corrupt.

"Well, yes. But there wasn't that much of a market for petroleum products," she went on. "There's the tailpipe tax, of course, and we also lost most of the necessary infrastructure during the war—highways, pipelines, all of it."

"I'm surprised your government didn't subsidize rebuilding."

"We don't do things that way here," she said.

I gave her a long startled look. "Obviously I have a lot to learn," I said finally.

She nodded. "Outsiders generally do."

I filed away the word *outsider* for future reference. "One thing I've been wondering since I crossed the border," I said then. "Or rather two. You really don't have metanet service in the Lakeland Republic?"

"That's correct," she replied at once. "We actually have jamming stations to block satellite transmissions, though it's been fifteen or sixteen years since we last had to use them."

"Hold it," I said. "Jamming stations?"

"Mr. Carr," Berger said, "since Partition we've fought off three attempts at regime change and one full-blown military invasion. All the regime change campaigns were one hundred per cent coordinated via the metanet—saturation propaganda via social media, flashmobs, swarming attacks, you know the drill. The third one fizzled because we'd rigged a kill switch in what little metanet infrastructure we still had by then and shut it down, and after that the legislature voted to scrap what was left. Then when Brazil and the Confederacy invaded in '49, one reason they pulled back a bloody stump was that military doctrine these days—theirs, yours, everybody else's—fixates on disrupting network infrastructure and realtime comm-comm, and we don't have those, so they literally had no clue how to

23

fight us. So, yes, we have jamming stations. If you'd like to visit one I can arrange that."

I took that in. "That won't be necessary," I said then. "Just out of curiosity, do you jam anything else?"

"Not any more. We used to jam radio broadcasts from the Confederacy, but that's because they jammed ours. We got that settled six years ago."

"Television?"

"Waste of time. Only about three per cent of the Republic's within range of a ground station, and the satellite situation— well, I'm sure you know at least as much about that as I do."

I was by no means sure of that, but let it pass. "Okay, and that leads to my second question. How on earth do you take notes when you don't have veepads?"

Instead of answering, she directed a rueful look at Vanich, who nodded once, as though my words had settled something.

"I'm guessing," I said then, "that somebody just won a bet."

"And it wasn't me," Berger said. "There are four questions that outsiders always ask, and there's always a certain amount of speculation, shall we say, about which one gets asked first." She held up one finger. "How do you take notes?" A second. "How do you find out what's happening in the world?" A third. "What do you do to contact people?" A fourth. "And how do you pay your bar tab?"

I laughed. "I've got a fifth," I said. "How do you look up facts without Metapedia?"

"That's an uncommon one, Mr. Carr," Vanich said. His voice was as bland and featureless as his face. If he wasn't a spy, I decided, the Lakeland Republic was misusing his talents. "I've heard it now and then, but it's uncommon."

"To answer your question," Berger said then, "most people use paper notebooks." She pulled a flat rectangular shape out of her purse, fanned it open to show pages with neat angular handwriting on them, put it away again. "Available at any

24

stationery store, but you won't have to worry about that. There's one waiting at your hotel room."

"Thank you," I said, trying to wrap my head around writing down notes on sheets of paper. It sounded about as primitive as carving them with a chisel on stone. "Just out of curiosity, what about the others? I was planning on asking those sometime soon."

"Fair enough," she said. "You find out what's happening by reading a newspaper or listening to the radio. You contact people by phone, if you're in a county with phone service, or by writing a letter or sending a radiotelegram anywhere. You pay your bar tab with cash, and any larger purchases with a check—we've got all that set up for you; you'll just have to visit a bank, and there's one a block and a half from the hotel. You look up facts in books—your own, if you've got them, or a public library's if you don't. There's a branch five blocks from your hotel."

"Not as convenient as accessing the metanet," I noted.

"True, but there are more important things than convenience."

"Like national survival?"

I meant the words as an olive branch, and she took them that way. "Among other things."

She looked out the window, then, and turned in her seat to face me. "We're almost to your hotel. I'm going to have to go back to the Capitol right away and see if I can shake some sense into the Restos, and Fred has his own work to get done. One way or another, there'll be someone to take you around tomorrow. If you like, after you've settled in and had some lunch, I can have somebody come out and show you the tourist sights, or whatever else you'd like to see."

"Thank you," I said, "but I'd suggest something else. I hear your streets are pretty safe."

She nodded. "I know the kind of thing you have to deal with in Philadelphia. We don't have that sort of trouble here."

25

"In that case, I'd like to wander around a bit on my own, check out the landscape—maybe visit the public library you mentioned."

It was a long shot; I figured the Lakeland government would want me under the watchful eye of a handler the whole time I was in the country. To my surprise, she looked relieved. "If that works for you, it works for us," she said. "I'll have somebody call you first thing tomorrow—eight o'clock, if that's not too early."

"That'll be fine."

"With any luck this whole business will have blown over by then and President Meeker can see you right away."

"Here's hoping," I said.

The cab came to a halt. The driver got my suitcase from in back and opened the door to let me out. I took the suitcase, thanked him, shook hands with Berger and Vanich, and headed through the big double door into the main lobby of the Capitol Hotel.

I'd already guessed that the lobby probably wouldn't look much like the ones I was used to seeing elsewhere, and so I wasn't surprised. Instead of the glaring lights, security cameras, angular metal wall art, and automated check-in kiosks I was used to, it was a comfortable space with sofas and chairs around the edges, ornate chandeliers overhead, landscape paintings on the walls, and a couple of desks staffed by actual human beings over to one side. Off to the other side, glass doors framed in wood led into a restaurant. A bellhop—was that the right word?—came trotting over to take my suitcase as soon as I came through the door, said something pleasant, and followed me over to the check-in desk.

"I've got a reservation," I said to the clerk. "The name's Peter Carr."

I'd been wondering whether the hotel would turn out to use an old-fashioned computer system with a keyboard and screen, but apparently even that was too high-tech for local standards.

26

Instead, the clerk pulled out a three-ring binder, opened it, and found my reservation in about as much time as it would have taken to input a name on a veepad and wait for a response to come out of the cloud. "Welcome to the Capitol Hotel, Mr. Carr. We have you down for fourteen nights."

"That's right."

"Looks like everything's paid for in advance. If you'll sign here." She handed me a clipboard with a sheet of paper on it and an old-fashioned ballpoint pen. Fortunately I hadn't quite forgotten how to produce a non-digital signature, and signed at the bottom. "Anything you order in the restaurant here—" She motioned toward the doors on the far side of the room. "—or for room service can be billed to the room account. How many keys will you want?"

"Just one."

She opened a drawer, pulled out an honest-to-Pete metal key with a ring and a tag with the room number on it. "Here you go. Stairs are right down the hall; if you need the elevator it's to the left. Is there anything else I can do for you? Enjoy your stay, Mr. Carr."

I thanked her and headed for the hall with the bellhop in tow. My room was on the third floor and the stairs didn't look too challenging, so I asked, "Do you mind if we take the stairs?"

"Not a bit," he said. "Comes with the job."

We started up the stairs. "Do you get a lot of people here from outside?"

"All the time. Capitol's just four blocks away, and Embassy Row's a little further. We had the foreign minister of Québec here just last week."

"No kidding." There had been rumors for years that the Québecois started tacitly ignoring the embargo even before Canada broke up. We had decent relations with Québec these days, but that hadn't always been the case, and so any news about what was going on between Québec and the Lakeland Republic were worth my attention. "Big official visit, or what?"

"Pretty much, yeah," said the bellhop. "Really nice lady."

We got to the third floor, left the stair, and went down the hall to my room. "Just leave it inside the door," I said, meaning the suitcase. "Thanks."

"Sure thing."

I didn't have any Lakeland money to tip him, but guessed the couple of Atlantic bills I had would do. Fortunately I was right; he grinned, thanked me, and headed back toward the stair.

The room was bigger than I'd expected, with a queen-sized bed on one side, a desk and dresser on the other, and a couple of old-fashioned paintings on the walls—you could tell what they were paintings of, they were that outdated—that looked as though someone had actually made them with a brush and paints. I knew there wouldn't be a veebox, and wondered there might be a screen or even an old-fashioned television in the room, but no dice. The only things even vaguely electronic were a telephone on the desk and a boxy thing on the dresser that had a loudspeaker and some dials on it: a radio, I guessed, and decided to leave turning it on for later. Curtained windows on the far wall let through diffuse light.

I went over and pulled the curtains open, and discovered that the bellhop hadn't been kidding. There was the Capitol dome, half-complete, rising up above an uneven roofline right in front of me. That would be convenient, I decided, and let the curtains fall again.

I got my things settled and then went to the desk and the big envelope of yellowish paper sitting on top of it. Inside was the notebook Melanie Berger had mentioned, a couple of pens, a packet of papers that had BANK OF TOLEDO printed across the top of each sheet, an identification card with my name and photo on it, a wallet that was pretty clearly meant to hold money and the ID card, and a letter on government stationery welcoming me to Toledo in the usual bland terms, over President Meeker's signature. Then there were half a dozen pages of instructions on how to get by in the Lakeland

Republic, which covered everything from customary tips (I'd overtipped the bellhop, though not extravagantly) to who to contact in this or that kind of emergency. I nodded; clearly the bellhop hadn't been exaggerating when he mentioned plenty of foreign guests.

I dropped my veepad in a desk drawer and got the wallet and some of the papers settled into the empty pocket. First things first, I decided: visit the bank and get the money thing sorted out, then get some lunch and do a bit of wandering.

Down in the lobby, the concierge was behind his desk. "Can I help you?"

"Please. I need to know where to find the Bank—" All at once I couldn't remember the name, and reached for the papers in my pocket.

"Out the door," said the concierge, "hang a left, go a block and a half straight ahead, and you'll be standing right in front of it."

I considered him. "You don't need to know which bank?"

"There's only one in town."

That startled me, though I managed not to show it. "Okay, thanks."

"Have a great day," he said.

I headed out the doors, turned left, started along the sidewalk. A cold damp wind was rushing past, pushing shreds of cloud across the sky, and it didn't take me long to figure out why most of the other people on the sidewalk were wearing hats and long coats; they looked much warmer than I felt. Still, Philadelphia has plenty of cold weather, and I was used to the way the chill came through bioplastic business wear. What annoyed me a little, or more than a little, was the way that my clothing made me stick out like a sore thumb.

In retrospect, it was amusing. Everybody else on the sidewalk looked like extras from half a dozen random history vids, everything from fedoras and trench coats to the kind of thing that was last in style when Toledo was a frontier town, and

29

there I was, the only person in town in modern clothing—and you can guess for yourself who was the conspicuous one. The adults gave me startled looks and then pretended that nothing was up, but the kids stared wide-eyed as though I had two extra heads or something. As I said, it was amusing in retrospect, but at the time it made me acutely uncomfortable, and I was glad to get to the bank.

That was a three-story brick building on a street corner. Fortunately it had BANK OF TOLEDO—CAPITOL BRANCH above the doors, or I'd probably have missed it, since it didn't look anything like the banks I was used to. Inside was even weirder: no security cameras, no automated kiosks, no guards in helmets and flak jackets pacing the balcony waiting for trouble, just a lobby with a greeter inside the door and a short line of patrons waiting for tellers. The greeter met me with a cheery "Hi, how can we help you today?" I got out the bank papers, and a minute or two later got shown into one of three little office spaces off the main lobby.

On the other side of the desk was a middle-aged African-American man with a neatly trimmed beard. "I'm Larry Jones," he said, getting up to shake my hand. "Pleased to meet you, Mr.—"

"Carr," I said. "Peter Carr." We got the formalities out of the way and sat down; I handed him the papers; he checked them, we discussed some of the details, and he then unlocked a drawer in his desk and pulled out a big envelope.

"Okay," he said. "Everything's good. The only question I have at this point is whether you've ever used cash or checks before."

"I'm guessing," I said, "that you ask that question fairly often."

"These days, yes," he replied. "Bit of a change since before the Treaty."

"I bet. The answer, though, is cash, yes; checks—well, I've seen a few of them."

"Okay, fair enough." He looked relieved, and I wondered how many people from the cashless countries he'd had to walk through the details of counting out coins. "Here's your checkbook," he said, pulling the thing out of the envelope, and then opened it and showed me how to write a check. "Up here," he said, flipping open a notebookish thing in front, "is where you keep track of how much you've spent." He must have caught my expression, because he broke into a broad smile and said, "Long time since you've done math with a pen, I bet."

"Depends on how long it's been since never," I told him.

He laughed. "Gotcha. Glad to say we can help you out there, too." He opened a different drawer in his desk, handed me a flat little shape of brass with a stylus clipped to the side. "This is a mechanical calculator," he said. "Adds and subtracts for you."

I took the thing, gave it a baffled look. "I didn't know you could do that without electronics."

"I think we're the only country on earth that still makes these." He showed me how to use the stylus to slide the digits up and down. Once I had it figured out, I thanked him and tucked the calculator and checkbook into my pocket.

"Do you have a minute?" I asked then. "I've got a couple of questions about the way you do things here—about banking, mostly."

"Sure thing," he said. "Ask away."

"The concierge at the hotel said there's only one bank here in Toledo. Is that true everywhere in the Lakeland Republic?"

"Yes, if you're talking about consumer banking."

"Is it the same bank everywhere?"

"Good heavens, no. Each county and each city of any size has its own bank, like it has its own water and sewer district and so on."

"That makes it sound like a public utility," I said, baffled.

"That's exactly what it is. Again, that's just consumer banking. We've got privately owned commercial banks here, but those do investment banking only—they're not allowed to offer savings and checking accounts, consumer loans, small business services, that sort of thing, just like we're not allowed to do any kind of investment banking."

I shook my head, baffled. "Why the restriction?"

"Well, that used to be law in the United States, from the 1930s to the 1980s or so, and it worked pretty well—it was after they changed the law that the US economy really started running off the rails, you know. So our legislature changed the law back after Partition, and it's worked pretty well for us, too."

"I don't think banks were public utilities back then," I objected.

"No, that was mostly further back, and only some banks," he agreed. "The thing is, the way we see it, there are some things that private industry does really well and some things that it doesn't do well at all, and public utilities like water, sewer service, electricity, public transit, consumer banking, that sort of thing—those work better when you don't let private interests milk them for profits. I know you do things different back home."

"True enough. But isn't it more efficient to leave those things to private industry?"

"That depends, Mr. Carr, on what you mean by efficiency."

That intrigued me. "Please go on."

Unexpectedly, he laughed. "I give a talk on that every year at one of the homeschool associations here in town. Efficiency is always a ratio—more or less efficient at producing an output in terms of a given input. A chemical process is efficient if it turns out more product for the same amount of raw materials, or the same amount of energy, or what have you. We get people from outside all the time talking about how this or that would be more efficient than what we do, and you know what? None of them seem to be able to answer a simple question: efficient for what output, in terms of what input?"

I could see where this was going, and decided to head onto a different tack. "And having consumer banks as public utilities," I said. "Is that more efficient for some output in terms of some input?"

"We don't worry so much about that," the banker said. "The question that matters to most people here is much simpler: does it work or doesn't it?"

"How do you tell?"

"History, Mr. Carr," he said. He was smiling again. "History."

CHAPTER 3

I went back to the hotel for lunch. The wind had picked up further and was tossing stray raindrops at anything in its path; my clothing was waterproof but not particularly warm, and I frankly envied the passersby their hats. For that matter, I still wasn't happy about the way that my bioplastic clothes made everyone give me startled looks. Still, it was only a block and a half, and then I ducked back inside the lobby, went to the glass doors to the restaurant, stepped inside.

Maybe a minute later I was settling into a chair in a comfortable corner, and the greeter was on his way back to the door, having promised the imminent arrival of a waitress. Stray notes of piano music rippled through the air, resolved themselves into an unobtrusive jazz number. It took me a moment to notice that the piano was actually there in the restaurant, tucked over in a nook to one side. The player was a skinny kid in his twenties, Italian-American by the look of him, and he was really pretty good.

Jazz is a thing of mine. Back home there isn't much of it outside of a few clubs in Philadelphia and a couple of other towns, and most people don't know a thing about it—back home, if you're not into something, it's usually nowhere on your image field—but I took an interest in it back in my teen years and never lost the habit. The kid at the piano made me glad of that. Some musicians play jazz laid-back because the fire's gone out or they never had any in the first place, but now and again you hear one who's got the fire and keeps it under perfect control while playing soft and low, and it's like watching somebody take a leisurely stroll on a tightrope strung between skyscrapers. This kid was one of those. I wondered what he'd sound like with a bunch of other musicians and a room full of people who wanted to dance.

As it was, I leaned back in the chair, read the menu and enjoyed the music and the absence of the wind. The waitress showed up as prophesied, and I ordered my usual, soup and sandwich and a cup of chicory coffee—you can get that anywhere in the post-US republics, just one more legacy of the debt crisis and the hard years that followed. I know plenty of people in Philadelphia who won't touch the stuff any more, but I got to like it and it still goes down easier than straight coffee.

Lunch was good, the music was good, and I'd missed the lunch rush so the service was better than good; I charged the meal to my room but left a tip well on the upside of enough. Then it was back outside into the wind as the kid at the piano launched into a take on "Ruby, My Dear" that wouldn't have embarrassed a young Thelonious Monk. I had plenty of questions about the Lakeland Republic, some things that I'd been asked to look into and some that were more or less a matter of my own curiosity, and sitting in a hotel restaurant wasn't going to get me any closer to the answers.

Outside there were still plenty of people on the sidewalks, but not so many as earlier; I gathered that lunch hour was over and everyone who worked ordinary hours, whatever those were here, was back on the job. I went around the block the hotel was on, noting landmarks, and then started wandering, lookng for shops, restaurants, and other places that might be useful during my stay: something I like to do in any unfamiliar city when I have the chance. There were plenty of retail businesses—the ground floor of every building I passed had as many as would fit—but none of them were big, and none of them had the sort of generic logo-look that tells you you're looking at a chain outlet. Everything I knew about business said that little mom-and-pop stores like that were hopelessly inefficient, but I could imagine what the banker I'd talked with would say in response to that, and I didn't want to go there.

The other thing that startled me as I wandered the streets was how little advertising there was. Don't get me wrong, most of the stores had signage in the windows advertising this or that product or doing the 10% OFF THIS DAY ONLY routine; what was missing was the sort of display advertising you see on every available surface in most cities. I'd figured already that there wouldn't be digital billboards, but there weren't any billboards at all; the shelters at the streetcar stops didn't have display ads all over them, and neither did the streetcars. I thought back to the morning's trip, and realized that I basically hadn't seen any ads at all since the train crossed the border. I shook my head, wondered how the Lakeland Republic managed that, and then remembered the notebook in my pocket and put my first note into it: *Why no ads? Ask.*

I was maybe six blocks from the hotel, by then, looping back after I'd checked out the streets on the west side of the capitol district, and that's when I tore my shoe. It was my own fault, really. There was a middle-aged blind woman strolling down the street ahead of me with her guide dog, going the same direction I was but not as fast. I veered over to the curb to get around them, misjudged my step, and a sharp bit of curbing caught the side of my shoe as I stumbled and ripped the bioplastic wide open. Fortunately it didn't rip me, but I hadn't brought a spare pair—these were good shoes, the sort that usually last for a couple of months before you have to throw them out. So there I was, looking at the shredded side of the shoe, and then I looked up and the first store I saw was a shoe store, I kid you not.

I managed to keep the ripped shoe on my foot long enough to get in the door. The clerk, a middle-aged guy whose hair was that pink color you get when a flaming redhead starts to go gray, spotted me and started into the "Hi, how can I help you?" routine right as what was left of the shoe flopped right off my foot. He started laughing, and so did I; I picked the thing up, and he said, "Well, I don't need to ask that, do I? Let's get you measured and put something a little less flimsy on your feet."

"I take a men's medium-large," I said.

He nodded, and gave me the kind of look you give to someone who really doesn't get it. "We like to be a little more precise here. Go ahead and have a seat."

So I sat down; he took the remains of the shoe and threw it away, and then proceeded to use this odd metal device with sliding bits on it to measure both my feet. "9D," he said, "with a high arch. I bet your feet ache right in the middle when you're on 'em too long."

"Yeah," I said. "I take pills for that."

"A good pair of shoes will do a better job. Let's see, now—that's business wear, isn't it? You expect to do a lot of walking? Any formal or semi-formal events coming up?" I nodded yes to each, and he said, "Okay, I got just the thing for you."

He went away, came back with a box, and extracted a pair of dark brown leather shoes from it. "This brown'll match the putty color of those clothes of yours pretty well, and these won't take any breaking in. Let's give it a try." The shoes went on. "There you go. Walk around a bit, see how they feel on you."

I got up and walked around the store. My feet felt remarkably odd. It took me a moment to realize that this was because the shoes actually fit them. "These are pretty good," I told him.

"Beat the pants off the things you were wearing, don't they?"

"True enough," I admitted. He rang up the sale on some kind of old-fashioned mechanical cash register and wrote out a bill of sale by hand; I wrote a check and headed out the door.

Half a block down the same street was a store selling men's clothes. I looked at it for a moment, and then the rain spattered down at me again and made up my mind for me. I came out something like an hour later dressed like one of the locals— wool jacket, slacks and vest, hempcloth button-up shirt and tie; with a long raincoat over the top, and my ordinary clothes in a shopping bag.

I'd already more than half decided to pick up something less conspicuous to wear before my shoe got torn, and money wasn't a problem, so I bought enough to keep me for the dura- tion of my stay, and had everything else sent back to the hotel. The bill was large enough that the clerk checked my ID and then called the bank to make sure I had enough in my account to cover it. Still, that was the only hitch, and quickly past.

From the clothes store I headed back the way I'd come, turned a corner and went three blocks into a neighborhood of narrow little shops with hand-written signs in the windows. The sign I was looking for, on the recommendation of the clothes store clerk, was barely visible on the glass of a door: S. EHRENSTEIN HABERDASHER. I went in; the space inside was only about twice as wide as the door, with shelves packed with boxes on both walls and a little counter and cash register at the far end.

S. Ehrenstein turned out to be a short wiry man with hair the color of steel wool and a nose like a hawk's beak. "Good after- noon," he said, and then considered me for a moment. "You're from outside—Atlantic Republic, or maybe East Canada. Not Québec or New England. Am I right?"

"Atlantic," I said. "How'd you know?"

"Your clothes and your shoes are brand new—I'd be sur- prised if you told me you've been in 'em for as much as an hour. That says you just came from outside—that and no hat, and five o'clock shadow this early in the day; I don't know why it is, but nobody outside seems to know how to get a proper shave. The rest, well, I pay attention to lots of little things. How'd you hear about my shop?"

I told him the name of the clothing store, and he nodded, pleased. "Well, there you are. That's Fred Hayakawa's store; his family's been in the business since half an hour before Eve bit the apple, and his clerks know a good hat, which is more than I could say for some. So are you in business, or—"

"Politics," I said.

"Then I have just the hat for you. Let's get your head measured." A measuring tape came out of his pocket and looped around my head. "Okay, good. Seven and a quarter, I should have in stock." He ducked past me, clambered onto a stepladder, pulled down a box. "Try it on. The mirror's there."

With the hat on, my resemblance to a minor character from a Bogart vid was complete. "Absolutely classic," the haberdasher said from behind me. "Fedoras, homburgs, sure, they're fine, but a porkpie like this, you can wear it anywhere and look real classy."

"I like it," I agreed.

"Well, there you are. Let me show you something." He took the hat, slipped a cord out from under the ribbon. "In windy weather you put this loop over your coat button, so you don't lose it if it blows off. If I were you I'd do that before I set one foot outside that door."

I paid up, accepted the business card he pressed on me, and got the loop in place before I went back outside. The wind had died down, so the hat stayed comfortably in place—and the adverb's deliberate; it kept my head warm, and the rest of the clothes were pleasant in a way that bioplastic just isn't.

You know what it's like when some annoying noise is so much part of the background that you don't notice it at all, until it stops, and then all of a sudden you realize just how much it irritated you? Getting out of bioplastic was the same sort of thing. In most countries these days, everything from clothes to sheets to curtains is bioplastic, because it's so cheap to make and turn into products that the big corporations that sell it drove everything else off the market years ago. It's waterproof, it's easy to clean—there's quite a litany, and of course it was all over the metanet and the other media back when you could still buy anything else. Of course the ads didn't mention that it's flimsy and slippery, and feels clammy pretty much all the time, but that's the way it goes; what's in the stores depends on what makes the biggest profit for the big dogs in industry, and the rest of us just have to learn to live with it.

The Lakeland Republic apparently didn't play by the same rules, though. The embargo had something to do with it, I guessed, but apparently they still weren't letting the multi-nationals compete with local producers. The clothes I'd bought were more expensive than bioplastic would have been, and I figured it would take trade barriers to keep them on the market.

I kept walking. Two blocks later, about the time I caught sight of the capitol dome again, I passed a barbershop and happened to notice a handwritten sign in the window advertising a shave and trim. I thought about what S. Ehrenstein had said about a proper shave, laughed, and decided to give it a try.

The barber was a big balding guy with a ready grin. "What can I do for you?"

"Shave and trim, please."

"Your timing's good. Another half hour and you'd have to wait a bit, but as it is—" He waved me to the coatrack and the empty chair. "Get yourself comfy and have a seat."

I shed my coat, hat, and jacket, and sat down. He covered me up with the same loose poncho thing that barbers use everywhere, tied something snug around my neck, and went to work. "New in town?"

"Just visiting, from Philadelphia."

"No kidding. Welcome to Toledo. Here on business?" Instead of the buzz of an electric trimmer, the clicking of scissors sounded back behind my right ear.

"More or less. I'm going to talk to some people up at the Capitol, make some contacts, ask some questions about the way you do things here."

"Might have to wait a day or two. Did you hear about this latest thing?"

"Just that there's some kind of crisis."

The scissor-sound moved around the back of my head from right to left. "Well, sort of. Tempest in a teapot is more like it. Something in the budget bill for next year set off the all-out Restos, and so one of the parties that's had Meeker's back says they'll bolt unless whatever it is gets taken out."

"Restos?"

"Nah, you don't have those out your way, do you? Here the two political blocs are Conservatives and Restorationists; Conservatives want to keep things pretty much the way they are now, Restos want to take things back to the way they used to be a long time ago. Okay, lay your head back." I did, and he draped a hot damp towel over the lower half of my face, then went back to trimming. "Used to be about half and half, but these days the Restos have the bigger half, with so many of the rural counties going to lower tiers."

"Hmm?" I managed to say.

"Oh, that's right. You probably don't know about the tier system."

"Mm-mh."

"It works like this. There are five tiers, and counties vote on what tier they want to be in. The lower the tier, the lower your taxes, but the less you get in terms of infrastructure. Toledo's tier five—we got electricity, we got phones in every house, good paving on the streets so you can drive a car if you can afford one, but we pay for it through the nose when it comes to tax time."

"Mm-hmm."

He took off the towel, started brushing hot lather onto my face. "So tier five has a base date of 1950—that means we got

42

about the same sort of infrastructure and services they had here that year. The other tiers go down from there—tier four's base date is 1920, for tier three it's 1890, tier two's 1860, and tier one's 1830. You live in a tier one county, you got police and fire departments, you got dirt roads, not a lot else. Of course your taxes are way, way down, too." He put away the brush, snapped open an old-fashioned straight razor, and went to work on my stubble. "That's the thing. Nobody's technology gets a subsidy—that's in the constitution. You want it, you pay all the costs, cradle to grave. You don't get to dump 'em on anybody else. That's what the Restos are all up in arms about. They think something in the budget is a hidden subsidy for I forget what high-tier technology, and that's a red line for them."

"Mm-hmm," I said again.

"They'll get it worked out. Go like this." He drew his lips to one side, and I imitated the movement. "Meeker's handled that sort of thing more'n a dozen times already—he's good. If we let our presidents have second terms he'd get one. Now go like this." I moved my lips the other way. "So they'll drop whatever it is out of the budget, or put in a user fee, or come up with some other gimmick so that everybody's happy. It's not a big deal. Nothing like the fight over the treaty, or the time ten years ago when Mary Chenkin was president, when the all-out Restos tried to get rid of tier five, just like that. That was a real donnybrook. This close to the Capitol, you better believe I got to hear all sides of it."

He finished shaving, washed the last bits of soap off my face with another hot wet towel, then splashed on some kind of bay-scented aftershave that stung a bit. A brush darted around my shoulders, and then he took off the neckcloth and the poncho thing. "There you go."

I got up, checked the trim in the big mirror on the wall, ran my fingers across my cheek; it was astonishingly smooth. "Very nice," I said. While I got out my wallet, I asked the barber, "Do you think Toledo's ever going to go to a lower tier?"

"People are talking about it," he said. "I mean, it's nice to have some of the services, but then tax time comes around and everyone says 'Ouch.' Me, I could live with tier four easy, and my business—" He gestured at the shop. "Other than the lights, might as well be tier one. A lot of businesses run things that way—it just makes more sense." He handed me my change with a grin. "And more money."

From the barber shop I swung past my hotel, dropped off the bag with my bioplastic clothes, and went back out onto Toledo's streets. That makes it sound easier than it was; some kind of event—a wedding reception, I guessed from the decor—was getting started in one of the second floor ballrooms, and the lobby and the sidewalk outside were both crammed with people in formal wear heading in. It took some work to get through it all, but after not too many minutes I was strolling up an uncrowded sidewalk toward the unfinished white dome of the Capitol.

The Legislative Building back home in Philadelphia doesn't have a dome. It's an angular blob of glass and metal, designed by I forget which hotshot European architectural firm, and when it opened twenty-two years ago you could hardly access the metanet without being barraged by oohs and ahs about how exciting, innovative, and futuristic it was. You don't hear much of that any more. They've spent twenty-two years now trying to get the roof to stop leaking and coming up with work-arounds for all the innovative features that never did work too well, and the design looks embarrassingly dated these days, the way avant-garde architecture always does a couple of decades down the road. I was curious to see what the Lakeland Republic had done instead.

It took two blocks to get to a place where I had a clear view of the building, and when I did, I wasn't in for any particular surprise. They'd modeled it on state capitol buildings in the old United States, with a tall white dome in the center above the rotunda and the big formal entrance, and a wing for each house of the legislature on either side. The Lakeland

Republic flag—blue above and green below, with a circle of seven gold stars for the seven states that joined together at Partition—fluttered from a flagpole out front. Long rows of windows on each wing showed that there was plenty of room for offices and meeting rooms along with the legislative chambers. The walls were white marble with classical decor, and the peaked roofs to either side of the dome didn't look as though they were likely to leak much. I thought about what the banker had said about history, and kept going.

Another block brought me to an open storefront with a big gaudy handpainted sign above it yelling KAUFER'S NEWS in big red letters. Down below were more newspapers and magazines—the kind that are printed on paper—than I'd ever seen in one place. I remembered what Melanie Berger had said about newspapers, and decided to check it out.

Inside, magazines lined the three walls and newspapers filled a big island unit in the middle. Signs with bright red lettering on the island unit gave me some guidance: one yelled TOLEDO PAPERS, another LAKELAND PAPERS, and a third FOREIGN PAPERS. That narrowed it down a bit, but there were still fifteen different newspapers in the Toledo section.

The proprietor was sitting on a tall stool next to the entrance. She was a scruffy-looking woman in her thirties with blonde hair spilling out from under a floppy cap, wearing an apron with KAUFER'S NEWS printed on it that had seen many better days. By the time I turned toward her, she'd already unfolded herself from the stool and came over. "Can I help you?"

"Please," I said. "I'm new in town and I don't know the local papers."

"No problem." She pointed to the stacked newspapers. "The *Blade* and the *Journal* are the two dailies—the *Blade*'s the paper of record, the *Journal*'s the community paper and a lot more lively. The rest of 'em are weeklies—neighborhood, ethnic, religious, what have you. The *Blade*'s a buck twenty-five, the *Journal*'s seventy-five cents, the others are twenty-five,

45

except for the *Wholly Toledo*—that's the arts and nightlife rag and doesn't cost a thing."

It's always amused me that everywhere in the former United States, the basic unit of the local currency is still called a buck—that's true even in California, where what trade goes on around the edges of the civil war is mostly in Chinese currency when it isn't just barter. I pulled out a couple of Lakeland bills, and got that day's *Toledo Blade* and the latest *Wholly Toledo* along with some change. "Thanks," I said.

"Sure thing." She turned to another customer who had a magazine open. "You want to read that, Mac, you gotta buy it. This ain't the library, you know."

The other guy looked sheepish, closed the magazine, paid for it and left the newsstand.

"Speaking of which," I said, "how do I get to the library from here?"

"Two blocks that way, hang a left, three blocks straight ahead and you're there."

I thanked her again, tipped her one of the quarters she'd given me in change, and left.

The library wasn't first on my list, though. The *Blade* had a couple of articles on the front page I wanted to read. The wind was picking up, so the idea of plopping down on one of the park benches out in front of the Capitol didn't particularly appeal; the question in my mind was where indoors I could sit down and read the thing. As it happened, I'd gone less than a block when I passed a little hole-in-the-wall café, and in the window seat was an old brown-skinned woman in a heavy wool coat with a cup of coffee in her hand and a copy of the *Journal* open in front of her. I took the hint, ducked inside, and a couple of minutes later was perched on a slightly rickety chair with a cup of coffee and the front page of the *Blade* to keep me company.

The lead article was on the political crisis that had blown up that morning. I'd guessed that the paper would have more details than you'd find in the 140-character stories you get from most metanet news sites, and I was right. For that matter, it had more detail than what you saw on the old internet, back in the day. I'd seen classified briefing papers on political issues that didn't cover as much ground. By the time I'd finished the first paragraph I knew the basics—the group that was threatening to bolt out of Meeker's coalition was the Social Alternative party, and the issue was whether lowering the natural resource tariff on three industrial metals counted as a government subsidy for technology—but the rest of the story, part of it on the front page and part of it back in the middle of the first section, filled in the details: who was backing the tariff reduction, who was opposing it, what the various arguments were, what the Senate and the justices of the Constitutional Court had to say, and so on. By the time I'd finished reading it I had a pretty fair snapshot of the way politics worked in the Republic.

There were other other articles worth reading—an update on this year's agricultural shortfalls, news from the civil war in California, another round of grumbling between Texas and the Confederacy over offshore oil drilling in the Gulf, another chunk of southern Florida lost to the sea—but the one that caught my eye was a follow-up piece on the destruction of the *Progresso IV* satellite a week before. That was news, and not just for spaceheads, since it was the first satellite to get taken out by orbital junk in a midrange orbit, and it was big enough that its fragments could turn into a real problem for other satellites in that range. The article quoted the head of the Brazilian space agency and an assortment of experts, with opinions ranging from sanguine to sobering.

None of the facts were new to me—I'd been following the satellite situation since my first stint in government a dozen years back—but the story put it all into context effortlessly in a page and a half of newsprint, all the way from the first warnings back in the 1970s, through the slow motion Kessler-syndrome disaster that got going in low earth orbit in 2029, to the increasing pace of satellite failures in geosynchronous orbits in the last half dozen years. Since the 2030s, I knew, the midrange orbits had gotten really crowded; the last thing anybody needed was a Kessler syndrome there, too.

I got a refill of my coffee, flipped through the rest of the paper. The business section was going to take careful study, I saw that at a glance. Some of it was pretty straightforward—several counties issuing bonds, commodity prices in the Chicago exchange veering this way and that, and two full pages that looked like ordinary stock market data, except that I didn't know any of the companies that were listed—but some of it was right out there in left field. The one that stuck in my mind was a corporation that was being wound up: not going bankrupt, being bought, or any of the other ways that corporations die back home, but winding up its affairs, distributing its remaining assets, and closing its doors. I shook my head, kept reading. The sports section seemed pretty much normal, except that I didn't know any of the teams and there were a lot of them, enough that I wondered whether every town in the Lakeland Republic had its own. The arts and entertainment section in back had everything from concerts to theater listings to a page of radio programs. I nodded, slid the paper into one of the big outside patch pockets of my raincoat, paid my tab and headed out into the fading afternoon light.

The library was easy enough to find. It was a big two-story brick building with arched windows and a wide porch over the entrance, and a couple of cloth banners out front with CAPITOL BRANCH—TOLEDO PUBLIC LIBRARY on them. The lobby was spacious, with a bulletin board full of flyers. To the left, the door was propped open, and I heard a woman's voice telling some story or other about a mole and a water rat in a boat; a glance upwards met the sign saying CHILDREN'S ROOM. I turned right, and went through the door into what I hoped was the adult section.

It didn't take me long to figure out that I'd guessed right, even though it didn't look like any library I'd ever seen. Instead of rows of long bare tables studded with keyboards and screens, it had shelves upon shelves upon shelves of printed books, more of them than I think I'd ever seen in one place before. Tables and chairs clustered in the middle of the room, with people sitting bent over books, and over toward the windows were a few sofas and overstuffed chairs with their own contingent of readers. Heavy carpet covered the floor and a historical mural covered the vaulted ceiling, spanning the distance from the native tribes on one end to a half-built Capitol on the other.

I really had no idea what to make of it all. In place of the clatter of keys and the babble of voices that gave the libraries I knew their soundtrack, the room was as hushed as a funeral parlor. I watched one of the patrons go up to the big desk where the librarians stood to ask a question, and the conversation that followed took place in murmurs. Lacking anything better to do, I crossed the room to the shelves of books. There was some kind of numerical code on the spines of the books, which didn't tell me much of anything, but from the titles I figured out quickly enough that numbers in the low three hundreds, or at least these numbers, had to do with politics. I pulled out a couple of books, glanced at them, and was about to go to another shelf when I spotted a slim volume titled *Changing Tiers*.

I pulled the book out, opened it, and found that it was exactly what I'd guessed, a guide for Lakelanders who were moving from one county to another at a different tier. I paged through it for a few minutes, decided that I needed to read it, and went looking for a free chair.

I realized pretty quickly that I'd found the book I needed, because it started out with a chapter on the history of the tier system, and that gave me the key to the whole arrangement. During the Second Civil War, the book explained, the states

49

that became the Lakeland Republic got pounded most of the way back to the Stone Age by Federal airstrikes and two years of town-by-town fighting. When Washington finally fell and the fighting ended, nearly every bit of infrastructure in those states—roads, railways, power grids, water and sewer systems, you name it—was in ruins, and once Partition and the beginning of the debt crisis put paid to the last hope of a fast recovery, Lakelanders had to figure out how to rebuild and how to pay for it. The differences of opinion were drastic enough, and funds and other resources short enough, that the provisional government decided to make each county responsible for deciding what kind of infrastructure it wanted, and taxing itself to pay the costs.

From that beginning, over a decade or so of contentious local decisions and gradual rebuilding, the tier system evolved. A second chapter sketched out the legal framework—certain clauses in the constitution and its amendments, two important decisions by the Constitutional Court, and the various laws that regulated what counties could and couldn't do, and what they could and couldn't enforce. It was all very clear, and I got out my notebook and filled most of four pages with notes. More to the point, I ended up with some sense of the logic of the tier system and the reasons why it made sense to Lakelanders.

By the time I'd finished those two chapters the last daylight was gone and the window in front of me looked out on a night scene lit by streetlamps and occasional windows. I decided not to read the rest of the book, put it back on the shelves, and headed out into the cold wind.

I don't get lost easily, or I'd probably have ended up wandering off in some random direction until I could find a cab or something. As it was, I wasn't sure of my bearings until I got close to the Capitol. The sidewalks were anything but deserted—I gathered that Toledo had a lively nightlife scene, and I heard live folk music coming out of one café I passed and some really gutsy blues coming out of another—but I didn't pay a lot of attention to the people I passed just then. I was thinking about the book I'd read and the newspaper in my pocket, and the difference between the fragmentary bits of information I was used to getting off the metanet and the knowledge I'd gathered from the longer, more context-rich pieces I'd just taken in. It was a sobering comparison. I decided I'd have to check out Lakeland schools and colleges, and see if the difference applied there as well.

When I got to the hotel where I was staying, though, I had to pay attention to the people, because there was no way in; the crowd from the wedding reception was out in front, lining a narrow path from the door to the edge of the sidewalk, where an ornate horsedrawn carriage waited. I didn't have too much trouble figuring out what was about to happen, so I stood there on the outer edge of the crowd, waiting for the happy couple. Some of the guests had taken the time to put on coats and hats before heading out into the night air, and I blended in well enough that a young woman pushing her way through the crowd handed me a little bag of rice to throw. I took it, amused, and waited with the rest.

A few minutes later, the guests of honor came out—two young men in their early twenties, laughing and holding hands and obviously very much in love. I pelted them with rice along with everyone else, and stood there while they climbed into the carriage and waved. The driver snapped his reins and the horses broke into a smart trot; the usual cheering and waving followed, and away they went.

The crowd began to scatter. I turned toward the door and found myself facing the pianist who'd been playing in the hotel restaurant during lunch that same day. Of course he didn't know me from George Washington's off ox; he turned to go back inside, and since that was the way I was headed, too, I followed him. The lobby wasn't too bad, but the stair was a river of people headed for the doors, and so the pianist and

I ended up standing next to each other at the foot of the stair, waiting for the crowd to pass by and let us through.

"That was pretty good jazz you were playing," I said to him, "here at lunchtime."

He gave me a grin. "Thank you!" Then: "You're one of Sandy's political friends?"

"No, just staying at the hotel." He nodded, and I went on. "You play anywhere else?"

"Yeah, that's just my day gig. Friday and Saturday nights I'm at the Harbor Club, north end of downtown." He reached into his jacket, pulled out a piece of stiff paper and handed it to me. I realized after a blank moment that it was an old-fashioned business card. Fancy script spelled out:

Sam Capoferro
and his Frogtown Five

Down below in little print was contact info.

"Show that at the door and there's no cover charge," he told me. "See you there sometime."

A gap opened up in the crowd, and he headed up the stair. I pocketed the business card and waited for another opening.

CHAPTER 4

The phone rang at 8 am sharp, a shrill mechanical sound that made me wonder if there was actually a bell inside the thing. I put down that morning's Toledo *Blade* and got it on the second ring. "Hello?"

"Mr. Carr? This is Melanie Berger. I've got—well, not exactly good news, but it could be worse."

I laughed. "Okay, I'll bite. What's up?"

"We've managed to get everyone to sit down and work out a compromise, but the President's got to be involved in that. With any luck this whole business will be out of the way by lunchtime, and he'll be able to meet with you this afternoon, if that's acceptable."

"That'll be fine," I said.

"Good. In the meantime, we thought you might want to make some of the visits we discussed with your boss earlier. If that works for you—"

"It does."

"Can you handle being shown around by an intern? He's a bit of a wooly lamb, but well-informed." I indicated that that would be fine, and she went on. "His name's Michael Finch. I can have him meet you at the Capitol Hotel lobby whenever you like."

"Would half an hour from now be too soon?"

53

"Not at all. I'll let him know."

We said the usual polite things, and I hung up. Twenty-five minutes later I was down in the lobby, and right on time a young man in a trenchcoat and a fedora came through the doors. I could see why Berger had called him a wooly lamb; he had blond curly hair and the kind of permanently startled expression you find most often in ingenues and axe murderers. He looked around blankly even though I was standing in plain sight.

"Mr. Finch?" I said, crossing the lobby toward him. "I'm Peter Carr."

His expression went even more startled than usual for a moment, and then he grinned. "Pleased to meet you, Mr. Carr. You surprised me—I was expecting to see someone dressed in that plastic stuff."

"I'm not fond of being stared at," I said with a shrug.

He nodded, as though that explained everything. "Ms. Berger told me you wanted to visit some of our industrial plants and the Toledo stock market. Unless you have something already lined up, we can head down to the Mikkelson factory first and go from there. We could take a cab if you like, or just catch the streetcar—the Green line goes within a block of the plant. Whatever you like."

I considered that, decided that a close look at Lakeland public transit was in order. "Let's catch the streetcar."

"Sure thing."

We left the lobby, and I followed Finch's lead along the sidewalk to the right. The morning was crisp and bright, with an edge of frost, and plenty of people were walking to work. A fair number of horsedrawn cabs rolled by, along with a very few automobiles. I thought about that as we walked. Toledo's tier had a base date of 1950, or so the barber told me the day before, but I didn't think that cars were anything like so scarce on American streets in that year.

54

We turned right and came to the streetcar stop, where a dozen people were already waiting. I turned to Finch. "The Mikkelson factory. What do they make?"

For answer he pointed up the street. Two blocks up, the front end of a streetcar was coming into sight as it rounded the corner. "Rolling stock for streetcar lines. We've got three streetcar manufacturers in the Republic, but Mikkelson's the biggest. The Toledo system runs their cars exclusively."

The streetcar finished the turn, sped up, and then rolled to a stop in front of us. Strictly speaking, I suppose I should say "streetcars," since there were four cars linked together, all of them painted forest green and yellow with brass trim. We lined up with the others, climbed aboard when our turn came, and Finch pushed a couple of bills down into the fare box and got a couple of paper slips—"day passes," he explained—from the conductor. There were still seats available, and I settled into the window seat as the conductor rang a bell, ding-di-ding-di-ding, and the streetcar hummed into motion.

It was an interesting ride, in an odd way. I travel a lot, like most people in my line of work, and I've ridden top-of-the-line automated light rail systems in New Beijing and Brasilia. I could tell at a glance that the streetcar I was on cost a tiny fraction of the money that went into those high-end systems, but the ride was just as comfortable and nearly as fast. There were two employees of the streetcar system on board, a driver and a conductor, and I wondered how much of the labor cost was offset by the lower price of the hardware.

The streetscape rolled past. We got out of the retail district near my hotel and into a residential district, a mix of apartment buildings and row houses, with solar water heaters gleaming in the sun on every south-facing roof. Here and there we passed other buildings: an elementary school with a playground outside, two churches, a public library, a synagogue, and then a big square building with a dome on top and a symbol above the door I recognized at once. I turned to Finch. "I wondered whether there were Atheist Assemblies here."

"Oh, yes. Are you an Atheist, Mr. Carr?"

I didn't see any reason to temporize. "Yes."

"Wonderful! So am I. If you're free this coming Sunday, you'd be more than welcome at the Capitol Assembly—that's this one here." He motioned at the building we were passing.

"I'll certainly consider it," I said, and he beamed.

More houses went by, more people got on, and then the streetcar rolled up and over a bridge. Underneath was a canal with a towpath next to it, and a canal boat sliding along toward the river, pulled by another honest-to-god mule. On the far side of the canal, warehouses and the kind of stores you get in industrial districts started elbowing aside the houses, until we were in the middle of a busy manufacturing district.

By the time we got to the factory the streetcar was crammed to the bursting point, mostly with people who looked like office staff, and the sidewalks were full of men and women heading toward the factory gates for the day shift. We got off with almost everyone else, and I followed Finch down another sidewalk to the front entrance of the business office, a sturdy-looking two-story structure with MIKKELSON MANUFAC-TURING in big letters above the second story windows and in gold paint on the glass of the front door.

The receptionist was already on duty, and picked up a telephone to announce us. A few minutes later a middle-aged woman in a dark suit came out to shake our hands. "Mr. Carr, pleased to meet you. I'm Elaine Chu. So you'd like to see our factory?"

A few minutes later we'd exchanged our hats, coats and jackets for safety helmets and loose coveralls of tough gray cloth. "Just under half the streetcars manufactured in the Lakeland Republic are made right here," Chu explained as we walked down a long corridor. "We've also got plants in Louisville and Rockford, but those supply the railroad industry—Rockford makes locomotives and Louisville's our plant for rolling stock. Every Mikkelson streetcar comes from this plant."

We passed through double doors onto the shop floor. I was expecting a roar of machine noise, but there weren't a lot of machines, just workers in the same gray coveralls we were wearing, picking up what looked like hand tools and getting to work. There were streetcar tracks running down the middle of the shop floor, and I watched as a team of workers bolted two wheels, an axle, and a gear together and sent it rolling down the track to the next team. Metal parts clanged and clattered, voices echoed off the metal girders that held up the roof, and now and then some part got pulled from the line and chucked into a big cart on its own set of tracks.

"Quality control," Chu said. "Each team checks each part or assembly as it comes down the line, and anything that's not up to spec gets pulled and either disassembled or recycled. That's one of the reasons we have so large a share of the market. Our streetcars average twenty per cent less downtime for repairs than anybody else's."

We left the wheel assemblies behind and walked down the shop floor, past the team that assembled them into four-wheel bogies, through the teams that built a chassis with electric motors and wiring atop each pair of bogies, to the point where the body was hauled in on a heavily-built overhead suspension track and bolted onto the chassis. From there we went back up another long corridor to the assembly line that built the bodies. It was all a hum of activity, with dozens of tools I didn't recognize at all, but every part of it was powered by human muscle and worked by human hands.

I think we'd been there for about two hours when we got to the end of the line, and watched a brand new Mikkelson streetcar get hooked up to overhead power lines, tested one last time, and driven away on tracks to the siding where it would be loaded aboard a train and shipped to its destination—Sault Ste. Marie, Chu explained, which was expanding its streetcar system now that the borders were open and trade with East Canada had the local economy booming. "So that's the line from beginning to end," she said. "If you'd like to come this way?"

We went back into the business office, shed helmets and coveralls, and proceeded to her office. "I'm sure you have plenty of questions," she said.

"One in particular," I replied. "The lack of automation. Nearly everything you do with human labor gets done in other industrial countries by machines. I'm curious as to how that works—economically as well as practically—and whether it's a matter of government mandates or of something else."

I gathered from her expression that she was used to the question. "Do you have a background in business, Mr. Carr?"

I nodded, and she went on. "In the Atlantic Republic, if I understand correctly—and please let me know if I'm wrong—when a company spends money to buy machines, those count as assets. That's how they appear on the books, and there are tax benefits from depreciation and so on. When a company spends the same money to do the same task by hiring employees, they don't count as assets, and you don't get any of the same benefits. Is that correct?"

I nodded again.

"On the other hand, if a company hires employees, it has to spend much more than the cost of wages or salaries. It has to pay into the social security system, public health care, unemployment, and so on and so forth, for each person it hires. If the company buys machines instead, it doesn't have to pay any of those things for each machine. Nor is there any kind of tax to cover the cost to society of replacing the jobs that went away because of automation, or to pay for any increased generating capacity the electrical grid might need to power the machines, or any of the other costs that automation places on the rest of the community. Is that also correct?"

"Essentially, yes," I said.

58

"So, in other words, tax codes and other government regulations subsidize automation and penalize employment. You probably were taught in business school that automation is more economical than hiring people. Did anyone mention all the ways that public policy contributes to making one more economical than the other?"

"No," I admitted. "I suppose you do things differently here."

"Very much so," she said with a crisp nod. "To begin with, if we hire somebody to do a job, the only cost to Mikkelson Manufacturing is wages or salary, and any money we put into training counts as a credit against other taxes, since that helps give the Republic a better trained work force. Social security, health care, the rest of it, all of that comes out of other taxes—it's not funded by punishing employers for hiring people."

"And if you automate?"

"Then the costs really start piling up. First off, there's a tax on automation to pay the cost to the community of coping with an increase in unemployment. Then there's the cost of machinery, which is considerable, and then there's the resource and pollution taxes—if it comes out of the ground or goes into the air, the water, or the soil, it's taxed, and not lightly, either; the taxes cover the total cost of replacement or remediation—nobody gets to push those costs off onto the government or the general public.

"Then there's the price of energy. Electricity's not cheap here; the Lakeland Republic has only a modest supply of renewable energy, all things considered, and it hasn't got any fossil fuels to speak of, so the only kind of energy that's cheap and abundant is the kind that comes from muscles." She shook her head. "If we tried to automate our assembly line, given the additional costs, the other two firms would eat us alive. It's a competitive business."

"I suppose you can't just import manufactured products from abroad."

"No, the resource and pollution taxes apply no matter what the point of origin is. You may have noticed that there aren't a lot of cars on the streets here."

"I did notice that," I said.

"Fossil fuels here don't get the massive government subsidies here that they get almost everywhere else, and there are the resource and pollution taxes on top of that. Petroleum products are pretty much unaffordable here; we use biodiesel, and that's cheaper but it's still not cheap. You can have a car if you want one, but you'll pay plenty for the privilege, and you'll pay even more for the fuel if you want to drive it."

I nodded. It all made a weird sort of sense, especially when I thought back to some of the other things I'd heard earlier. "So nobody's technology gets a subsidy," I said.

"Exactly. Here in the Lakeland Republic, we're short on quite a few resources, but one thing there's no shortage of is people who are willing to put in an honest day's work for an honest day's wage. So we tax the things we want to discourage rather than the things we want to encourage, and use the resource we've got in abundance, rather than becoming dependent on things we don't have."

"And would have to import from abroad."

"Exactly. As I'm sure you're aware, Mr. Carr, that involves considerable risks."

I wondered if she had any idea just how acutely I was aware of those. I put a bland expression on my face and nodded. "So I've heard," I said.

By the time Michael Finch and I left, it was pushing eleven. "Where next?" I asked.

"We're about four blocks from one of the municipal power plants," the intern said. "I called ahead and arranged for a tour—that'll take about an hour, and should still give us plenty of time for lunch. Ms. Berger said you wanted a look at our electrical infrastructure."

I nodded. "Please. Electricity's an ongoing problem back home."

"It hasn't always been that easy here, either," Finch admitted. "Would you like to take a cab, or—"

"Four blocks? No, that's walking distance." From his expression, I gathered that wasn't always the case with visitors from outside, but he brightened and led the way east toward the Maumee River. North of us I could see bridges arching across the river, and the unfinished dome of the Capitol rising up white above the brown and gray rooftops. We passed a paper mill with big bales of industrial hemp sitting on the loading dock, and a couple of warehouses, and then we got to the power plant.

That was another big brick building like the streetcar factory, and I looked in vain for smokestacks anywhere on top of it. Finch led me in through the office entrance, a double door in an ornate archway, and introduced us to the receptionist inside. A few moments later we were shown into the office of the plant manager, a stocky brown-skinned man with gray hair who came over to shake my hand.

"Jim Singletary," he said. "Pleased to meet you. I don't imagine you have anything like our facility over in the Atlantic Republic, so if there's anything you want to know, ask, okay?"

I assured him I would, and he led us out of the office. The corridor outside went straight back into the heart of the plant; at its far end, we went through a door onto a glassed-in balcony overlooking an open room the size of a commercial aircraft hangar, where six big complex machines rose up from a concrete floor.

"Down on the floor, you couldn't hear a thing but the turbines," he said. "That's the business end of the plant—six combined cycle gas turbines driving our generators. We get almost sixty-two per cent efficiency in terms of electrical generation, and more than that when you factor in the heat recycling to the facility. You know how a combined cycle turbine works?"

"More or less—you put the gases from the turbine through a heat exchanger, and use that to boil water to run a steam turbine that runs off the leftover heat, don't you?"

"Exactly. What comes out of the other end of the steam turbines runs around 300 degrees Fahrenheit, which is more than enough to do something with. Here, a lot of it goes to heat the fermentation tanks."

I wondered what he meant by that, but it didn't take long to find out. Singletary led us along the balcony to another set of doors, and through them into another glassed-in balcony overlooking a double row of what looked a little like the top ends of a row of gargantuan pressure cookers.

"The fermentation tanks," he said. "Feedstock goes in, methane and slurry come out. At any given time, eighteen tanks are in operation and the other six are being loaded or unloaded. This way, please."

The balcony ended at another door, and a corridor led to the left. At its end was a balcony, this time open to the outside air. Below was the Maumee River, and a line of big blocky riverboats tied up along a quay. The one closest to us was having something unloaded from it through a big pipe.

"And there's the feedstock that makes the whole thing work," said Singletary. "I don't recommend going down to the quayside—it's pretty ripe."

"What's the feedstock?" I asked, even though I'd begun to guess the answer.

"Manure," he said. "Cow, horse, sheep, human—you name it. We buy manure from an eight county region to supplement what gets produced here in Toledo." I gave him a startled look, and he grinned. "Yep. If you've used the toilet since you got here, you've contributed to Toledo's electricity supply."

I laughed to cover my discomfort at the thought, and he grinned and went on. "We use a three-stage fermentation process to extract nearly eighty per cent of the carbon from the feedstock while the nitrogen, phosphorus, and potassium stay

62

in the sludge. By the time it's finished in the tanks it's sterile enough you could rub it on an open wound. After the steam heats the fermentation tanks it goes to dry the sludge, and ship it back to farmers as fertilizer. Meanwhile we get enough electricity out of it to power Toledo and environs—of course we use a lot less electricity per capita than most cities in North America, mostly just lights and streetcars, so that keeps our demand for feedstock in check. One way or another, everyone's happy."

We went back to his office. On the way, I thought about the electricity problems we had back home: the constant struggle to get enough natural gas for the power plants we had, the snake oil salesmen from the nuclear industry trying to push us into buying reactors that would never pay for themselves, and the rest of it. Nobody anywhere I knew of had looked into methane from manure, and I suddenly wondered why.

Once we were back in Singletary's office, I got a rundown on the economics of the plant. "How close do you get to breaking even between feedstock costs and fertilizer sales?" I asked.

"Not as close as I'd like," Singletary admitted. "Electricity's not cheap here. Ever since the Maumee and Ohio canal got reopened, the farmers south of us can sell their feedstock to Dayton or Springfield just as easily as to us—Lima's tier three so it's not in the market. North of us we've got Detroit and Ann Arbor to bid against; east there's Cleveland, and the canal system west of the Maumee is still being rebuilt, so that's out of the picture at the moment."

"You depend on canals that much?"

"We can't afford not to. Back in the early days, we used to ship in some feedstock by rail, but the costs are just too high. For any kind of bulk cargo, if you don't have to worry about speed, canal shipping's really the way to go."

I asked a few more questions, and then we all shook hands and Finch and I headed out into the crisp fall air. "Interested in lunch?" he asked me; we discussed restaurants while waiting for the streetcar, and then rode it north into downtown. A bar and grill around the corner from the streetcar stop where we got off served up a very passable BLT sandwich, and then we wove our way through crowded sidewalks to the big stone building that housed the Toledo Stock Market.

"Vinny Patzek," said the young man with black slicked-back hair who greeted us in a crowded office not far from the trading floor. "Pleased to meet you." He had his jacket off and his sleeves rolled up, and looked like he spent a lot of his time running flat out from one corner of the building to another. "Any chance you know something about stock markets, Mr. Carr?"

"Actually, yes—I did two years on the NYSE floor before it moved to Albany," I said.

His face lit up. "Sweet. Okay, this is gonna be a lot less confusing to you than it is to most people we see here from outside. It's not quite the same as what you're used to, but the differences are mostly the technology, not the underlying setup. Come on."

"I'll leave you with Mr. Patzek for now," Finch told me. "I promised Ms. Berger I'd check in after lunch and see how things are going at the Capitol."

"Fair enough," I said, and he left through one door while Patzek herded me out through another, down a corridor, and onto the trading floor of the stock exchange.

All things considered, it wasn't much quieter than the turbine room of the power plant, but since I'd worked on a trading floor the noise and bustle actually meant something to me. There was a reader board, a big one, covering most of the far wall; it was mechanical, not digital, and flipped black or eye-burning yellow in little rectangular patches to spell out the latest prices. There were trading posts scattered across the floor, where specialists handled the buying and selling of shares. There were floor traders and floor brokers, enough of them to make the floor look crowded, and the featureless roar made up of hundreds of voices shouting bids and offers.

"You probably still use computers in New York, right?" Patzek said in something that wasn't quite a yell. "Here it's all old-fashioned open outcry, with the same kind of hand signals you'd see in the Chi-town commodity pits. Lemme show you. All we need is an order."

"I'll take one share of Mikkelson Manufacturing," I said.

He grinned. "You're on."

"You get a lot of small orders like that?"

"All the time. You get little old ladies, working guys, you name it, who save up the cash to buy a share or two once a month, that sort of thing, and come on down here to buy it in person." He looked up at the reader board. "Mikkelson's MIK—see it? Seventy-two even a share. Let's go."

We plunged into the crowd, and I managed to follow Patzek through the middle of it to one of the trading posts, where the traders and brokers looked even busier than they were elsewhere on the floor. Right in the middle of it, the yelling was loud enough I couldn't make out a single word, just Patzek gesturing with a closed hand and then a raised index finger and shouting something that didn't sound much like Mikkelson Industries. It only took about a minute, though, for the market to do what markets are supposed to do, and Patzek came out of the scrum with a big grin and an order written up on a pad of paper he'd extracted from one of his vest pockets.

"We're good," he said. "Seventy-two and a quarter—it's pretty lively. I'd be surprised if it doesn't hit seventy-four by closing. Let's settle up back at the office; they'll be sending the certificate there."

We went back the way we'd came. The office, busy as it was, seemed unnervingly quiet after the roar of the trading floor. "So that's how it's done," said Patzek. "A little different, I bet."

"Not as much as it used to be," I said. "When I first got on the NYSE floor, there were only a couple of dozen floor traders left, and it was as quiet as a library most days. With the satellite situation and some of the other problems lately, a lot of brokerages are putting trades back on the floor again. But of course it's still done with handheld computers, not the sort of thing you've got in there."

Patzek nodded. "The way I heard it, there were handhelds on the floor in the early days after Partition, but the first time the outside tried regime change here they hacked the system and crashed it, and the exchange just let it drop. Computers are just too easy to hack. Floor traders? Not so much."

"I bet," I said, laughing.

I wrote a check for the price of the share, then, and filled out a couple of forms covering my side of the transaction. When I got to the form for dividend payouts, though, I looked up at Patzek. "I'll have to make some arrangements back home before I can finish this." He nodded, and I went on. "What kind of dividends does Mikkelson pay these days?"

"Five, maybe six percent a year. Not bad, especially since it's tax free."

That startled me. "Mikkelson, or dividends in general?"

"Dividends in general. They count as earned income, like wages, salaries, royalties, that sort of thing. Most other investments, you're gonna pay tax, and if you sell that share and make a profit on it, that's speculative income and you're gonna get whacked."

"So earned income is tax free, but investment income isn't."

"Yeah—again, except for dividends."

I remembered what Elaine Chu had said about taxes back at the Mikkelson plant. "So you tax what you want to discourage, not what you want to encourage."

"Heck if I know," said Patzek. "You gotta ask the politicians about that."

A moment later a messenger came in through the door we'd used, plopped a manila folder on one of the desks, and ducked back out. Half a dozen people converged on the folder; Patzek waited his turn, and came back with a sheet of stiff paper printed in ornate script.

"Here you go," he said. "One share of Mikkelson Manufacturing. Congratulations—you're now a limited partner with Janice Mikkelson."

I gave him a startled look, then glanced at the certificate. I'd read about printed stock certificates, but never actually handled one, so it took me a bit to sort through the fancy printing and read the line that mattered. Sure enough, it read MIKKELSON MANUFACTURING LLP.

"Limited liability partnership," I guessed. "So it's not a corporation?"

"Nah, it's a little different here. Back in the day—and we're talking before the First Civil War, forget about the Second—corporations had to be chartered by the legislature, for some fixed number of years, and only for some kind of public benefit, not just because somebody wanted to make a few bucks. After all the problems the old United States had with corporations claiming to be people and demanding political rights nobody in their right mind would give them, we up and drew a line under that, and went back to the original laws. Here, if a business wants to sell stock, it becomes a limited liability partnership. The limited partners are only on the hook to the value of their stock holdings, but the managing partner or partners—their butts are on the line. If Mikkelson Manufacturing ever goes bust, Janice Mikkelson can kiss her mansion goodbye, and if the company breaks the law, she's the one who goes to jail."

I took that in. "Does that actually happen?"

"Not so much any more. Back when I was a kid, there were some really juicy cases, and yeah, some rich people lost their shirts and landed behind bars. These days, you're in business, you watch the laws as close as you watch the bottom line—there's too many politicians who'd be happy to buy their constituents a new streetcar line with the proceeds from a court case."

That didn't sound much like the politics I was used to back home. I was still processing it when the other door came open and Michael Finch came in. "Mr. Carr," he said, "I just talked to Ms. Berger. They got everything settled around lunchtime. If you're ready, the President will be happy to see you this afternoon."

I glanced at Patzek who grinned and made a scooting motion with one hand. We shook hands and said the usual, and I followed Finch out the door.

He flagged down a cab as soon as we got out onto the sidewalk, and within a minute or two we were rolling through downtown at however many miles an hour a horse makes at a steady trot. Before too many more minutes had gone by, we were out from among the big downtown buildings, and the unfinished dome of the Capitol appeared on the skyline. Finch was in high spirits, talking about the compromise Meeker had brokered with the Restos, but I was too keyed up to pay much attention. A day and a half in the Lakeland Republic had answered a few of my questions and raised a good many more that I hadn't expected to ask at all, and the meeting ahead would probably settle whether I'd be able to get the answers that mattered.

The cab finally rolled to a halt, and the cabbie climbed down from his perch up front and opened the door for us. I'd been so deep in my own thoughts for the last few blocks that I hadn't noticed where we'd ended up, and I was startled to see the main entrance to the Capitol in front of me. I turned to Finch. "Here, rather than the President's mansion?"

The intern gave me a blank look. "You mean like the old White House? We don't have one of those. President Meeker has a house in town, just like any other politician, and his office is here in the Capitol." I must have looked startled, because he went on earnestly: "We dumped the whole imperial-executive thing after Partition. I'm surprised so many of the other republics kept it, after everything that happened."

I nodded noncommittally as we walked up to the main entrance, climbed the stair, and went in. There were a couple of uniformed guards inside the outer doors, the first I'd seen anywhere in the Lakeland Republic, but they simply nodded a greeting to the two of us as we walked by.

We pushed open the inner doors and went into the rotunda. There was a temporary ceiling about forty feet overhead, and someone had taken the trouble to paint on it a trompe l'oeil view of the way the dome would look from beneath. In the middle of the floor was a block of marble maybe three feet on a side; I could barely see it because a dozen or so people were standing around it. One of them, a stout and freckled blonde woman in a pale blue gingham dress, was saying something in a loud clear voice as we came through the doors:

"... do solemnly swear that, should I be elected to any official position, I will faithfully execute the laws of the Lakeland Republic regardless of my personal beliefs, and should I be unable to do so in good conscience, I will immediately resign my office, so help me my Lord and Savior Jesus." Three sudden blue-white flashes told of photos being taken, a little patter of applause echoed off the temporary ceiling, and then some of the people present got to work signing papers on the marble cube.

Finch led me around the group to a door on the far side of the rotunda. "What was that about?" I asked him with a motion of my head toward the group around the cube.

"A candidate," he explained as we went through the doors. "Probably running for some town or county office. A lot of them like to do the ceremony here at the Capitol and get the pictures in their local papers. You can't run for any elected position here unless you take that oath first—well, with or without the Jesus bit, or whatever else you prefer in place of it. There was a lot of trouble before the Second Civil War with people in government positions claiming that their personal beliefs trumped the duties of their office—"

"I've read about it."

"So that went into our constitution. If you break the oath, you get kicked out of the office and do jail time for perjury."

I took that in as we went down a corridor. On the far end was what looked like an ordinary front office with a young man perched behind a desk. "Hi, Gabe," Finch said.

"Hi, Mike. This is Mr. Carr?"

"Yes. Mr. Carr, this is Gabriel Menendez, the President's assistant secretary."

We shook hands, and Menendez picked up a phone on his desk and asked, "Cheryl, is the boss free? Mr. Carr's here." A pause, then: "Yes. I'll send him right in." He put down the phone and waved us to the door at the far end of the room. "He'll see you now."

We shed coats and hats at the coatrack on one side of the office, and went through the door. On the other side was another corridor, and beyond that was a circular room with doors opening off it in various directions. Off to the left an ornate spiral stair swept up and down to whatever was on the floors above and below. To the right was another desk; the woman sitting at it nodded greetings to us and gestured to the central door. I followed Finch as he walked to the door, opened it, and said, "Mr. President? Mr. Carr."

Isaiah Meeker, President of the Lakeland Republic, was standing at the far side of the room, looking out the window over the Toledo streetscape below. He turned and came toward us as soon as Finch spoke. He looked older than the pictures I'd seen, the close-trimmed hair and iconic short beard almost white against the dark brown of his face. "Mr. Carr," he said as we shook hands. "Pleased to meet you. I hope you haven't been completely at loose ends this last day or so." He gestured toward the side of the room. "Please have a seat."

It wasn't until I turned the direction he'd indicated that I realized there were more than the three of us in the room. A circle of chairs surrounded a low table there. Melanie Berger and Fred Vanich, whom I'd met in the train station, were already seated there, and so were two other people I didn't know. "Stuart Macallan from the State Department," Meeker said, making introductions. "Jaya Patel, from Commerce. Of course you've already met Melanie and Fred."

Hands got shaken and I took a seat. Macallan was the assistant secretary of state for North American affairs, I knew, and Patel had an equivalent position on the trade end of things. "I apologize for the delay," Meeker went on. "I imagine you know how it goes, though."

"Of course."

"And you seem to have put the time to good use—at least for our garment industry."

That got a general chuckle, which I joined. "When in Rome," I said. "I take it that's not one of the things visitors usually do, though; Mr. Finch here looked right past me this morning."

Finch turned pink. "It really does vary," Patel said. "Some of the diplomats and business executives we've worked with have taken to buying all their clothes here—we've even fielded inquiries about exporting garments for sale abroad. Still, most of our visitors seem to prefer their bioplastic." Her fractional shrug showed, politely but eloquently, what she thought of that.

"To each their own," said the President. "But you've had the chance to see a little of Toledo, and learn a few details of the ways we do things here. I'd be interested to know your first reactions."

I considered that, decided that a certain degree of frankness wasn't out of place. "In some ways, impressed," I said, "and in some ways disquieted. You certainly seem to have come through the embargo years in better shape than I expected—though I'm curious about how things will go now that the borders are open."

"That's been a matter of some concern here as well," Meeker allowed. "That said, so far things seem to be going smoothly."

Macallan paused just long enough to make sure his boss wasn't going to say more, and then cleared his throat and spoke. "One of the things we hope might come out of your visit is a better relationship with the Atlantic Republic. I'm

71

sure you know how fraught things were with Barfield and the Dem-Reps generally. If Ms. Montrose is willing to see things ratchet down to a more normal level, we're ready to meet her halfway—potentially more than halfway."

"That was quite an upset she pulled off in the election," Meeker observed. "I hope you'll pass on my personal congratulations."

"I'll gladly do that," I said to the President, and then to Macallan: "It's certainly possible. I don't happen to know her thoughts on that, but a lot of people on our side of the border are interested in seeing things change, and she's got a stronger mandate than any president we've had since Partition. Still—" I shrugged. "We'll have to see what happens after the inauguration."

"Of course," Macallan said.

"One thing we'd be particularly interested in seeing," said Patel, "is a widening of the opportunities for trade. Obviously that's going to be delicate—it's a core policy of ours that the Republic has to be able to meet all its essential needs from within its own borders, and I know that stance isn't exactly popular in global-trade circles. We're not interested in global trade, but there are things your country produces that we'd like to be able to buy, and things we produce that you might like to buy in exchange."

"Again," I said, "we'll have to see what happens—but I don't know of any reason why that wouldn't be a possibility."

She nodded, and a brief silence passed. Vanich's featureless voice broke it. "Mr. Carr," he said, "you mentioned that you found some of the ways we do things here disquieting. I think we'd all be interested in hearing more about that, if you're willing."

Startled, I glanced across the table at him, but his face was as impenetrable as it had been the first time I'd seen him. I looked at the President, who seemed amused, and then nodded. "If you like," I said. "At first it was mostly the—" I floundered for a term. "—deliberately retro, I suppose, quality of so much

72

of what I've seen: the clothing, the technology, the architecture, all of it. I have to assume that that's an intentional choice, connected to whatever's inspired your Resto parties in politics."

Meeker nodded. "Very much so."

"But that's not actually the thing I find most disquieting. What has me scratching my head is that your republic seems to have gone out of its way to ignore every single scrap of advice you must have gotten from the World Bank, the International Monetary Fund, the other global financial institutions—in fact, from the entire economics profession—and despite that, you've apparently thrived."

Meeker's face broke into a broad smile. "Excellent," he said. "Excellent. I'll offer just one correction: we haven't succeeded as well as we have despite ignoring the economic advice of the World Bank and so forth. We've done so precisely *because* we've ignored their advice."

I gave him a long wary look, but his smile didn't waver.

"Mr. Carr," Melanie Berger said then, "Since the end of the embargo we've been approached four times by the World Bank and the IMF. I've been involved in the discussions that followed. Each time, their economists have made long speeches about how the way we do things is hopelessly inefficient, and how we've got to follow their advice and become more efficient. Each time, I've asked them to answer a simple question: 'more efficient for what output in terms of what input?' Not one of them has ever been able, or willing, to give me a straight answer."

"I had a lecture on that subject yesterday from a bank officer," I told her.

Her eyebrows went up, and then she smiled. "Not surprising. It's something most people here know about, if they know anything at all about money."

I nodded, taking that in. "So what you're suggesting," I said, as much to Meeker as to her, "is that the rest of the world doesn't have a clue about economics."

"Not quite," said the President. "It's just that our history has forced us to look at things in a somewhat different light, and prioritize different things."

It was a graceful answer, and I nodded. "The question that comes to mind at this point," he went on, "is whether there's anything else you'd like to see, now that you know a little more about our republic."

"As it happens, yes," I said. "There is."

He motioned me to go on.

"When I drew up the list we sent to your people right after the election, I didn't know about the tier system, and I've got some serious questions about what things are like at the bottom rung of that ladder. I've read a little bit about the system, but I'm frankly skeptical that anybody in this day and age would voluntarily choose to live in the conditions of 1830."

"That's actually a common misconception," Jaya Patel said, with the same you-don't-get-it smile I'd seen more than once since my arrival. "The only thing the tier system determines is what infrastructure and services gets paid for out of tax revenues."

"I saw a fair number of horsedrawn wagons on the train ride here," I pointed out. "That's not a matter of infrastructure."

"Actually, it is," she said. "Without a road system built to stand up to auto traffic, cars and trucks aren't as efficient as wagons—" Her smile suddenly broadened. "—in terms of the total cost of haulage per ton per mile. That doesn't keep people in tier one counties from having whatever personal technologies they want to have, and are willing and able to pay for."

"Got it," I said. "I'd still like to see how it works out in practice."

"That's easy enough," the President said. "Anything else?"

"Yes," I said, "though I know this may be further than you're willing to go. I'd like to see something of your military."

The room got very quiet. "I'd be interested," Meeker said, "in knowing why."

74

I nodded. "It seems to me that whatever you've achieved by this retro policy of yours comes at the cost of some frightful vulnerabilities. Ms. Berger told me a little about the war with the Confederacy and Brazil, and of course I knew a certain amount about that in advance. Obviously you won that round—but we both know that the Confederacy wasn't in the best of shape in '49, and I really wonder about your ability to stand up to a modern high-tech military."

"Like the Atlantic Republic's?" Meeker asked, with a raised eyebrow.

I responded with a derisive snort. "With all due respect, I'm sure you know better than that. I'm thinking about what would happen if we ended up with a war zone or a failed state on our western borders."

"Fair enough," he said after a moment, "and I think we can satisfy you about that."

"I have a suggestion," Berger said to the President. "Defiance County is first tier."

He glanced at her. "You're thinking Hicksville?"

"Yes."

"We'll have to find someone."

"Tom Pappas comes to mind," she said.

The President's face took on a slightly glazed expression, and then he laughed. "Yes, Tom will do. Thank you, Melanie." He turned to me. "Have you made any plans for tomorrow?"

"Not yet."

"Good. The day after tomorrow, there's a—military exercise, I think you would call it—in a first tier county a few hours from here by train. If you're willing, I can have my staff arrange for you to go there tomorrow, have a look around, stay the night, see how our military does things the next day, do some more looking around, and then come back. Is that workable?"

"I'd welcome that," I told him, wondering what I'd just gotten myself into.

CHAPTER 5

The phone rang at eight a.m. sharp the next morning. I was in the bathroom, trying to get my electric shaver to give me a shave half as good as the one I got at the barbershop, and failing. I turned the thing off, put it down, and got to the phone on the third ring. "Hello?"

"Mr. Carr? Melanie Berger. We've got everything lined up for your trip today. Can you be at the train station by nine o'clock?"

"Sure thing," I said.

"Good. Your tickets will be waiting for you, and Colonel Tom Pappas will meet you there. You can't miss him; look for a wheelchair and a handlebar mustache."

The wheelchair didn't sound too promising—I had no idea what kind of accommodations the Lakeland Republic's lower tiers made for people with disabilities—but I figured Meeker's people knew what they were doing. "I'll do that."

"You'll be back Saturday evening," Berger said then. "The president would like to see you again Monday afternoon, if you're free."

"I'll put it on the schedule," I assured her; we said the usual, and I hung up.

It took me only a few minutes to pack for the trip, and then it was out the door, down the stairs, and through the lobby to the street to wave down a taxi. As I got out onto the sidewalk, a kid with a bag of rolled newspapers hanging from one shoulder turned toward me expectantly and said, "Morning *Blade*? 'Nother satellite got hit."

That sounded worth the price of a paper; I handed over a bill and a coin, got the paper in return, thanked the kid, and went to the street's edge. A couple of minutes later I was sitting in a two-wheel cab headed for the train station, listening to the clip-clop of the horse's hooves ahead and reading the top story on the newspaper's front page.

The kid who'd sold me the paper hadn't been exaggerating. A chunk of the *Progresso IV* satellite that got taken out by space junk a week before had plowed into a big Russian telecom satellite during the night, spraying fragments at twenty-one thousand miles an hour across any number of midrange orbits. Nothing else had been hit yet, but the odds of a full-blown Kessler syndrome had just gone up by a factor I didn't want to think about.

Aside from the fact itself, only one thing caught my attention in the article: a comment from a professor of astronomy at the University of Toledo, mentioning that her department was calculating the orbits of as many fragments as they'd been able to track. I didn't know a lot about astronomy, but I'd learned just enough that the thought of trying to work out an orbit using pen and paper made my head hurt. I wondered if they'd scraped together the money to buy a bootleg computer from a Chicago smuggling ring or something like that.

I'd finished the first section of the paper when the taxi pulled up to the sidewalk in front of the train station. I paid the cabbie, stuffed the newspaper into my coat pocket, and headed inside. The big clock above the ticket counters said eight-thirty; there wasn't much of a line, so by eight-forty I had my round trip ticket in an inner pocket and was heading through the doors marked Platform Four.

I'd just about gotten my bearings when I spotted a burly man in a wheelchair halfway down the platform. He turned around and saw me a moment later, made a little casual half-salute with one hand, and wheeled over to meet me. Berger hadn't been kidding about the handlebar mustache; it was big, black, and curled at the tips. That and bushy eyebrows made up for the lack of a single visible hair anywhere else on his head. He was wearing the first hip-length jacket I'd seen anywhere in the Lakeland Republic, over an olive-drab military uniform.

"Peter Carr?" he said. "I'm Tom Pappas. Call me Tom; everyone else does."

"Pleased to meet you," I said, shaking his hand. The guy had hands the size of hams and a grip that would put a gorilla to shame.

"Melanie tells me you rattled the boss good and proper yesterday," he said with a chuckle. "You probably know we've been getting a lot of semi-official visitors from outside governments since the borders opened. Of course they all want to know about our military. Care to guess how many of them asked about that right up front, to the President's face?"

"I can't be the only one," I protested.

"Not quite. Ever met T. Crawford Batchley?"

I burst out laughing. "Yes, I've met him. Don't tell me he's the only other."

"Got it in one. Of course he blustered about it in the grand Texan style, and more or less implied that every single soldier in the army of the Republic of Texas was drooling over the prospect of invading us."

I shook my head, still laughing. "I bet he did. I was on a trade mission to Austin a while back, and we got a typical Batchley lecture to the effect that everyone in Philadelphia was going to starve to death if they didn't get shipments of Texas beef that week."

"Sounds about right."

The train came up to the platform just then, and the roar of the locomotive erased any possibility of further conversation for the moment. The conductor took our tickets and waved us toward one of the cars. I wondered how Pappas was going to climb the foot or so from the platform to the door, but about the time I'd finished formulating the thought, one of the car attendants popped out, grabbed a handle I hadn't noticed under the step, and slid out a steel ramp. Pappas rolled up into the car, the attendant pushed the ramp back into its place, they said a few words to each other, and then Pappas wheeled his way over to a place at the back of the car, flipped one of the two seats up, and got a couple of tiedown straps fastened onto his chair. By the time I'd followed him the straps looked snug and so did he.

I took the seat next to him. "Do they have this sort of thing in all the trains here?"

"Wheelchair spots? You bet. We had a lot of disabled vets after the Second Civil War, of course, and got a bunch more in '49. That's how I ended up in this thing—got stupid during the siege of Paducah, and took some shrapnel down low in my back."

The train filled up around us. "I'm sorry to hear that," I said.

"Oh, it doesn't slow me down that much. The only complaint I've got is that I'm stuck in a desk job in Toledo now, instead of out there in the field." He shook his head. "How much did they tell you about our military?"

"Here, or back home?"

"Either one."

"Here, nothing. Back home—" I considered the briefings I'd been given, edited out the classified parts. "They're pretty much baffled. We know you've got universal military service on the Swiss model, but no modern military tech at all—plenty of light infantry and field artillery, but no armor, no drones, no air force worth mentioning, and what amounts to a glorified coast guard on the Great Lakes, half of it in sailing ships."

80

He nodded as the train lurched into motion. "That's about right. And you're wondering how we can get away with that."

"It's a concern," I said. "As I told President Meeker, we don't want a failed state or a war zone on our western border."

Pappas laughed, as though I'd made a joke. "I bet. What if I told you that we're less likely to end up that way than any other country on this continent?"

I gave him a wry look. "You'd have to to some very fast talking to convince me of that. With that kind of armament, I don't see how you could expect to defeat a country with modern military technology."

"We don't have to defeat them," he said at once. "All we have to do is bankrupt them."

I stared at him.

"War's not cheap," he went on. "Modern high-tech warfare, square and cube that. Half the reason the old United States collapsed was the amount of money it poured into trying to stay ahead of everybody else's military technology. I'm not going to ask you how much the Atlantic Republic has to pay each year for drones, robot tanks, helicopter gunships, cruise missiles, and the information systems you need to run all of it; you know as well as I do that it's a big chunk of the national budget, and I'd be willing to make a bet that you have to skimp on the rest of your military budget to make up for it—meaning that your ordinary grunts don't have anything like the training or the morale they ought to have."

I didn't answer. Outside the window, commercial buildings gave way to a residential neighborhood dotted with gardens and parks.

"So you've got a whole lot of money sunk in military hardware. Let's say you guys decided to invade us."

"Not going to happen," I told him.

"Just for example." He waved the objection away with one massive hand. "You send in your drones and robot tanks and helicopter gunships, seize Toledo and wherever else your general staff thinks is strategic enough to merit it, and dump a bunch of infantry to hold onto those places. You've won, right? Except that that's when the fun begins.

"All that light infantry and field artillery you mentioned—it's still there, distributed all over the country, and it's not dependent on any kind of central command. It's got first-rate training, and most of the training is oriented to one thing and one thing only: insurgent operations. So thirty minutes after your drones cross the border, you're dealing with a full-on, heavily armed insurgency with prepared positions and more firepower than you want to think about, in every single county of the Lakeland Republic. However long you want to hold on, we can hold on longer, and every day of it costs you a lot more than it costs us. Oh, and a lot of the training our troops get focuses on taking out your high-tech assets with inexpensive munitions. So it's the same kind of black hole the old United States kept getting itself into—no way to win, and the bills just keep piling up until you go home."

"I'm a little surprised you're telling me all this," I said after a moment.

"Don't be. We want people outside to know exactly what they're facing if they invade."

"Okay," I said. "But what if it's China or Brazil or somebody, and they decide to use their nuclear arsenal?"

"They're not that stupid," Pappas replied at once. "The reason there are only eight nuclear powers in the world these days, and not a hundred and eight, is that the countries that have nukes don't use them on the countries that don't. That's why Brazil didn't help the Confederacy out with a couple of mushroom clouds in the war in '49. You know as well as I do that if they'd done that, every nation in the Western Hemisphere would have scraped together a nuclear deterrent of their own just as soon as they could—and that's the last thing Brazil needs. Or anyone else, for that matter." He gestured out the window. "Check that out."

We were still in the residential part of Toledo, the same patchwork of houses, gardens, and little business districts I'd seen on the way from Pittsburgh, but something else cut across the landscape: a canal. It didn't have water in it yet, and so I could see that the sides were lined with big slabs of concrete that must have been salvaged from a prewar freeway.

"We're putting those in everywhere that the landscape permits," Pappas said. "Partly that's economic—canals are cheaper to run than any other transport—but it's also military. You want to try to take a robot tank across one of those, be my guest. There's a lot of that sort of thing. Every county has its own military organization with its own budget, and builds bunkers, prepared positions, tank traps, you name it. Since we're not interested in invading anybody else, we can put a lot of resources into that."

I decided to take a risk. "If you're not interested in invading anybody else, why did your people put so much work into getting topo maps of our territory before the border opened?"

The bushy eyebrows went up. "You know about that."

I nodded. "We got lucky."

"Gotcha," Pappas said. "Did you hear much about the other side of our dust-up with the Confederacy in '49?" I motioned for him to go on, and he grinned. "We sent teams across the border into their territory to mess with their infrastructure. Bridges, power lines, levees, you name it—anything that would raise the price tag. We even got a couple of teams into Brazil to do the same thing; we would have done more of that if the war hadn't ended when it did."

"So it's all about economics," I said.

"Of course. You know how Clausewitz said that war's a continuation of politics by other means? He got that half right. It's also a continuation of economics—and the last guy standing is the one who can afford to keep fighting longest."

I nodded. Outside the window, the first of the farms and fields were coming into view, brown with stubble or green with cover crops for overwintering.

"All across this country," Pappas said then, "we've got young men and women doing their two year stints in the army, and showing up for two weeks a year afterwards as long as they can still shoulder a gun—and there's a good reason for that. This country got the short end of the stick for decades back before the Second Civil War, then got the crap pounded out of it during the fighting, and then—well, I could go on. We found out the hard way what happens when you let some jerk in a fancy white house a thousand miles away decide for you how you're going to run your life. That's why President Meeker's not much more than a referee to ride herd on the parties in the legislature; that's why each county makes so many of its own decisions by vote—and it's why all the people you're going to see tomorrow are putting a nice fall weekend into shooting at drones."

"Is that what's on the schedule for tomorrow?"

The bushy eyebrows went up again. "Melanie didn't tell you?" Suddenly he chuckled, rubbed his big hands together. "Oh man. You're going to get an education."

We changed trains in Defiance. The station wasn't much more than a raised platform running along each side of the tracks, with a shelter of cast iron and glass over each platform to keep off any rain that might happen along. The day was shaping up clear and cool; the town looked like old county seats I'd seen in parts of upstate New York that hadn't been flattened during the endgame of the Second Civil War, a patchwork of clapboard and brick with the county courthouse rising above the nearby roofs. I could see only two obvious differences—first, that the only vehicles on the streets were pulled by horses, and second, that all the houses looked lived in and all the businesses I could see seemed to be open.

The train west to Hicksville came after we'd waited about fifteen minutes. Colonel Pappas and I weren't the only people waiting for it, either. Something close to a hundred people got off the train from Toledo with us, some in olive drab Lakeland Army uniforms, some in civilian clothing, all of them with luggage and most with long flat cases that I guessed held guns. Once Pappas rolled up the ramp onto one of the cars and I followed him, I found that the train was already more than half full, and it was the same mix, some soldiers, some civilians, plenty of firepower.

I sat down next to Pappas, who gestured expansively at the train. "Not what you'd usually see going to Hicksville," he said. "Every other time of the year this is a twice a day milk run that hits every farm town between Bowling Green and Warsaw. This weekend it's six or eight runs this size every day."

The train jolted into motion, and I watched Defiance slide past: brick commercial buildings, clapboard-covered houses, and then an open-air baseball field with bleachers around it and a proud sign, HOME OF THE DEFIANCE SPARTANS—NORTHEAST LEAGUE CHAMPIONS '45, '56, '59. After maybe a mile, we were rolling through farmland dotted with houses and barns. Some of the houses had wind turbines above them and solar water heaters on the roofs, while others didn't; tall antennas I guessed were meant to catch radio signals rose above most of them, but not all. The dirt roads looked well tended and the bridges were in good repair. I shook my head, trying to make sense of it.

"Checking out tier one?" Pappas asked me.

I glanced at him. "Pretty much. I wasn't expecting to see the wind and solar gear."

"You're thinking it's tier one, how come they have tech that wasn't around in 1830, right?" When I nodded, he laughed. "Outsiders always get hung up on that. Tier level just says what infrastructure gets paid for by county taxes. You can get whatever tech you want if it's your own money."

"What about a veepad?"

"Sure, as long as you don't expect somebody else to pay for a metanet to make it work."

I nodded again, conceding the point. "I get the sense that a lot of people here wouldn't buy modern technology even if they could."

85

"True enough. Some of that's religious—we've got a lot of Amish and Mennonites here, and there're also some newer sects along the same lines, Keelyites, New Shakers, that sort of thing. Some of it's political—most of the people in the full-on Resto parties are just as much into low-tech in their own lives as they are in their politics. They learned that lesson from the environmentalists before the war—you know about those?"

It was my turn to laugh. "Yeah. I had some of them in my family when I was a kid. 'I want to save the Earth, but not enough to stop driving my SUV.'"

"Bingo—and you know how much good that did. The Restos aren't into that sort of hypocrisy, so a lot of them end up in low-tier counties and stick to simple tech."

"What do you think of that?"

"Me? I'm a city kid. I like nightlife, public transit—" He slapped one of the tires of his wheelchair. "—smooth sidewalks. Tier one's fun to visit but I'd rather live tier four or five."

The train rattled through farmland for an hour or so, stopping once at a little place named Sherwood, before we reached Hicksville. The station there was even more rudimentary than the one at Defiance, just a raised platform and a long single-story building with a peaked roof alongside the track, but Pappas had no trouble maneuvering his wheelchair on the platform once we got off the train. "We'll wait here," he told me. "Once the crowd clears someone'll meet us."

He was right, of course. After a couple of minutes, as the train rolled westwards out of the station and the crowd started to thin, a young man in army uniform with corporal's stripes on his sleeves wove his way toward us and saluted Pappas. "Colonel, sir," he said, "good to see you." To me: "You're Mr. Carr, right? Pleased to meet you. The jeep's this way."

He wasn't kidding. Sitting on the street next to the station, incongruous amid a press of horsedrawn carts and wagons, was what looked like a jeep straight out of a World War Two history vid. Pappas saw the expression on my face, and laughed.

"The army's got a lot of those," he told me. "It's not actually a Willys Jeep, but we borrowed the best parts of the design: its good, cheap, sturdy, and it handles unpaved roads like nobody's business."

"What fuel does it use?" I asked.

"Oh, it's diesel. Everything we use in the army runs on vegetable oil if it doesn't eat corned beef or hay."

Pappas hauled himself into the jeep's front passenger seat while I tried to parse that. The corporal helped him get his wheelchair folded and stowed, then waved me to a seat in back and went to the driver's seat. I got in next to the wheelchair, found a place for my suitcase, and got a firm grip on the grab bar as the engine roared to life.

Six blocks later we were on the edge of Hicksville. "Tomorrow's action is twelve miles north of town," Pappas told me. "We'll be staying right near there—all the farmhouses around here rent out rooms to visitors. Melanie told me you want to see how people live in tier one; you'll get an eyeful."

It took us half an hour to get to the farm Pappas had in mind, driving on what pretty clearly wasn't the main road—now and then I could see dust rising off to the east, and a couple of times spotted what had to be a line of wagons and carts carrying people and luggage toward whatever was going to happen the next day. I speculated about why I wasn't part of that line—Pappas' rank, maybe? Or a courtesy toward a guest from outside who wasn't used to the pace of horsedrawn travel? That latter irked me a bit, even though I was grateful for the quick trip.

Finally the jeep swerved off the road, rattled along a rough driveway maybe a half mile long, and clattered to a stop in front of a big clapboard-sided building three stories tall. Two others and a huge barn stood nearby, and fields, pastures, and gardens spread out in all directions around them.

"Welcome to Harmony Gathering," Pappas said, turning half around in his seat. "I mentioned the New Shakers earlier, remember? You're about to meet some of 'em."

By the time he finished speaking the front door of the building swung open and a big gray-bearded man in overalls and a plain blue short-sleeved shirt came out. "Good day, Tom," he called out. "And—Mr. Carr, I believe."

I got out of the jeep. "Peter Carr," I said, shaking his hand.

"I'm Brother Orren. Be welcome to our Gathering." He turned to the corporal. "Joe, do you need help with any of that?"

"Nah, I've got it." The corporal came around, got the wheelchair unfolded, and Pappas slid into it. I got my suitcase; the gray-bearded man turned back to the door and nodded once, and a boy of ten or so dressed the same way he was came out at a trot, took the suitcase from me, gave me a big smile, and vanished back into the building with it.

"Things hopping yet, Orren?" Pappas asked him.

"Very much so. You have plenty of company." He motioned toward the door. "Shall we?"

Inside the walls were bare and white, the furniture plain and sturdy, the air thick with the smell of baking bread. "Tom tells me that you're from the Atlantic Republic," the bearded man said to me. "I don't believe our church has put down roots there yet. If you have questions—why, ask me, or anyone."

"Thanks," I said. "I'll take you up on that once I figure out what to ask."

He beamed. "I'll welcome that. Of course you'll want to get the dust off first, and lunch will be ready shortly." He turned and called out: "Sister Susannah? Could you show our guests to their rooms?"

An old woman with improbably green eyes, dressed in a plain blue dress, came into the room from a corridor I hadn't noticed. "Of course. Come with me, please."

"Don't worry about me, Sue," Pappas said. "I know the way."

That got a quiet laugh and a nod. Pappas rolled away down a different corridor, and the old woman led me up a nearby stair and down a long hall lined with doors. "This is yours," she said, opening one. "Give me just a moment." She smiled, went on further down the hall.

The room was a simple cubicle with a bed on one side, a dresser and desk on the other, and a window on the far end. The bare white walls and the plain sturdy furniture were scrupulously clean, and the bed had a colorful quilt on it. My suitcase had been set down neatly beside the dresser.

A moment later the old woman was back with two pitchers and a bowl. "Here you are," she said, setting them on the desk. "If you need anything else, please ring the bell and someone will be up to help you right away." She smiled again and left, closing the door behind her.

The pitchers turned out to contain hot and cold water. Towels and a washcloth hung on a rack near the door, and a little shelf next to it had a bar of soap on it that didn't look as though it had ever seen the inside of a factory. Two bags hanging from the back of the door had hand-embroidered labels on them, *towels and linen* and *guest clothing;* over to one side was an oddly shaped chair that turned out on inspection to be some sort of portable toilet, with a big porcelain pot underneath that sealed with a tightly fitting lid when it wasn't in use. Tier one, I thought, and decided to make the best of it.

The funny thing was that the primitive accommodations weren't actually that much more awkward or difficult to use than the facilities you'd find in a good hotel in Philadelphia. I wasn't sure what I would be in for if I decided to take a bath, but I managed to get cleaned up and presentable in short order, and went out into the hall feeling distinctly ready for the lunch the old man had mentioned. I wondered for a moment if I should ring the bell, but that didn't turn out to be necessary; as soon as I stepped out into the hall, the same boy who'd taken my suitcase up to the room came down the hall and gave me directions. As I left, he was hauling away the water pitchers.

Lunch—sandwiches on homebaked whole-grain bread and big bowls of hearty chicken soup—was served in a big plain

89

room in back, where big wooden tables and benches ran in long rows, and the benches were full of men in Lakeland Republic uniforms; the only people who wore New Shaker blue were a couple of young men who brought out the food. "The people who live here eat in their own dining hall," Pappas told me when I asked him about that. "You're welcome to join them, if you don't mind eating in perfect silence while somebody reads out loud from the Bible."

"I'll pass," I said.

He laughed. "Me too. Sundays at Holy Trinity is enough religion for me, but I guess it works for them. They start a new Gathering every few years, they're growing that fast."

I racked my brains for the little I knew about the Shakers. "Do they swear off sex?"

"No, that was the old Shakers. The New Shakers marry, or some of them do—Orren and Sue are a couple, for example. The brothers and sisters don't own anything, not even a toothbrush, and live together like the old Shakers did."

"And the other sect you mentioned?"

"The Keelyites? They're like the Amish, they own their own homes and farms, but they've got their own beliefs and their prophet Eleanor Keely put a third testament into their Bibles. They'll tell you that when God said we have to live by the sweat of our brows, He meant that anything that's not powered by human muscles is sinful."

"We've got Third Order Amish back home who say that," I told him.

Pappas considered that. "I don't think we have them here yet," he said. "Now that the border's opened, who knows? I bet they'll start talking theology with the Keelyites. God knows what they'll come up with."

About the time I'd polished off lunch, Brother Orren came in and asked if I'd be interested in a tour of the Gathering— I gathered he'd been briefed by somebody—and I spent the afternoon trotting around the place with a soft-spoken guy in his early twenties named Micah, who had brown skin and a mane of frizzy red-brown hair. "My parents got killed in an air raid during the war of '49," he told me as we walked toward the barn, "and the Gathering took me in. Any child who comes to us finds a home."

"Did you ever consider leaving?" I asked.

"I left when I was nineteen," he told me. "Spent three years out in the world, two of them in the army. But I came back once I realized that this was where I belong."

"Do you miss anything from outside the Gathering?"

"Oh, now and again. Still, there's a song we inherited from the old Shakers; the first line is 'Tis a gift to be simple'—and that's true, at least for me. It's a gift, and as we say, a grace, and I'm happier here than I ever was out there in the world."

I thought about that as we walked through the barn, the greenhouses, and the rest of the Gathering. In its own way, it was impressive—a community of around two hundred people that met all its own needs from its own fields and workshops, and produced enough of a surplus to make it an asset to the local economy—but something about it troubled me, and I sat up late that night, by the glow of the one candle each room was allotted, trying to figure out what it was.

CHAPTER 6

A rooster yelling at the top of its lungs woke me before dawn the next morning. It didn't seem likely to shut up any time soon, and I doubted the New Shakers would be happy if I threw anything at their livestock, so I got up instead. I rang the bell as I'd been told, and a couple of minutes later, a quiet knock on the door announced the arrival of a middle-aged woman with two pitchers and a bowl. I took them and thanked her; she smiled and curtseyed, and headed off to somewhere else.

I started washing up, and only then realized two things. The first was that there weren't any outlets for electricity in the room; the second was that the only thing I had to shave with was an electric shaver with no batteries. I finished washing and got dressed, hoping a day's growth of beard wouldn't be a faux pas by Lakeland standards. Maybe an hour later, I was sitting behind Colonel Pappas in the jeep as it rattled over a dirt road on its way to the Lakeland Republic's annual drone shoot.

"How much do you know about modern drones?" Pappas had asked me the night before; when I admitted my ignorance, he laughed. "Fair enough. You start talking about drones, a lot of people think of the old first and second generation machines, the ones that used to launch rockets from a mile or so in the air.

Those haven't been in service anywhere since the 'thirties—ever hear of the battle of Mosul?"

I tried to remember. "That was in the second Kurdistan war, wasn't it?"

"Bingo. Both sides had drones, but the Kurds figured out that you can target them with old-fashioned antiaircraft guns, got a bunch of those in place without anybody being the wiser, and took out most of the Turkish drone force in an afternoon. After that, you had militaries all over the place figuring out ways to target drones, and that's when the sort of drones you see these days started popping up on the drawing boards—observation drones way up where artillery can't hit them, and attack drones flying at treetop level where they can hide from radar. Of course then they've got other vulnerabilities."

"Can't they reprogram their attack drones to fly high if they're going to attack you?"

"Sure." He grinned. "We've got plenty of old-fashioned antiaircraft guns, too."

So there I was, jolting along a rough road with brown fields of stubble to the left and a line of trees to the right, and a moving dot up above the trees caught my eye. I turned to look; Pappas saw me move, turned in his seat, and handed me a pair of binoculars. Despite the joggling of the jeep, I managed to get the thing in focus: a lean angular shape with broad straight wings, flying low and fast.

As I watched, shards suddenly flew up from the middle of one wing. A moment later the outer half of the wing tumbled one way and the rest of the drone tumbled the other. I managed to follow it most of the way to the trees, then handed the binoculars back to Pappas.

"Wing hit?" he asked, pitching his voice to be heard above the jeep's engine. I nodded. "That's the easy one," he went on. "Good shots aim for the engine or the fuel tank."

A quarter mile or so on, as another drone came into sight, the road veered suddenly to the right, ducked through the trees, and stopped in an impromptu parking lot where jeeps were more or less lined up. Just past the parking lots was a cluster of olive-drab tents, and past those a fair-sized crowd. Off to the left, though, a bunch of horses were munching grass in a fenced-off field, and as I watched, a dozen or so people in Lakeland Army uniforms rode up on horses, got out of the saddles, and led the animals into the field.

The jeep stopped. "What's with that?" I asked Pappas. "Cavalry in this day and age?"

"Nah, dragoons." He figured out from my face that I didn't know the word, and went on: "Mounted infantry—they ride to the battlefield and then dismount to fight. Most countries had lots of 'em until the end of the nineteenth century, and we tried 'em out in the war of '49 with good results. Transport's a lot easier on the logistical end if the only fuel you need is hay."

I got out of the jeep. Pappas hauled himself into his wheelchair, then handed me a pair of earplugs. "You'll need these," he said. "Drone rifles are .50 caliber, and they're good and loud."

We wove our way through the tents, through the crowd, and out to the places where the guns were firing. There were maybe two dozen of them in a big arc, each with twenty or so stations for shooters, though things were just getting under way and most of the stations didn't have anyone at them yet. "Those are first timers doing their qualifying rounds," Pappas said, pointing to one set of stations filling up quicker than the others; the earplugs muffled his voice but I could still hear him. "Over here, the expert marksmen—you'll see some of the best shots in the Republic here today. Check this one out."

"This one" was a short middle-aged woman in jeans and a buffalo plaid wool shirt, cradling a rifle that must have been as long as she was tall. Past her, I could see a dot against the morning sky. She lined up the shot with practiced ease. Even through the earplugs, the crack of the rifle was loud enough to sting.

95

A moment later, off in the distance, the dot vanished in a little red-orange flash.

"Sweet," Pappas said. "Right in the fuel tank. That's Maude Duesenberg—I don't know how many drone shoot trophies she's got on her mantle, but it's got to be getting crowded."

"Where do you get all the drones?" I asked him.

"Oh, most of 'em we make ourselves. Expert class and proof-of-concept shooters get real drones—we buy them through smugglers in Chicago. You probably don't want to know how many officers in how many countries sell us a couple of drones every year, list 'em as crashed, and pocket the proceeds."

I knew enough about the military back home to guess that the Atlantic Republic was on that list. Still, something else had sparked my curiosity. "What's proof of concept shooting?"

"New or revived technologies. They're over on this side—let's check 'em out."

Instead of the shooter's stations elsewhere on the arc, the place for proof-of-concept shooters was an open patch of mostly flattened grass with a long straight view ahead of it. There wasn't much of a crowd there, just a couple of officers in the ubiquitous Lakeland trench coats, and several dozen kids watching with hopeful looks on their faces. Out on the grass were maybe twenty soldiers who looked even scruffier than I felt, manhandling what looked like a cannon on an oddly shaped mount.

"Oh my God," Pappas said. "I know these guys—the 34th Infantry from Covington. I wonder what they're up to; that can't be an ordinary howitzer."

I gave him a startled look. One of the officers standing there laughed, and said, "Good morning, sir. Yeah, Carlos and I have been wondering about that since they started setting the thing up."

Introductions followed; Michael Berconi and Carlos Lopez Ruiz were captains in the Lakeland Army, down from Toledo to watch the proof-of-concept tests. "You probably don't know about the 34th," Lopez said to me. "They're a bunch of maniacs. Every year they come up with some new stunt."

"That's for sure," said Berconi. "You should have been here last year. We were standing here, and all of a sudden a bright red triplane—you know, like the Red Baron's plane—comes over the trees there and starts blasting drones from above with a couple of machine guns. I heard later they spent two years building the damn thing."

"I'm surprised the drones didn't dodge it," I said.

"They couldn't see it," Pappas told me. "Military frequency radar doesn't reflect off of wood and fabric, and military drones only have video looking forward and down—though I under-stand that's being changed. You're not the only visitor from outside at these events." He grinned, though there was an edge to it. "Though most of the others don't announce themselves."

The soldiers out on the open grass had finished setting up their cannon, and one of them spread his arms in what was pretty obviously a signal. "Here goes," Pappas said. "You may want to put your hands over your ears; a 75-mm howitzer makes more noise than your earplugs'll handle."

I covered my ears. Off in the distance, a dot rose up into the air and came toward us in a zigzag pattern. About the time it got close enough that I could see more of it than a dot, the cannon went off, and Pappas wasn't kidding; even with my hands over my ears, it packed a wallop. Something blurred the air downrange from where we stood; an instant passed, and then the drone shattered as though it had slammed into an unseen wall. The watching kids whooped; so did the soldiers, and then reloaded.

"What the ringtailed rambling—" Pappas began to say, then covered his ears; he'd spotted the next drone a moment after I had. The same process repeated, except that the second drone only lost half of one wing; that was enough to send it tumbling down onto the range, but the chief of the gun crew regaled the others with a string of profanity that would have gotten a standing ovation from Marines I knew back home. Then it was hands-over-ears time; they let the final drone get good and close before firing, and so I got a fine view as something slammed into it and sent the fragments tumbling down to the grass below.

Before the soldiers had finished whooping Pappas wheeled out toward them, shouting, "What the *hell* are you maniacs putting in that thing?" He was apparently no stranger to the 34th Infantry; they greeted him with sloppy salutes and big grins, and the crew chief and one of the others stood talking with him while the others started breaking the cannon down for transport.

A woman's voice sounded behind me just then: "Excuse me, is this the place for proof-of-concept tests?"

I turned around. She was a twenty-something blonde in a big brown barn coat. "Yes," I said. "They're just packing up from the last test."

"Oh, good." She turned and waved, and someone hauling a cart with two bicycle wheels came out of the crowd. He turned out to be a young man of about the same age, in a fedora and trench coat that had seen quite a bit of hard wear; one of his shoulders was noticeably higher than the other.

"Are you with the soldiers?" she asked me.

"No, just visiting. I'm Peter Carr."

"I'm Emily Franken, and this is my husband Jim." Hands got shaken all around. The cart was full of what looked like antique radio gear—a couple of big metal boxes with dials, switches, and gauges all over the front, and something that I swear looked like a death-ray gun from some old skiffy vid. The kids craned their necks to look at it all, but had the common sense not to touch anything.

"Should I ask about that?" I motioned to the contents of the cart.

"Sure," she replied. "It's a maser—a microwave laser. It's old tech—they made them in the 1950s, but nobody could figure out how to get real power out of them." In response to my look of surprise: "There's a lot of things like that—interesting bits of technology nobody followed up on."

"What Emily's not saying," Jim interjected, "is that she spent two years studying quantum mechanics to find something that would mase steadily at room temperature, and published a couple of papers on the subject that are going to turn two or three branches of physics on their heads."

"Oh, stop it," she said, blushing.

"Not a chance. When we were in engineering school, Mr. Carr, Emily was the only person in class who came up with anything really interesting for me to build."

"And Jim was the only one in the class who could build the things I needed for my projects—so of course we got married right after graduation." Laughing: "When he proposed, he said I had to marry him, so I'd almost have the right last name to be a mad scientist, and a hunchbacked lab assistant too."

He grinned, pushed his shoulder up further, and gave me a bug-eyed look. I laughed.

Out on the grass, the soldiers had the cannon and mount set up for transport, and hauled it back toward the parking lot and the jeeps. I wished the Frankens good luck, and they hauled the cart of electronic gear out onto the field. They passed Pappas as he came wheeling back, shaking his head.

"Even for the 34th, that's pretty good," he said when he reached me and the two captains. "You know what they were shooting? Grapeshot."

Lopez and I looked blank, but Berconi let out a startled laugh. "Seriously?"

"God's honest truth." To the rest of us: "It's something artillery used to use back in the Civil War and before—basically, the world's biggest shotgun shell, with pellets half an inch across. We may actually want to give that a good hard look; it'd do the same thing to a helicopter." With a motion of his head in the direction of the Frankens, who were busy setting up their gear: "What's that all about?"

"Some kind of twentieth century microwave laser," I said.

Pappas gave me a startled look, then turned to Berconi. "What's on the schedule?"

"Standard three trials—but they've requested one with live ordnance."

Pappas let out a long whistle. "This could get colorful."

Out on the grass, the two had finished setting up their gear: a row of batteries, the two boxes, the death-ray-thing on a tripod, and cables connecting them. Emily Franken signaled that they were ready, and then got behind the ray-thing and aimed it downrange while her husband hunched over the two boxes and fiddled with the dials. The first drone appeared in the distance. I'm not sure what I was expecting—flashes and bangs, a beam of light, or what have you—but all that happened was that the drone suddenly dropped out of the air as though the Frankens had flipped the off switch at a distance.

A second drone met the same fate a few minutes later. "The third—" Pappas said.

"That'll be the one with heat on board," Berconi told him.

By the time the third drone went up people were beginning to drift over to the proof-of-concept range, wondering what was going on. As it came close enough to be more than a distant dot, I could see two missiles under each wing. Emily Franken crouched behind the device she was aiming, Jim twisted dials and fiddled with switches, and all of a sudden the drone vanished in a flash and a bubble of red fire. The sharp crack of the explosion, muffled by the earplugs I was wearing, arrived an instant later. The watching kids whooped in delight.

Berconi and Lopez hurried across the grass to the Frankens the moment the flaming wreckage of the drone was on the ground. "What do you think?" Pappas asked me.

"I have no idea," I admitted. "What did they do, microwave the inside of the drones?"

"Good question. If I had to guess—well, you know how a radio antenna works? Radio waves hit a piece of metal the right length and set up a current in it? I wonder if they've tuned the thing so that it sets up electrical surges in the onboard computer chips and the fuses for the missiles."

I gave him a horrified look. "You could fry anything electronic with that."

"Not our gear. All our electronics use vacuum tubes—you hit those with a surge, they just shrug—but outside electronics? Pretty much, yeah."

I considered him for a long moment, thinking about the military implications of a weapon that could make electronics fail at a distance, and then wondered whether this whole business had been staged for my benefit. "You get a lot of mad scientists here in the Lakeland Republic?"

"You'd be surprised," he said with a grin. "Lots of technologies that got invented in the nineteenth and twentieth centuries were just plain abandoned even though they worked fine— there wasn't a market yet, or something else got there first, or somebody bribed the right officials so government subsidies favored some other technology instead. A lot of engineers here spend their time going through old technical journals and what have you, looking for things that the Republic can use."

"Like grapeshot," I said.

"Bingo. Or masers, or dragoons—or for that matter canals and canal boats."

By then the Frankens had their maser broken down and loaded on the cart, and they were hauling it away, still deep in conversation with Berconi. Lopez headed back our way, while a bunch of soldiers hauled something that looked like a hand-cranked Gatling gun out onto the grass. "Come on," Pappas said then. "Unless you want to see more here, of course. The expert competition ought to start pretty soon." I nodded, and followed him.

That's how the day went. It must have been midnight, or close to it, when Pappas and I got back to the New Shaker gathering. The shooting went on until four in the afternoon; during a lull in the gunfire, a little after noon, we got into line outside a big olive-green tent in the middle of things, filed in, and left with glasses of beer and sausages and sauerkraut on big fresh-baked rolls. After the last drone was blown out of the air, people milled around while the judges conferred, and then it was time for trophies to be handed out—Maude Duesenberg, who I'd seen shooting earlier, squeaked out another win by a couple of points over a scruffy-looking kid from the mountain country off east. They shook hands, and he grinned; you could tell he was already thinking about how to get ready for next year's shoot.

From there it turned into a big party, with plenty of food—somebody spent most of the day roasting a couple of pigs, just for starters—and no shortage of alcohol, either. Pappas and I ended up sipping moonshine around a fire with the guys from the 34th Infantry, who were already talking about what kind of stunt they were going to pull the following year. The 'shine was pure enough that I'm honestly surprised that the whole lot of us weren't lifted into the treetops by a sudden explosion, just from the vapors. As it was, I was tipsier than I usually let myself get by the time Pappas and I headed back to the jeep, and he was worse off than I was. Did you know a wheelchair can stagger? Trust me, I've seen it.

The next morning came too early, announced by the same overenthusiastic rooster as before. I got myself washed and dressed, and stumbled downstairs, to find Pappas looking as though he'd slept the clock around and was ready for anything. "I'm going to have to get the early train back," he told me, "but Melanie says you want to see first tier up close, so she found someone to show you around Hicksville—a city councilwoman, I think."

"If she can show me the nearest barber shop first," I said, "I'd be happy."

Pappas pulled out a pocket watch, glanced at it. "There's one on Main Street," he told me. "If we go now you'll have time to take care of that before she shows up."

That sounded like a good idea to me, so we said our good-byes to the New Shakers and piled into the jeep for the ride back into town. This time there weren't more than three or four wagons on the road that had been so crowded two days back; I gathered that most of the attendees were either sleeping off the consequences of the previous night or enjoying a leisurely morning. Fields and pastures eventually gave way to the outlying houses of the town, and then to the main street, which was paved—I hadn't expected that—and lined on both sides with the sort of shops and city buildings you'd expected to see in an Old West history vid.

"City Hall's there," Pappas said as the jeep pulled up a few yards from the promised barbershop. He pointed to a three-story building of what looked like local stone half a block up the street. "Right next to the library. Ask for Ruth Mellencamp. All set? Hey, it was a pleasure." We shook hands, I hauled my suitcase out of the jeep, and away it went.

The barbershop was a little hole in the wall place toward one end of the block. Just this side of it was another shop, no bigger, with LAKELAND RADIOTELEGRAPH SERVICE in bright yellow paint on the windows and a big antenna rising up above the roof. The sign on the door promised same day message delivery anyplace in the Lakeland Republic. That seemed pretty remarkable for a tier one county, but it suddenly occurred to me that they could do it by having a shop like this in every town of any size. Two customers stood inside, one writing something on a sheet of paper and the other standing at the counter talking with a clerk.

I shook my head and went into the barbershop, and found a half dozen guys ahead of me in line. I'd expected that; what I didn't expect is that four of them were singing. They had books open in their laps—copies of the same songbook, I gathered after a fast glance—and were belting out some song I didn't know, and doing it in pretty fair harmony. I sat down in the nearest available chair, tucked my suitcase back under the seat, and all of a sudden had to fight down an impulse to laugh. You can run into a phrase hundreds of times and never think about what it actually means; I must have read at least that many references to "barbershop quartets" without realizing that that's what guys did in barbershops while waiting for a shave, back in the days when there weren't loudspeakers in the ceiling blaring pop music everywhere and veepads sitting in everyone's lap to make up for any lack of distraction. In the Lakeland Republic, obviously, those days were back.

I'm pretty sure that if I'd picked up a copy of the songbook from the table in front and joined in, nobody would have blinked, and in fact that's what happened with two of the next three guys to come into the barber shop. The odd thing was that the songs weren't the sort of thing I dimly associated with barbershop quartets. I didn't know most of them, but like most people back home I've got pretty specific musical tastes—jazz on the one hand, and opera on the other. Still, they were pretty good. One that stuck in my memory had a rock beat, and something in the chorus about a girl named Lucy who was in the sky with diamonds. I made a note in my notebook to look it up once I got back home and could chase down the lyrics on the metanet.

It was a half hour or so later when I left the barbershop, feeling a lot less scruffy, and with another song's chorus, something about turning to face the strange ch-ch-changes, ringing in my head. It wasn't a bad introduction for the day I was about to have, for that matter.

I walked up the sidewalk that led to City Hall, went in, and asked for Ruth Mellencamp. She turned out to be short, plump, gray-haired, and businesslike, the kind of woman that looks like somebody's slightly batty granny until she starts talking and you realize there's a mind like a steel trap behind the cozy facade. "Pleased to meet you," she said, shaking my hand. "Yes, Ms. Berger called down from Toledo two days ago. It's not often we get visitors from outside here in Hicksville, and I admit I'm curious to see what you'll think of our little town."

"So far," I said, "I know that it has decent train service and you can get an excellent shave at a barbershop here."

She chuckled. "Well, that's certainly a good start! Why don't you stash your suitcase here and we can have a look at the town."

"I was a little surprised to see paved streets and sidewalks here," I said as we left the building. "I thought you didn't have those in a first tier county."

"They weren't paid for with tax money," she said. "About ten years ago, some of the business people in town got together, organized a corporation, got a charter from the legislature for it, and used that to raise money to pave six streets downtown. A lot of people contributed, and not just people who live in town. So the streets got built, a fund was set aside to repair them, and the corporation wound up its affairs and closed down."

"I imagine you know," I said, "just how odd that sounds to someone from outside."

"Of course." She gestured down the street, and we turned. "The thing is, that's what corporations were originally: schemes for public betterment that were chartered by one of the old state governments for a fixed term, and allowed to raise money by stock sales for that reason alone. It wasn't until clever lawyers twisted the laws out of shape in the interests of the railroad barons that corporations got turned into imaginary persons with more rights and fewer responsibilities than the rest of us."

I remembered what Vinny Patzek told me about corporations at the Toledo stock market. "So you went back to the older way of doing things."

"Exactly. We do that a lot here."

"I've gotten that impression," I said dryly, and she chuckled again.

Hicksville was a farm town's farm town, and you could tell. The biggest store in town was a feed-and-seed with big silos out back, next to a rail siding where freight cars could pull up to take on loads of grain, and the next biggest business was a whiskey distillery—"you won't find a better bourbon in the Republic," Mellencamp told me—which also had its own rail siding, and a loading dock stacked with cases of bottles ready to ship. Another large building belonged to an organization called the Freemasons, which confusingly enough didn't have anything to do with the building trades, and another belonged to something called the Grange, which I gathered was some kind of farmer's organization. I made notes in my notebook and hoped I'd have time to look things up when I got back to Toledo.

The thing that struck me hardest, though, was how lively everything was. Thinking about the tier system when I was in Toledo, I'd conjured up a picture of log cabins, dirt roads, and the kind of squalor you get in the poorer rural districts of the Atlantic Republic these days, but that's not what I saw all around me in Hicksville. What I saw instead was a bustling, prosperous community that somehow got by without the technologies everyone outside took for granted.

We'd just passed the Grange building when a policeman came strolling past us and smiled and said hi to us both. That didn't surprise me, since Ruth Mellencamp was what she was, but he said the same thing to every person he passed, and stopped here and there to talk to people, as though he was everybody's friend. It was only after he'd passed that it really sank in that he wasn't wearing a flak jacket or a helmet and he didn't have an assault rifle in his hands. Like the border guard I'd seen, he was wearing an old-fashioned uniform, this one of blue wool, and the only heat he had on him was a pistol at his hip. I shook my head, wondered how they managed. "I'm curious," I said to my guide, "about the crime rate here."

"In Hicksville, or the Lakeland Republic generally?"

"Both, actually."

106

"I can get you some hard numbers when we head back to City Hall. The short version is that it's lower than any other country in North America."

"Any idea why?"

"Sure. On the one hand, anybody who's willing to work can earn a living wage here, so you don't have the extreme poverty and joblessness that drives so much crime elsewhere. On the other, we have a lot fewer laws." I gave her a startled look, and she went on. "I'm not sure how much you know about the laws in the old United States."

"Not a lot," I admitted.

"Convoluted to the point of insanity," she said. "You could hardly turn around and draw a deep breath without violating some law or regulation or other. We got rid of most of it; the only things our criminal law covers are significant crimes against persons and property. Then there were the drug laws—I hope those have been scrapped in your country."

"No," I said. "You've legalized drugs here?"

"Prohibition is a recipe for failure," she replied at once. "It's never worked anywhere it's been tried, and it never will. When you come right down to it, the only thing you get from legal prohibition is a system of price supports for organized crime. Treat drug addiction as a medical issue rather than a legal one, the way most European countries do these days, and it's much more manageable—and you get a lot fewer people in prison." She shrugged. "Of course some people are going to break the law no matter what, but it's quite a bit easier to have a humane prison system when you aren't throwing millions of people into the prisons for things that don't actually need to be crimes."

I thought about that as we came up to another big building of local stone, with HICKSVILLE SCHOOL carved over the door. "I don't know whether you're interested at all in our education system," Mellencamp said.

"Actually, I am," I told her. "Ours has problems; maybe I can pick up some useful ideas." It was half a joke and half the understatement of the year—the public schools all over the Atlantic Republic are a disaster area, and the private schools charge more and more each year for an education that isn't all that much better.

She beamed. "Maybe you can. We're very proud of our school here."

We went inside. I probably shouldn't have been surprised that there were no armed guards in flak jackets in the halls, but it still rattled me. The place was clean and pleasant, without the medium-security prison look that schools have back home. We went to the office, a cubbyhole in front with a desk for the secretary and a bunch of filing cabinets, and Ellencamp introduced me; the secretary had me sign in, said something pleasant, and away we went.

"People come here all the time," Mellencamp explained. "People moving to the area who want to check out our schools, parents and grandparents who have free time and want to volunteer, that sort of thing. It's very much part of the community."

There were eight classrooms, one for each of the eight grades taught there. We slipped into the back of the second grade classroom, nodded a greeting to the teacher, and sat in wooden chairs up against the back wall. The room was about as plain as could be, a simple square space with a blackboard and a teacher's chair and desk up in front, a round clock over the door, four big windows letting in light on the left, a teacher's desk and chair up front, and rows of seats for the students, each with its little half-desk curving forward from one arm. Over on the wall opposite the windows, student art projects had been pinned up on a cork board; they looked bright and lively, and a couple showed some real talent.

The teacher was maybe thirty, brown-skinned, with her hair in a flurry of braids tied back loosely behind her neck. A blonde girl of sixteen or so was standing next to the desk, reading a story aloud, and the students were following along in their textbooks.

I leaned over to Mellencamp. "Who's she?" I whispered, meaning the girl who was reading.

"An apprentice," she whispered back, and motioned to a boy around the same age, brown-haired and red-cheeked, who was going from student to student, and now and then squatting down and murmuring something or pointing to some bit in the book. "So's that one."

I gave her a startled look, but decided not to risk interrupting.

The story wound to an end, and then the teacher started asking questions about it to one student after another—not the kind of simple thing you'd expect to see in a test back home, either. It sank in after a moment that she was actually asking the kids for their thoughts about this or that part of the story. I put my hand on my chin. It struck me as a very odd way to run a lesson—wasn't the point of schooling to make sure that everyone in the class came up with the right answer when it was called for? Not in the Lakeland Republic, I gathered.

The reading lesson ended at ten-thirty sharp—it took me a while to remember how to read a clock with hands, but I managed it—and once it was over, the students and both apprentices got up and trooped out the door in a ragged but tolerably well behaved line. Ruth Mellencamp got to her feet once the last of them were gone, gestured for me to follow, and went to the front of the room. "Angie," she said, "this is Peter Carr, who's visiting from outside. Mr. Carr, Angela McClintock."

We shook hands, said the usual polite things. "How long do you have before the next class?" I asked.

The teacher gave me a blank look, then smiled the you-don't-get-it smile I'd seen too often for my liking. "They'll be back in fifteen minutes, after morning recess." It was my turn to wear a blank look, and her eyebrows went up. "Good heavens, you can't expect second graders to sit still for an entire school day. Don't the early grades have recesses where you're from?"

"We probably should," I allowed.

"You certainly should. If I kept them in much longer they'd be so restless they wouldn't absorb a thing I taught them. This way, twenty minutes from now they'll be ready to sit back down and pay attention to the next set of lessons."

I nodded. "I was curious about the two young people who were helping you—apprentices?" She nodded, beaming, and I went on: "They look a little young to have gotten a teaching degree already—will they go to college and get that after their apprenticeship?"

That got me the blank look again, and this time it wasn't followed by the too-familiar smile. Ruth Mellencamp came to the rescue. "They used to send teachers to college before the war," she said. "I gather they still do that outside."

"And I gather you don't do that here," I said.

"Good heavens, no," said the teacher. "Why would we? You don't need a college degree to teach second graders how to read—just patience and a little bit of practice."

"But I'm sure you teach them more than reading," I objected.

"Yes, but the same thing's true of all the three C's," she said.

"That's what we call the curriculum," Mellencamp added, seeing the blank look start to appear on my face. "Literacy, numeracy, naturacy—those are the three C's."

I took that in. "So you teach them to read, and then—mathematics?"

"Literacy's more than just reading," McClintock said. "It's the whole set of language skills—reading, grammar, spelling, logical reasoning, composition and speaking, so they can learn whatever interests them, think intelligently about it, and share what they find with other people. Numeracy's the whole set of number skills—mathematics, sure, but also the trick of putting things in numerical terms and using math in the real world, so probability, statistics, everything you need to keep from being fooled or flummoxed by numbers."

"Okay," I said. "And—naturacy? I don't even know the word."

"The same principle," said the teacher. "The whole set of natural science skills: learning how to observe, how to compare your observations to what's already known or thought to be known, how to come up with hypotheses and figure out ways to test them—and also natural history, what living things you found here, how they interact with us, with their habitats, with other living things."

"I suppose you don't teach that in the schools back home," said Mellencamp.

"There are college classes," I said.

"Most of these kids will grow up to be farmers," McClintock told me. "Most of those that don't will be dealing with farmers and the farm economy here every day of their lives. How on Earth they'd be able to do that if they don't understand soil and weather and how plants grow, I'm sure I don't know."

"Back before the war," Mellencamp reminded her, "the big corporate farms tried to do without that."

"Yes, and look what happened." She shook her head. "I'm not sure we've learned everything we should have from the mistakes that were made back then, but that's one I think we picked up."

I thought about that on the train that afternoon all the way back to Toledo.

CHAPTER 7

I'd had lunch with Ruth Mellencamp at a pleasant little diner a block from the station before I caught the train, so I had nothing to do until I got to Defiance but watch farmland roll by and think about what I'd seen since I'd crossed the border less than a week before. My reactions were an odd mix of reluctant admiration and unwilling regret. The people of the Lakeland Republic had taken a situation that would have crushed most countries—an international embargo backed up with repeated attempts at regime change—and turned it into their advantage, using isolation from the capital flows and market pressures of the global economy to give them space to return to older ways of doing things that actually produced better results than the modern equivalents.

The problem with that, I told myself, was that it couldn't last. That was the thing that had bothered me, the night after I'd toured the New Shaker settlement, though it had taken another day to come into focus. The whole Lakeland Republic was like the New Shakers, the sort of fragile artificial construct that only worked because it isolated itself from the rest of the world. Now that the embargo was over and the borders with the other North American republics were open, the isolation was gone, and I didn't see any reason to think the Republic's back-to-the-past ideology would be strong enough by itself in the face of the overwhelming pressures the global economy could bring to bear.

That wasn't even the biggest challenge they faced, though. The real challenge was progress—the sheer onward momentum of science and technology in the rest of the world. Sure, I admitted, the Lakeland Republic had done some very clever things with old technology—the Frankens blowing drones out of the sky with a basement-workshop maser kept coming to mind—but sooner or later the habit of trying to push technology into reverse gear was going to collide catastrophically with the latest round of scientific or technical breakthroughs, with or without military involvement, and leave the Lakelanders with the hard choice between collapse and a return to the modern world.

A week earlier, I probably would have considered that a good thing. As the train rolled into Defiance, I wasn't so sure. The thing was, the Lakeland Republic really had managed some impressive things with their great leap backward, and in a certain sense, it was a shame that progress was going to steamroller them in due time. Most of the time, people say "progress" and they mean that things get better, but it was sinking in that this wasn't always true.

I picked up a copy of that day's Toledo *Blade* from a newsboy in the Defiance station, and used that as an excuse to think about something else once I boarded the train back to Toledo. The previous day's drone shoot was right there on page one, with a nice black and white picture of Maude Duesenberg getting her sixth best-of-shoot trophy, and a big feature back in the sports section with tables listing how all the competitors had done. I didn't pay attention to anything else at first, though, because another satellite had been hit.

The *Progresso IV* and the the Russian telecom satellite were bad enough, but this one was a good deal worse, because it was parked in a graveyard orbit—one of the orbital zones where everybody's been sticking their defunct satellites since it sank

114

in that leaving them in working orbits wasn't a good plan. Most of the graveyard-orbit zones are packed to the bursting point with dead hardware, and though they're some distance from the working orbits, that doesn't really matter once you get a Kessler syndrome started and scrap metal starts spalling in all directions at orbital speeds.

That was basically what was happening. A defunct weather satellite had taken a stray chunk of the *Progresso IV* right in the belly, and it had just enough fuel for its maneuvering thrusters left in the tanks to blow up. A couple of amateur astronomers spotted the flash, and the astronomy people at the University of Toledo announced that they'd given up trying to calculate where all the shrapnel was going; at this point, a professor said, it was just a matter of time before the whole midrange was shut down as completely as low earth orbit.

That was big news, not least because the assault drones I'd watched people potshotting out of the air depend on satellite links. There are other ways to go about controlling them, but they're clumsy compared to satellite, and you've also got the risk that somebody will take out your drones by blocking your signals—that's happened more than once in the last few decades, and I'll let you imagine what the results were for the side that suddenly lost its drones. Of course that wasn't the only thing in trouble: telecom, weather forecasting, military reconnaissance, you name it, with the low orbits gone and the geosynchronous ones going fast, the midrange orbits were the only thing left, and now that door was slamming shut one collision at a time.

It occurred to me that the Lakeland Republic was one of the few countries in the world that wasn't going to be inconvenienced by the worsening of the satellite crisis. Still, I told myself, that's a special case, and paged further back. The rest of the first section was ordinary news: the Chinese were trying to broker a ceasefire between the warring factions in California; the prime minister of Québec had left on a state visit to Europe;

President Bulford of Texas was in Geneva, bringing some kind of complaint about the Gulf oil fields to the United Nations; the windpower industry was in trouble because another rare earth metal was running short; the melting season in Antarctica was turning out worse than expected, with a big new iceflow from Marie Byrd Land dumping bergs way too fast—that meant more flooding in the coastal cities back home, of course. I shook my head, read on.

Further in was the arts and entertainment section. I flipped through that, and in there among the plays and music gigs and schedules for the local radio programs was something that caught my eye and then made me mutter something impolite under my breath. The Lakeland National Opera in Toledo was about to premier its new production of *Parsifal* the following week, and every performance was sold out. Sure, I mostly listen to jazz, but I have a soft spot for opera from way back—my grandmother was a fan and used to play CDs of her favorite operas all the time, and it would have been worth an evening to check it out. No such luck, though: from the article, I gathered that even the scalpers had run out of tickets. I turned the page.

I finished the paper maybe fifteen minutes before the train pulled into the Toledo station. A horsedrawn taxi took me back to my hotel; I spent a while reviewing my notes, got dinner, and made an early night of it, since I had plans the next morning.

At nine-thirty sharp—I'd checked the streetcar schedule with the concierge—I left the hotel and caught the same streetcar line I'd taken to the Mikkelson plant. This time I wasn't going anything like so far: a dozen blocks, just far enough to get out of the retail district. I hit the bell just before the streetcar got to the Capitol Atheist Assembly.

Half a dozen other people got off the streetcar with me, and as soon as we figured out that we were all going the same place, the usual friendly noises followed. We filed in through a pleasant lobby that had the usual pictures of famous Atheists

116

on the walls, and then into the main hall, where someone up front was doing a better than usual job with a Bach fugue on the piano, while members and guests of the Assembly milled around, greeted friends, and settled into their seats. Michael Finch, who'd told me about the Assembly, was there already—he excused himself from a conversation, came over and greeted me effusively.

We all got seated eventually. What followed was the same sort of Sunday service you'd get in any other Atheist Assembly in North America: the Litany, the lighting of the symbolic Lamp of Reason, and a couple of songs from the choir, backed by lively piano playing. There was a reading from one of Mark Twain's pieces on religion, followed by an entertaining talk on Twain himself—his birthday was coming up soon, I thought I remembered. Then we all stood and sang "Imagine," and headed for coffee and cookies in the social hall downstairs.

"Anything like what you get at the Assembly in Philadelphia?" Finch asked me as we sat at one of the big tables in the social hall.

"The music's a bit livelier," I said, "and the talk was frankly more interesting than we usually get in Philly. Other than that, pretty familiar."

"That's good to hear," said a brown-skinned guy about my age, who was just then settling into a chair on the other side of the table. "Even with the borders open, we don't have anything like the sort of contacts with Assemblies elsewhere that I'd like."

"Mr. Carr," Finch said, "this is Rajiv Mohandas—he's on the administrative council here. Rajiv, this is Peter Carr, who I told you about."

We shook hands, and Mohandas gave me a broad smile. "Michael tells me that you were out at the annual drone shoot Friday. That must have been quite an experience."

"In several senses of the word," I said, and he laughed.

We got to talking, about Assembly doings there in Toledo and back home in Philadelphia, and a couple of other people joined in. None of it was anything out of the ordinary until somebody, I forget who, mentioned in passing the Assembly's annual property tax bill.

"Hold it," I said. "You have to pay property taxes?" They nodded, and I went on: "Do you have trouble getting Assemblies recognized as churches, or something?"

"No, not at all," Mohandas said. "Are churches still tax-exempt in the Atlantic Republic? Here, they're not."

That startled me. "Seriously?"

Mohandas nodded, and an old woman with white hair and gold-rimmed glasses, a little further down the table, said, "Mr. Carr, are you familiar with the controversy over the separation of church and state back in the old United States?"

"More or less," I said. "It's still a live issue back home."

She nodded. "The way we see it, it simply didn't work out, because the churches weren't willing to stay on their side of the line. They were perfectly willing to take the tax exemption and all, and then turned around and tried to tell the government what to do."

"True enough," Mohandas said. "Didn't matter whether they were on the left or the right, politically speaking. Every religious organization back then seemed to think that the separation of church and state meant it had the right to use the political system to push its own agendas—"

"—but skies above help you if you asked any of them to help cover the costs of the system they were so eager to use," said the old woman.

"So the Lakeland Republic doesn't have the separation of church and state?" I asked.

"Depends on what you mean by that," the old woman said. "The constitution grants absolute freedom of belief to every citizen, forbids the enactment of any law that privileges any form of religious belief or unbelief over any other, and bars the

118

national government from spending tax money for religious purposes. There's plenty of legislation and case law backing that up, too. But we treat creedal associations—"

I must have given her quite the blank look over that phrase, because she laughed. "I know, it sounds silly. We must have spent six months in committee arguing back and forth over what phrase we could use that would include churches, synagogues, temples, mosques, covens, assemblies, and every other kind of religious and quasireligious body you care to think of. That was the best we could do."

"Mr. Carr," Finch said, "I should probably introduce you. This is Senator Mary Chenkin."

The old woman snorted. "'Mary' is quite good enough," she said.

I'd gotten most of the way around to recognizing her before Finch spoke. I'd read about Mary Chenkin in briefing papers I'd been given before this trip. She'd been a major player in Lakeland Republic politics since Partition, a delegate to their constitutional convention, a presence in both houses of the legislature, and the third President of the Republic. As for "Senator," I recalled that all their ex-presidents became at-large members of the upper house and kept the position until they died. "Very pleased to meet you," I said. "You were saying about creedal associations."

"Just that for legal purposes, they're like any other association. They pay taxes, they're subject to all the usual health and safety regulations, their spokespeople are legally accountable if they incite others to commit crimes—"

"Is that an issue?" I asked.

"Not for a good many years," Chenkin said. "There were a few cases early on—you probably know that some religious groups before the Second Civil War used to preach violence against people they didn't like, and then hide behind freedom-of-religion arguments to duck responsibility when their followers took them at their word and did something appalling.

119

They couldn't have gotten away with it if they hadn't been behind a pulpit—advocating the commission of a crime isn't protected free speech by anyone's definition—and they can't get away with it here at all. Once that sank in, things got a good deal more civil."

That made sense. "How's the Assembly doing financially, though, with taxes to pay?"

"Oh, not badly at all," said Mohandas. "We rent out the hall and the smaller meeting rooms quite a bit, of course, and this room—" He gestured around us. "—is a school lunchroom six days a week." In response to my questioning look: "Yes, we have a school—a lot of," he grinned, "creedal associations do. Between public schools, private schools like ours, and the homeschooling associations, there's quite a bit of competition, which is good for everybody. Our curriculum's very strong on science and math, strong enough that we get students from five and six counties away."

"That's impressive," I said. "I visited a public school out in Defiance County yesterday; it was—well, interesting is probably the right word."

"Well, then, you've got to come tour ours," Chenkin said. "I promise you, there's no spectator sport in the world that matches watching a class full of fourth-graders tearing into an essay that's been deliberately packed full of logical fallacies."

That got a general laugh, which I joined. "I bet," I said. "Okay, you've sold me. I'll have to see what my schedule is, but I'll certainly put a tour here on the list."

"Delighted to hear it," Mohandas said.

I wrote a note to myself in my pocket notebook. All the while, though, I was thinking about the future of the Lakeland Republic. Unless the science and math they taught was as antique as everything else in the Republic, how would the kids who graduated from the Assembly school—and equivalent schools in other cities, I guessed—handle being deprived of the kinds of technology bright, science-minded kids everywhere else took for granted?

I made some phone calls the next morning and got my schedule sorted out for the next few days. Now that President Meeker had gotten things sorted out with the Restos, I had a lot of things to discuss with the Lakeland government, and I knew they'd want to know as much as possible about what was going to change following the election back home.

By quarter to nine I was climbing the marble stairs in front of the Capitol, passing a midsized crowd of wide-eyed school-children on a field trip. The morning went into detailed discussions with government officials—Melanie Berger from Meeker's staff, Stuart Macallan from the State Department, and Jaya Patel from the Department of Commerce—about the potential reset in relations between their country and mine now that Barfield and the Dem-Reps were out on their collective ear.

They were frankly better prepared for the discussion than I was. I'd taken the precaution of printing out the position papers from Montrose's transition team before I got on the train in Pittsburgh, and reviewed them the night before, but it was pretty obvious that the Lakelanders weren't used to looking things up moment by moment on a veepad and I was. There was more to it than that, though—I got the impression that they had a much broader education than I did. They had all kinds of facts at their fingertips that I'd never have thought to bring into the discussion. I thought of the school I'd visited, and tried to keep up.

We had lunch downstairs in the Capitol's dining room, a big pleasant space with tall windows letting in the autumn sunlight, and then it was up to Meeker's office and a long afternoon talk with the President. I have no idea to this day if Isaiah Meeker plays poker, but if he does, I pity the other players; the skill with which he tried to lure me into saying more than I should, while gracefully evading any question of mine he didn't want to answer, was really quite impressive.

I'm pretty sure that he ended up with a clearer idea of the incoming administration's foreign-policy plans than anyone outside of Ellen Montrose's inner circle was entitled to have, though in exchange I think I got a good sense of how his administration was likely to respond to some of the impending changes in inter-American relations—including some I was pretty sure he didn't know about yet.

Dinner was at a really pleasant French place two blocks from the Capitol: Berger, Patel, her husband Ramaraj, and me—Macallan had to attend some kind of event at the Deseret embassy. The conversation stayed deftly on the edge between too little politics to be interesting and too much to be safe. When I finally got back to my hotel room that night, I sat at the desk writing down my impressions until well past midnight, and then fell into bed.

The next morning I'd scheduled a visit to the Capitol Atheist Assembly's school, and showed up at nine AM promptly just as classes were getting under way. The drill was nearly the same as at the school in Hicksville; I went to the office and signed in with the secretary, they found someone to show me around, and I sat in the back of the room and watched a couple of classes. I'd wanted to see their math and science classes, and I got my wish, but what I saw wasn't anything like the math and science I was used to. The kids weren't learning how to run programs to solve mathematical problems, or watching computer simulations of experiments—no, they were actually solving the problems and doing the experiments themselves. I watched a room full of sixth-graders work their way through a geometrical proof, and a class of eighth-graders hard at work setting up some kind of complicated apparatus on a big central table.

"The Millican oil drop experiment," the teacher explained to me as we stood on one side of the classroom and watched the students and a couple of teacher's apprentices get everything lined up. He was an old guy with flyaway white hair and disconcertingly blue eyes. "I don't know if they teach that outside, but it's one of the classic experiments in physics."

"I don't think I heard of it," I admitted. "I'm curious why you have them repeat it, rather than just telling them how it came out."

That got me the classic Lakeland you-don't-get-it look. "We actually have them replicate a whole series of classic scientific experiments," he said. "That way, they learn that science isn't some kind of revelation handed down from on high—it's a living, growing thing, and it lives and grows when people get their hands dirty running experiments, and replicating them." He gestured at the hardware. "And by making mistakes. The oil drop's a finicky one; the first time they do it, the kids almost always get a different result than Millican got, and once that happens they get to go back over what they did and figure out what happened."

Right then he got called over to help sort out some detail of setting up the apparatus, and my guide and I watched for a few more minutes and then headed for another class. All in all, it was an interesting morning; one thing I noticed is that the kids were never just sitting there being bored and restless, the way they were in every school I'd ever seen back home. I wondered how much that had to do with the fact that the students here were actually doing something active in every class I saw, instead of sitting there staring at screens by the hour.

I left when the students went to lunch. While I'd been inside, a rainstorm had come rolling in off the lake, and though it wasn't much more than five minutes before a streetcar came to the stop out front, I was pretty wet by the time I climbed on board. I had lunch at the hotel; by then the rain had stopped, and I dodged puddles up to the Capitol and then a block and a half past it, to the office building that housed the Lakeland Republic's Department of Commerce. I spent all afternoon there with Jaya Patel and half a dozen other Commerce staffers, looking into possible trade deals and sorting out how those would be affected by their tax and tariff policies. It was a productive session but a tiring one, and then we headed off to an Indian place for dinner; by the time I got back to my hotel room I was feeling pretty run down.

It wasn't until the next morning that I realized that there was more going on than simple tiredness. I felt awful, and the face that confronted me in the mirror looked even worse. I sat down on the side of the hotel bed and tried to figure out what to do. Back home, I'd simply have canceled everything for a week, taken some over-the-counter meds, and waited it out. You don't go to a doctor or a hospital in the Atlantic Republic if you can possibly help it—a checkup plus lab work and a simple prescription will cost you the better part of a month's income even after health insurance pays its cut, and you really don't want to know how many people end up sick or dead every year because somebody screwed up a diagnosis, or because trade treaties won't allow the government to pull medicines off the market even if they're ineffective or actually harmful. I've seen the numbers and they're pretty grim.

Still, I wasn't at home, and I couldn't afford to spend the next week doing nothing. After a bit I went over to the packet I'd gotten on arrival, and paged through the paper on getting by in the Lakeland Republic. There was one short paragraph on medical emergencies and another on ordinary health care; this didn't feel like an emergency, so I read the second one. It told me to call the concierge's desk, and so as soon as I'd called Melanie Berger and cancelled the day's meetings, that's what I did.

"No problem, sir," said the voice on the other end of the line. "I'll call Dr. Hammond, find out how soon he can get here, and call you right back. It'll be just a moment."

About the time I'd begun to wonder how long "just a moment" was—it probably wasn't more than five minutes, to be fair—the phone rang. "Mr. Carr? Dr. Hammond's on his way. He'll be up to see you in twenty minutes or so."

Up to see me? I wondered about that. Something I'd read on the metanet once mentioned that a long time ago, doctors used to actually go to people's homes—I think they called it "making house calls" or something like that. The idea sounded pretty far-fetched to me, but then plenty of things about the Lakeland Republic were pretty far-fetched by the standards I knew. Sure enough, right about twenty minutes after I'd gotten off the phone with the concierge, a crisp knock sounded on the door, and I went to open it.

Dr. Paul Hammond turned out to be a youngish African-American guy dressed like an ordinary Toledo businessman, with a big brown leather case in one hand. We did the usual, and then he sat me down, pulled over a chair, pulled a pen and a notebook out of the big leather case and started asking me questions about my health and the symptoms I'd noticed. After he'd finished with that, he got a thin glass thing that seemed to be some kind of thermometer in my mouth, checked my pulse, used some kind of rig with tubes that went from his ears to an odd-shaped disk to listen to my breathing, and then took the thermometer out, had me stick my tongue out and shone a flashlight down my throat.

"Pretty much what I expected, Mr. Carr," he said then. "There's a nasty little 24-hour flu going around, and I'm sorry to say you've got it. The good news is that you'll be over it tomorrow if you take it easy and let your body deal with it. You've got a mild fever, but that and the muscle aches are normal for this bug—all we have to do is keep any kind of secondary infection from getting going in your upper respiratory tract or your chest, and you'll be fine."

He reached into his case, pulled out a brown glass dropper bottle and what looked for all the world like a package of tea bags. "Twenty drops of this in water every two hours," he said, indicating the bottle, "and one of these in hot water whenever you feel like it—that's to treat the muscle aches."

125

I picked up the package, gave it a dubious look. Yes, they were tea bags, full of what looked like bits of leaves that I guessed came from a bunch of different plants.

Hammond watched me with an amused look on his face. "The concierge tells me that you're from outside," he said. "So you were expecting pills, right, rather than plants."

"Well, yes."

"Care to guess where a lot of the ingredients in those pills come from?"

I gave him a quizzical look.

"Plants. Aspirin comes from willow bark, digitalis from foxglove, opiates from poppies, and so on—there's a long list. And here's the thing—some of these plants have been bred for thousands of years to have the right mix of active compounds to treat this or that health problem. By and large, the kind of pharmaceuticals you're used to taking pull just one compound out of the mix and use that, because somebody or other decided that it was the 'active ingredient.'" He shook his head. "I can get you some pills if you really want them, but the tincture and the infusion will actually do you more good."

That seemed improbable to me, but I was feeling too out of sorts to argue. He wrote down some notes about what to eat, told me what symptoms to watch for, and handed me his card so I could call him if anything out of the ordinary happened. Then he told me he'd check on me the next morning, said goodbye, and headed out the door.

I put twenty drops of the stuff from the dropper bottle into half a glass of water from the tap. It tasted so bad that I filled the glass the rest of the way before choking it down. By then I was feeling really tired, so I crawled back into bed and proceeded to sleep like a stone until past noon. I called room service and got some food, along with hot water for the tea-ish stuff—I figured, what the heck, might as well give it a try. It had an aromatic smell I didn't recognize at all, but it went down easily enough and it seemed to make my muscles ache less.

I didn't feel sleepy after lunch, and wasn't thrilled with the thought of lying in bed staring at the ceiling for hours at a time, so when my eye fell on the radio on the dresser, I decided to give it a try. There was a sheet of paper underneath it that listed the Toledo stations—there were nineteen of them—with a few notes on programming; one was listed as a jazz station, which sounded promising. After a few false starts I got the radio on and tuned to the right number on the dial, and flopped back down on the bed as the opening bars of "Take the A Train" came through the loudspeaker.

I really wasn't sure what to expect, but what followed was a pleasant surprise: a mix of classic recordings, recent remakes by Lakeland jazz players, and just enough experimental stuff to keep things interesting. Every so often, a woman's voice told the listeners what had just played and what was coming up, mentioned the four letters that served as the station's name, and introduced the next track. At three o'clock there was fifteen minutes of news, and half an hour at six o'clock, covering most of the stories I'd read about a couple of days back in the *Blade*. I took the tincture and drank the tea as prescribed, and by seven o'clock, rather to my surprise, I was starting to feel noticeably better.

After a room service dinner I slept again for a while—I'm not sure how many people can doze off to the sound of Louis Armstrong playing "Basin Street Blues," but I managed it—and woke up to the sound of voices. The radio had taken a break from jazz; two men with English accents were talking in tense tones about a horse named Silver Blaze, and then someone else with a typical Lakeland voice announced something called Toledo Radio Theater. That seemed pretty silly to me. What, I wondered, were they going to run the soundtrack of a vid without the image track? Still, I was awake, and so I listened.

I was surprised by how good it was. I'd thought that without the image track, it would be less vivid than a vid, but I was wrong. The voices, sound effects, and bits of background music made it really compelling, enough so to keep me listening

127

closely, and I'm not that into murder mysteries. I wondered at first if it was set in the Lakeland Republic—the detective, some guy named Sherlock Holmes, and his sidekick Dr. Watson traveled by train, received telegrams, and read newspapers—but by about halfway through the story I'd figured out that it was in England back in the nineteenth century. At any rate, it kept me listening for an hour, and then I took one more dose of the tincture, turned off the radio, and went to sleep.

By the time morning came around I felt—not well, exactly, but the sort of weak-but-better feeling that tells you that you're going to be over an illness pretty soon. Dr. Hammond showed up again at nine-thirty sharp. He had someone else with him, a wiry kid of eighteen or so—Hammond introduced him as his apprentice Larry Soames. "So how are we feeling?" he asked, as he settled on the same chair he'd used the morning before.

"A lot better," I admitted. I fielded his questions and then got my temperature, pulse, and so on taken again, while the kid watched and listened and took notes in a little black notebook.

"Excellent," Hammond said finally. "You ought to take the rest of today off, too, but if you do that you should be back on your feet again tomorrow."

"Fair enough," I said, "and thank you. Now how much do I owe you?"

"You don't," he said, with a broad smile. "I gather nobody's told you how we do health care here." When I shook my head: "It's pretty simple, really. Doctors like me—general practitioners—contract with businesses, churches, neighborhoods, fraternal lodges, and citizen's groups to provide basic health care, and there are enough of us that everybody has access. That used to be common all over the old United States a century and a half ago. My contract's with the hotel; I get a flat monthly salary from them, and in return I provide all the primary health care for the employees and the guests."

"What if somebody gets something a general practitioner can't treat?"

"Well, of course, then I refer them to a specialist, and people have health insurance to cover that—but that's not really that common, all things considered."

That surprised me. Back home, if you want to risk going to a doctor, you pretty much have to go to a specialist in whatever's the matter, and if more than one part of your body is involved you'd better hope the specialists you get are willing to talk to each other or you're going to land in a world of hurt.

"You don't have a lot of general practitioners back home, I imagine," he said then.

"I don't think I've ever met one," I admitted.

"Well, there you are. Here, well over ninety per cent of the physicians are GPs, and if you want to get into medical school and become a specialist you pretty much have to go through an apprenticeship and then work as a GP for at least a few years first. That way you remember that your job's to treat patients, and not just a heart or an endocrine system or what have you."

"Hold it," I said. "You don't go to medical school to become a GP?"

"No." With another broad smile: "Back before Partition, the universities got really good at inserting themselves as a requirement into just about every job category you can think. It was a big moneymaker for the academic industry but it didn't work well for anybody else—you'd go to college and learn a bunch of things dreamed up by people who didn't actually work in the field, and then you'd graduate and have to unlearn most of it once you were on the job, and hope you didn't cause too many disasters. We ditched all that here in the Republic; outside of a very few scholarly fields, it's pretty much all apprenticeship."

He nodded at Larry. "Six years from now, when he's done with his apprenticeship, he'll have years of hands-on experience to go with what he's learning from the books, and once he passes his board exams he'll be ready to start treating patients on his own right away. That's the way it used to be done, you know—apprenticeship, followed by state board exams. Doctors, lawyers, teachers, architects, all the skilled professions used to be that way, and it worked better, so we went back to it."

He got up. "But that's neither here nor there. Take it easy for the rest of the day, and if you feel worse—or if you get any of the symptoms I mentioned—give me a call right away. Okay? Excellent. Well, Mr. Carr, have a great day."

They left, and I turned on the radio again, lay back down and dozed off.

CHAPTER 8

The next morning I felt pretty good, all things considered, and got up not too much later than usual. It was bright and clear, as nice an autumn day as you could ask for. I knew I was behind schedule and a lot of discussions and negotiations with the Lakeland Republic government still waited, but I'd been stuck in my room for two days and wanted to stretch my legs a bit before I headed back into another conference room at the Capitol. I compromised by calling Melanie Berger and arranging to meet with her and some other people from Meeker's staff after lunch. That done, once I'd finished my morning routine, I headed down the stairs and out onto the street.

I didn't have any particular destination in mind, just fresh air and a bit of exercise, and two or three random turns brought me within sight of the Capitol. That sent half a dozen trains of thought scurrying off in a bunch of directions, and one of them reminded me that it had been more than two days since I'd gotten any more news than the radio had to offer. Another couple of blocks and I got to Kaufer's News, where the same scruffy-looking woman was sitting on the same wooden stool, surrounded by the same snowstorm of newspapers and magazines. I bought that day's Toledo *Blade*, and since it was still way too early to put anything into my stomach, I crossed the street, found a park bench in front of the Capitol that had sunlight all over it, sat down and started reading.

There was plenty of news. The president of Texas had just denounced the Confederacy for drilling into fields on the Texas side of the border, and the Confederate government had issued the kind of curt response that might mean nothing and might mean trouble. The latest word from the Antarctic melting season was worse than before; Wilkes Land had chucked up a huge jokulhlaup—yeah, I had to look the word up the first time I saw it, too; it means a flood of meltwater from underneath a glacier—that tore loose maybe two thousand square miles of ice and had half the southern Indian Ocean full of bergs. I wondered how much more of New York City, Philadelphia, and the other coastal cities we were going to lose this time around.

There was another report out on the lithium crisis, from another bunch of experts who pointed out yet again that the world was going to run out of lithium for batteries in another half dozen years and all the alternatives were much more expensive; I knew better than to think that the report would get any more action than the last half dozen had. Back home, meanwhile, the leaders of the Dem-Reps had a laundry list of demands for the new administration, most of which involved Montrose ditching her platform and adopting theirs instead. There'd been no response from the Montrose transition team, which was probably just as well. I knew what Ellen would say to that and it wasn't fit to print.

Still, the thing I read first was an article on the satellite situation. There was a squib on the front page about that, and a big article with illustrations on pages four and five. It was as bad as I'd feared. The weather satellite that got hit on Friday had thrown big chunks of itself all over, and two more satellites had already been hit. The chain reaction was under way, and in a year or so putting a satellite into the midrange orbits would be a waste of money—a few days, a week at most, and some chunk of scrap metal will come whipping out of nowhere at twenty thousand miles an hour and turn your umpty-billion-yuan investment into a cloud of debris ready to share the love with anything else in orbit.

That reality was already hitting stock markets around the world—telecoms were plunging, and so was every other economic sector that depended too much on satellites. Most of the Chinese manufacturing sector was freaking out, too, because a lot of their exports go by way of the Indian Ocean, and satellite data's the only thing that keeps container ships out of the way of icebergs. Economists were trying to rough out the probable hit to global GDP, and though estimates were all over the map, none of them was pretty. The short version was that everybody was running around screaming.

Everybody outside the Lakeland Republic, that is. The satellite crisis was an academic concern here. I mean that literally; the paper quoted a professor of astronomy from Toledo University, a Dr. Marjorie Vanich, about the work she and her grad students were doing on the mathematics of orbital collisions, and that was the only consequence the whole mess was having inside the Lakeland borders. I shook my head. Progress was going to win out eventually, I told myself, but the Republic's retro policies certainly seemed to deflect a good many hassles in the short term.

I finished the first section, set down the paper. Sitting there in the sunlight of a clear autumn day, with a horsedrawn cab going clip-clop on the street in front of me, schoolchildren piling out of a streetcar and heading toward the Capitol for a field trip, pedestrians ducking into Kaufer's News or the little hole-in-the-wall café half a block from it, and the green-and-blue Lakeland Republic flag flapping leisurely above the whole scene, all the crises and commotions in the newspaper I'd just read might as well have been on the far side of the Moon. For the first time I found myself wishing that the Lakeland Republic could find some way to survive over the long term after all. The thought that there could be someplace on the

133

planet where all those troubles just didn't matter much was really rather comforting.

I got up, stuck the paper into one of the big patch pockets of my trench coat, and started walking, going nowhere in particular. A clock on the corner of a nearby building told me I still had better than an hour to kill before lunch. I looked around, and decided to walk all the way around the Capitol, checking out the big green park that surrounded it and the businesses and government offices nearby. I thought of the Legislative Building back home in Philadelphia, with its ugly walls of glass and metal and its perpetually leaky roof; I thought of the Presidential Mansion twelve blocks away, another ultramodern eyesore, where one set of movers hauling Bill Barfield's stuff out would be crossing paths just then with another set of movers hauling Ellen Montrose's stuff in; I thought of the huge bleak office blocks sprawling west and south from there, where people I knew were busy trying to figure out how to cope with a rising tide of challenges that didn't look as though it was ever going to ebb.

I got to one end of the park, turned the corner. A little in from the far corner was what looked like a monument of some sort, a big slab of dark red stone up on end, with something written on it. Shrubs formed a rough ring around it, and a couple of trees looked on from nearby. I wondered what it commemorated, started walking that way. When I got closer, I noticed that there was a ring of park benches inside the circle of shrubs, and one person sitting on one of the benches; it wasn't until I was weaving through the gap between two shrubs that I realized it was the same Senator Mary Chenkin I'd met at the Atheist Assembly the previous Sunday. By the time I'd noticed that, she'd spotted me and got to her feet, and so I went over and did and said the polite thing, and we got to talking.

The writing on the monument didn't enlighten me much. It had a date on it—29 APRIL 2024—and nothing else. I'd just about decided to ask Chenkin about it when she said, "I bet they didn't brief you about this little memento of ours—and they probably should have, if you're going to make any kind of sense of what we've done here in the Lakeland Republic. Do you have a few minutes?"

"Most of an hour," I said. "If you've got the time—"

"I should be at a committee meeting later on, but that should be plenty long enough." She waved me to the bench and then perched on the front of it, facing me.

"You probably know about DM-386 corn, Mr. Carr," she said. "The stuff that had genes from poisonous starfish spliced into it."

"Yeah." Ugly memories stirred. "I would have had a kid brother if it wasn't for that."

"You and a lot of others." She shook her head. "Gemotek, the corporation that made it, used to have its regional head-quarters right here." She gestured across the park toward the Capitol. "A big silver glass and steel skyscraper complex, with a plaza facing this way. It got torn down right after the war, the steel went to make rails for the Toledo streetcar system, and the site—well, you'll understand a little further on why we chose to put our Capitol there.

"But it was 2020, as I recall, when Gemotek scientists held a press conference right here to announce that DM-386 was going to save the world from hunger." Another shake of her head dismissed the words. "Did they plant much of it up where your family lived?"

"Not to speak of. We were in what used to be upstate New York, and corn wasn't a big crop near where we lived."

"Well, there you are. Here, we're the buckle on the corn belt: the old states of Ohio, Indiana, Illinois, and across into Iowa and Nebraska. Gemotek marketed DM-386 heavily via exclusive contracts with local seed stores, and it was literally everywhere. They insisted it was safe, the government insisted it was safe, the experts said the same thing—but nobody both-ered to test it on pregnant women."

135

"I remember," I said.

"And down here, it wasn't just in the food supply. The pollen had the toxin in it, and that was in the air every spring. After the first year's crop, what's more, it got into the water table in a lot of places. So there were some counties where the live birth rate dropped by more than half over a two year period."

She leaned toward me. "And here's the thing. Gemotek kept insisting that it couldn't possibly be their corn, and the government backed them. They brought in one highly paid expert after another to tell us that some new virus or other was causing the epidemic of stillbirths. It all sounded plausible, until you found out that the only countries in the world that had this supposed virus were countries that allowed DM-386 corn to cross their borders. The media wouldn't mention that, and if you said something about it on the old internet, or any other public venue, Gemotek would slap you with a libel suit. They'd win, too—they had all the expert opinion on their side that money could buy. All the farmers and the other people of the corn belt had on their side was unbiased epidemiology and too many dead babies.

"So by the fall and winter of 2023, the entire Midwest was a powderkeg. A lot of farmers stopped planting DM-386, even though Gemotek had a clause in the sales agreement that let them sue you for breach of contract if you did that. Seed stores that stocked it got burnt to the ground, and Gemotek sales staff who went out into farm country didn't always come back. There were federal troops here by then—not just Homeland Security, also regular Army with tanks and helicopters they'd brought up from the South after the trouble in Knoxville and Chattanooga the year before—and you had armed bands of young people and military vets springing up all over the countryside. It was pretty bad.

"By April, it was pretty clear that next to nobody in the region was planting Gemotek seeds—not just DM-386, anything from that company. Farmers were letting their farms go fallow if they couldn't get seed they thought was safe. That's when Michael Yates, who was the CEO of Gemotek, said he was going to come to Toledo and talk some sense into the idiots who thought there was something wrong with his product. By all accounts, yes, that's what he said."

All of a sudden I remembered how the story ended, but didn't say anything.

"So he came here—right where we're sitting now. The company made a big fuss in the media, put up a platform out in front of the building, put half a dozen security guards around it, and thought that would do the job. Yates was a celebrity CEO—" Unexpectedly, she laughed. "That phrase sounds so strange nowadays. Still, there were a lot of them before the Second Civil War: flashy, outspoken, hungry for publicity. He was like that. He flew in, and came out here, and started mouthing the same canned talking points Gemotek flacks had been rehashing since the first wave of stillbirths hit the media.

"I think he even believed them." She shrugged. "He wasn't an epidemiologist or even a geneticist, just a glorified salesman who thought his big paycheck made him smarter than anyone else, and he lived the sort of bicoastal lifestyle the rich favored in those days. If he'd ever set foot in the 'flyover states' before then, I never heard of it. But of course the crowd wasn't having any of it. Something like nine thousand people showed up. They were shouting at him, and he was trying to make himself heard, and somebody lunged for the platform and a security guard panicked and opened fire, and the crowd mobbed the platform. It was all over in maybe five minutes. As I recall, two of the guards survived. The other four were trampled and beaten to death, and nineteen people were shot—and Michael Yates was quite literally torn and trampled to bloody shreds. There was hardly enough left of him to bury.

"So that's what happened on April 29th, 2024. The crowd scattered as soon as it was all over, before Homeland Security troops could get here from their barracks; the feds declared a state of emergency and shut Toledo down, and then two days later the riots started down in Birmingham and the National Guard units sent to stop them joined the rioters. Your historians probably say that that's where and when the Second Civil War started, and they're right—but this is where the seed that grew into the Lakeland Republic got planted."

"Hell of a seed," I said, for want of anything better.

"I won't argue. But this—" Her gesture indicated the monument, and the shadow of a vanished building. "—this is a big part of why the whole Midwest went up like a rocket once the Birmingham riots turned serious, and why nothing the federal government did to get people to lay down their arms did a bit of good. Every family I knew back in those days had either lost a child or knew someone who had—but it wasn't just that. There had been plenty of other cases where the old government put the financial interests of big corporations ahead of the welfare of its people—hundreds of them, really—but this thing was that one straw too many.

"And then, when the fighting was over, the constitutional convention was meeting, and people from the World Bank and the IMF flew in to offer us big loans for reconstruction, care to guess what one of their very first conditions was?"

I didn't have to answer; she saw on my face that I knew the story. "Exactly, Mr. Carr. The provisional government had already passed a law banning genetically modified organisms until adequate safety tests could be done, and the World Bank demanded that we repeal it. To them it was just a trade barrier. Of course all of us in the provisional government knew perfectly well that if we agreed to that, we'd be facing Michael Yates' fate in short order, so we called for a referendum."

She shook her head, laughed reminiscently. "The World Bank people went ballistic. I had one of their economists with his face all of six inches from mine, shouting threats for fifteen minutes in half-coherent English without a break. But we held the referendum, the no vote came in at 89%, we told the IMF and the World Bank to pack their bags and go home, and the rest of our history unfolded as you've seen—and a lot of it was because of a pavement streaked with blood, right here."

Something in her voice just then made me consider her face closely, and read something in her face that I don't think she'd intended me to see. "You were there, weren't you?" I asked.

She glanced up at me, looked away, and after a long moment nodded.

Another long moment passed. The clop-clop of a horsedrawn taxi came close, went on into the distance. "Here's the thing," she said finally. "All of us who were alive then—well, those who didn't help tear Michael Yates to pieces helped tear the United States of America to pieces. It was the same in both cases: people who had been hurt and deceived and cheated until they couldn't bear it any longer, who finally lashed out in blind rage and then looked down and saw the blood on their hands. After something like that, you have to come to terms with the fact that what's done can never be undone, and try to figure out what you can do that will make it turn out to be worthwhile after all."

She took a watch out of her purse, then, glanced at it, and said, "Oh dear. They've been waiting for me in the committee room for five minutes now. Thank you for listening, Mr. Carr—will I see you at the Assembly next Sunday?"

"That's the plan," I told her. She got up, we made the usual polite noises, and she hurried away toward the Capitol. Maybe she was late for her meeting, and maybe she'd said more than she'd intended to say and wanted to end the conversation. I didn't greatly care, as I wanted a little solitude myself just then.

I'd known about DM-386 corn, of course, and my family wasn't the only one I knew that lost a kid to the fatal lung defects the starfish stuff caused if the mother got exposed to it in the wrong trimester. For that matter, plenty of other miracle products then and later turned out to have side effects nasty enough to rack up a big body count. No, it was thinking of the pleasant old lady I'd just been sitting with as a young woman with blood dripping from her hands.

Most nations start that way. The Atlantic Republic certainly did—I knew people back home who'd been guerrillas in the Adirondacks and the Alleghenies, and they'd talk sometimes about things they'd seen and done that made my blood run cold. The old United States got its start the same way, two and a half centuries further back. I knew that, but I hadn't been thinking about it when I'd sat on the park bench musing about how calm the Lakeland Republic seemed in the middle of all the consternation outside its borders. It hadn't occurred to me what had gone into making that calm happen.

The breeze whispering past the stone monument seemed just then to have a distant scent of blood on it. I turned and walked away.

I got lunch at the little café across the street from the Capitol, and then went to talk to Melanie Berger and a dozen other people from Meeker's staff. We had a lot of ground to cover and I'd lost two and a half days to the flu, so we buckled down to work and kept at it until we were all good and tired. It was eight o'clock, I think, before we finally broke for dinner and headed for a steak place, and after that I went back to my hotel and slept hard for ten hours straight.

The next morning we were back at it again. Ellen Montrose wanted a draft trade agreement, a draft memorandum on border security, and at least a rough draft of a treaty allowing inland-waterway transport from our territory down the Ohio River to the Mississippi and points south, and she wanted them before her inauguration, so she could hit the ground running once her term began. I figured she also meant to announce them in her inauguration speech and throw the Dem-Reps onto the defensive immediately, so they'd be too busy trying to block her agenda to come up with an agenda of their own.

The Lakelanders knew about the proposals—they'd been briefed while my trip was still in the planning stage—and they were willing to meet her halfway, but they had a shopping list of their own. The trade agreement in particular required a lot of finagling, so the Restos wouldn't shoot it down when it came up for ratification by the legislature, and I had to weigh everything against what Montrose's people and the legislature in Philadelphia would be willing to tolerate. Fortunately the Lakelanders were just as clear on the political realities as I was; everybody approached the negotiations with "how do we make this work?" as the first priority, and we got a lot done.

By lunchtime we'd gotten the framework of the trade agreement settled—there would be plenty of fiddling once the formal negotiations got started, but the basic arrangements looked good—and the memorandum on border security was a piece of cake, the way it usually is when neither side is looking for an excuse to start a fight. The inland-waterway treaty was another matter. We wanted access to the Mississippi, with an eye toward markets in the Missouri Republic, the Gulf, and points further south; they wanted to be able to ship goods to the Atlantic via the New York canal system, to keep Québec from getting expansive ideas about transit fees on the St. Lawrence Seaway. In principle, those were both workable, but the details were tenanted with more than the usual quota of devils.

So we got lunch in the dining room downstairs in the Capitol, sat over in a corner, and kept on hashing out details between bites of sandwich and spoonsful of bean soup. Once lunch was over, we trooped back up to the conference room downstairs from Meeker's office and kept going. The one big question we still had to tackle by that point was how to handle the difference in technology—our tugs and barges rely on high-tech gear that the Lakeland waterways aren't set up for, and theirs don't have the equipment our regulations require—and we talked through I don't know how many different ways to handle that, before finally agreeing that each side's tugs would stay on their own side of the border, their barges would rent portable computer rigs when they were on our side, and our barges would hire extra crew to do the same work on theirs.

Once that was out of the way, the rest of it came together quickly enough, but by then the sun was down and we were all pretty tired. It was a Friday night, so the only people left in the Capitol besides us by then were janitors and security guards, and most of the others had someplace or other to go and somebody to meet. In the end, it was just me and Melanie Berger who walked two blocks north to the Indian place we'd been earlier that week.

We got settled in a little booth, ordered drinks and dinner, sat there for a few minutes without saying much. She looked as tired as I felt. Drinks and a basket of onion naan put in an appearance, though, and took the edge off two very long days.

"Well, that was a marathon," Berger said, sipping at something that was supposed to be a martini—I'd never heard of one that just had gin, vermouth, and an olive in it, but I figured it was a local habit. "Still, no regrets." With a sudden smile: "I bet Fred Vanich that we could get the three agreements roughed out before you left for Philadelphia, and this time I get to collect."

I laughed. "Glad to oblige."

We busied ourselves with the naan for a bit. "You're leaving Wednesday, right?" she said then. When I nodded: "I admit I'm wondering what you think about—" Her gesture took in the restaurant, the other patrons in their old-fahioned clothing, the streetcar rolling purposefully past on the street outside, the unfinished dome of the Capitol rising above the buildings on the other side of the street. "You've been here long enough to get over the initial shock, and I'd be interested in hearing what all this looks like from an outsider's perspective."

Looking back on it all, it probably would have been more professional to fob her off with a few trivial comments, but I didn't do that. Partly I was tired enough that I wasn't thinking clearly, partly I'd been wishing for days that I could talk

142

to someone intelligent about the insight I'd had on the way back from Defiance County, and it probably didn't help that there was some definite chemistry between me and Melanie Berger, which seemed to be mutual. So I got stupid and said, "My reaction's kind of complex."

She motioned for me to go on, but just then the waiter came back with our entrees, noted our empty glasses, and returned promptly from the bar with another round of drinks. I waited until he'd gone sailing smoothly over to another table before continuing.

"On the one hand," I said, "you've played a weak hand astonishingly well. No, it's more than that—you've taken what I'd have considered crushing disadvantages and turned them into advantages. I'd be willing to bet that the World Bank and the IMF figured that after a couple of years shut out of global credit markets and foreign trade, you'd crawl on your knees over broken glass to be let back in."

Berger nodded. "I've heard that they told President More something like that to his face."

"But you took every lemon they threw at you and made lemonade out of it. No foreign trade? You used that as an opportunity to build up an industrial plant aimed at local markets. No access to credit? You made banking a public utility and launched what looks like a thriving stock market. No technology imports? You rebuilt your economy to use human labor and local resources instead—and it hasn't escaped my attention how enthusiastic your population is about all three of those moves."

"You can hardly blame them," she said. "Lots of jobs at decent pay, and banks that pay a decent rate of interest and don't go belly up—what's not to like?"

"I'm not arguing. And here's the thing—so far, it's insulated you from a lot of trouble. This satellite business is a good example." I gestured with my fork. "The last three days have been a complete mess in the rest of the world. Stock markets are

143

down hard, and everybody from military planners to weather forecasters are trying to figure out what the hell they're going to do without satellite data. Here? I know exactly how much time Tom Pappas is going to spend worrying about getting by without satellites—"

She burst into laughter. "Just under zero seconds."

"If that," I said, laughing with her. "And the Toledo stock market had three decent days. I don't even want to think about how my other investments are doing, but here I made two dollars and fifty cents."

That got me a surprised look. "I didn't know you had money invested here."

"One share of Mikkelson Industries. It was a good way to see the market in action."

She laughed again. "I'll have to tell Janice that the next time I see her. She'll be tickled." Then: "But there's another side to your reaction."

"Yes, there is." All of a sudden I wished I didn't have to go on, but I'd backed myself into a corner good and proper. "The downside is that it can't last. You're going one way but the rest of the world is going the other, and all it's going to take is one round too many of technological innovation out there and you'll be left twisting in the wind. Right now, what you've got looks pretty good compared to what's on the other side of the borders, but when the global economy finally gets straightened out and the next big wave of innovation and growth hits, what then? Regime change using technologies you can't counter, maybe, or maybe just the sort of slow collapse that happens to a country that's tried to stay stuck in the past a little too long."

She was smiling when I finished. "I was wondering if you'd bring that up."

That stopped me cold. I used a forkful of tandoori chicken as a distraction, then said, "I take it you've heard someone else mention it."

144

"Fairly often. When someone from outside gets past the initial shock, and actually thinks about what we've done here—and of course quite a few of them never get around to that—that's usually the next point they bring up."

I considered that. "And I suppose you have an answer for it."

"Well, yes." She jabbed at the palak paneer. "When the global economy finally gets straightened out, when the next big wave of innovation and growth hits. Are you sure those are going to happen?"

I put down my fork and stared at her. "It's got to happen sooner or later."

"Why?"

I tried to think of something to say, and couldn't.

"The Second Civil War ended thirty-two years ago," she pointed out. "The Sino-Japanese war was over and done with twenty-seven years ago. Ever since then, economists every-where outside our borders have been insisting that things would turn up any day now, and they haven't. You know as well as I do that real global GDP has been flat to negative twenty-six of the last thirty years, and the last decade's shown zero improvement—quite the contrary. That's not going to change, either, because every other country in the world is chasing a policy goal that's actively making things worse."

"And that is?"

"Progress," she said.

Once again, I was left speechless.

"Here are some examples." She held up one finger. "The consumer sector of your economy has been in the tank ever since Partition. Why? Because you've got really bad maldistri-bution of income."

"There's more to it than that," I protested.

"Yes, but that's the core of it—if consumers don't have money to spend, they're not going to be able to buy consumer goods, and your consumer sector is going to suffer accordingly.

Why don't they have money to spend? Because you've automated most working class jobs out of existence, and if you want to try to tell me that technology creates more jobs than it eliminates, you're going to have to argue with some very hard figures. You've got appalling rates of permanent unemployment and underemployment, and yet everybody on your side of the border seems to think that a problem that was caused by automation is going to be solved by even more automation."

She raised a second finger. "That's one example. Here's another. As technology gets more complex and interconnected, you're guaranteed to see more situations where a problem in one system loads costs on other systems. Look at the satellite situation—it's because so many economic sectors rely on satellite technology that that's going to be such an economic headache. That's an obvious example, but there are plenty of others; our estimate is that cascading problems driven by excess technological interaction knocked a good eight to ten per cent off global GDP last year, and it's getting worse, because everybody outside seems to believe that the problems of complexity can only be fixed by adding more complexity.

"A third." Another finger went up. "Resource costs. The more complex your technology gets, the more it costs to build it, maintain it, power it, and so on, because you need more resources for all those things. Any time an analysis says otherwise, some of the costs are being pushed under the rug—and that rug's getting very lumpy nowadays. Direct and indirect resource costs of technology are like a tax on all other economic activity, and since most of what you do with complex tech used to be done in less resource-intensive ways already, the economic return on tech doesn't make up for the resource costs. Try telling that to a World Bank economist sometime, though—it's quite entertaining to watch.

"And here's a fourth." She raised another finger. "Systemic malinvestment. Since each generation of tech costs more on a whole system basis than the one before, tech eats up more and more of your GDP each year, and everything else gets to fight over the scraps. After the Second Civil War, your country and mine were pretty much equally flattened. We put our investment into basic infrastructure; you put yours into high technology. We got rebuilt cities and towns, canals, railways, schools, libraries, and the rest of it. You got a domestic infrastructure so far in decay I'm amazed you put up with it, because the money that could have fixed your roads and bridges and housing stock went down a collection of high tech ratholes instead. Sure, you've got the metanet; does that make up for everything you do without?

"I could go on. There was a time when progress meant prosperity, but we passed that point in the late twentieth century, and since then, every further increment of progress has cost more than it's worth—and yet the rest of the world stays stuck in the past, pursuing an ideology of progress that doesn't work any more. Until that changes, the global economy isn't going to straighten out and the next big boom is going to turn into one more bust; it's not going to change until someone else notices that progress has become the enemy of prosperity."

I was shaking my head by the time she was finished. "With all due respect," I said, "that's crazy."

It was a clumsy thing to say and I regretted saying it the moment the words were out. "That attitude," she snapped back, "is why we don't have to worry about technological innovation and the rest of it. One more round of innovation, one more economic boom and bust, and the rest of the world is going to progress itself straight into the ground."

I opened my mouth to reply, and then shut it again. One more word, and we would have had a quarrel right there in the restaurant, but I wasn't going to let that happen, and neither was she. So we finished dinner in silence, didn't get another round of drinks, paid up and went to the door.

She flagged down a taxi. "I'll have someone contact you Monday," she said, looking away from me. "Good night."

I wished her a good night, stood there while the clop-clop of the horse faded into the other street noises, and then started walking back to my hotel. The things she'd said chased each other around and around in my mind. None of it made any sort of sense—except that it did, in an uncomfortable sort of way, and when I tried to tease out the holes in her logic I had a hard time finding any. I figured that I was just too tired, and—let's be honest—too upset.

Progress as the enemy of prosperity, I thought, shaking my head. What a bizarre idea.

Something very bright streaked across the sky above me, and I looked up. A little uneven shape of brilliant light with a long streaming tail behind it went tumbling across the stars, faster than a jet. As I watched, it broke in two, and then the two pieces disintegrated one after another into sprays of tiny glowing points that flared and went dark. I tried to tell myself that it was just a meteor, but I knew better.

CHAPTER 9

The next day was Saturday, and for a change, I didn't have anything on the schedule. The marathon sessions of negotiation with President Meeker's staff, exhausting though they'd been, had taken up less of my time in Toledo than I'd expected; even if I sat on my rump in my room until it was time to catch the train home Wednesday, I'd still get back to Philadelphia with everything taken care of that I'd officially been asked to do—and the unofficial side of my trip would wait. That was comforting, or it should have been.

As it was, I woke up in a foul mood, and things didn't get any better as I went through my morning routine and then stared at the window, trying to decide what to do with the day. Partly, I was annoyed at the way the evening had gone, annoyed with myself for almost getting into a fight with Melanie Berger, and with her for almost getting into a fight with me. The worst of it, though, was the bizarre logic she'd used to brush aside my concerns about the Lakeland Republic's survival. Her notion that progress had somehow turned into the enemy of prosperity and the source of most of the world's problems—I could barely frame the idea in my mind without shaking my head and laughing, it was so obviously wrong.

The difficulty was that I couldn't come up with a straight-forward argument against it. You know the kind of paradox that looks simple and turns out to be diabolically complicated once you start trying to poke holes in it? This was the same sort of thing. I started by trying to come up with a mental list of new technologies that obviously had more benefits than drawbacks, but that turned into a tangled mess, because I'd spent enough time in the private sector to know that most of the costs of any new technology get swept under the rug in one way or another, and most of the benefits the public gets told about are basically made up by somebody's marketing department.

For that matter, most of the new technologies that I'd seen hitting the market—bioplastics, veepads, the metanet, and so on—actually offered fewer benefits than the things they replaced, and I knew perfectly well that the publicly admitted costs weren't the only ones there were. Technologies come onto the market because somebody thinks they can make a profit off them, period, end of sentence. You can spend your entire life in corporate boardrooms and one thing I can promise you you'll never hear is someone asking, "But is it actually *better*?"

I tried half a dozen other gambits and got absolutely nowhere. Finally I decided to go for a walk and check out the latest news. I was tired enough after the last few days that I'd slept in late, and it was past ten in the morning before I went out the front door and headed for Kaufer's News. The day was brisk and blustery, with torn scraps of gray cloud rushing past overhead, and the blue and green Lakeland Republic flag out in front of the Capitol snapped and billowed in a cold wind.

There was a crowd around Kaufer's. I wondered what that meant, until I got close enough to hear the woman who ran it saying, in a loud voice: "Ladies, gentlemen, listen up. I'm out of today's *Blade*, but there's more on the way. No, I don't know how soon—depends on traffic. Hang on and it'll be here."

I'd figured out by the time she started talking that something important must have happened, but I didn't want to stand there, so I walked the five blocks to the public library. I thought I remembered that they had newspapers, though if

150

the big story was big enough I guessed there might be a line there too. They did, and there was, but there were half a dozen copies of the *Blade* and one copy each of a dozen daily papers from nearby cities, and they all had the same thing on the top headline. Since I didn't care which paper I got, it took just a couple of minutes before I got handed a copy of the Cleveland *Plain Dealer* and settled down on a chair to read the news.

The short version was that the business between Texas and the Confederacy was getting ugly in a hurry. Right around the time Melanie Berger and I were trying not to quarrel, the president of Texas gave a speech in Houston claiming that Confederate oil companies, with Richmond's covert backing, were using horizontal drilling to poach oil from offshore fields on the Texan side of the treaty line—and he said he had hard data to prove it. The Confederate secretary of energy held a press conference an hour later calling the claims an attempt to cover up Texan mismanagement of offshore oil reserves. President Bulford was right back on the podium fifteen minutes later warning of "consequences" if he didn't get a satisfactory response; Richmond responded by putting its armed forces on alert.

The *Plain Dealer* had the sort of detailed situation report you basically have to belong to government to get in the Atlantic Republic. Of course there were photos of President Bulford, his face red and angry under the mandatory Stetson, and Secretary Lyall, with the icy expression that Confederate gentlefolk use the way rattlesnakes use their rattles, to warn you that someone's about to die. The pages further in, though, gave all kinds of hard data: a map of the treaty line off the Gulf coast with drilling platforms marked in, a sidebar talking about the quarrels over the Gulf boundary before the Treaty of Richmond, one long article about the Texan accusations and the Confederate response, another long article about the troubled history of the Gulf oil fields, a third trying to gauge international reaction.

I read the whole thing carefully, because it wouldn't take much to turn the situation into a world-class headache for the Atlantic Republic. There were still a few wells pumping in Pennsylvania, but most of the oil and gas that kept things running back home was bought from the Confederacy, and there wasn't enough spare capacity elsewhere to make up the difference if anything ugly happened and the Confederate and Texan oil and gas fields got shut in. That meant yet another spike in fuel prices, more turmoil on stock markets worldwide, and a messy balance-of-payments problem for the new administration in Philadelphia to deal with.

The most annoying thing about it all, though, was that it brought me right back up against Melanie Berger's paradox about progress. The one country in North America that had pretty much nothing to lose if the Confederacy and Texas started lobbing ordnance at each other was the Lakeland Republic. While the rest of the continent was going to be flailing around trying to keep their transport networks from coming unglued, the Lakelanders didn't have to care; their trains, streetcars, canals, horsedrawn buggies, and the rest of it would keep on running. It frankly seemed unfair.

By the time I was finished with the *Plain Dealer* it was getting on for lunchtime. I found a pleasant little Greek place a couple of blocks past the library, had lunch, and then headed back to the hotel to regroup. Right out front was a kid with a TOLEDO MUDHENS cap on his head—I gathered that was some kind of sports team—and a canvas bag of rolled newspapers on his shoulder. He was calling out, "Extra! Latest news on the mess down south!" That sounded worth another buck and a quarter. I had to dig in my wallet for a one, though, and in the process a card went fluttering to the ground. The kid scooped it up and handed it back to me, so I tipped him an extra quarter. The card turned out to be the one the musician handed to me my first day in Toledo, the one advertising Sam Capoferro and His Frogtown Five; I glanced at it, pocketed it, took my paper and headed up to my room.

I'd seen newsboys shouting "Extra! Extra!" in old vids, but didn't have a clue what they were yelling about. Now I knew, and I also knew one of the ways that people in the Lakeland Republic got news about fast-breaking stories. The extra issue was a single thick section, all about "the mess down south;" they'd apparently thrown every reporter in town at the story, gotten plenty of quotes from Lakeland officials and assorted experts, not to mention the Confederate and Texan embassies in Toledo, and a couple of stringers down on the Gulf coast. I ended up putting in a good chunk of the afternoon reading and taking notes. Wednesday night I'd be back in Philly, and unless this blew over fast I was going to be in Ellen Montrose's office Thursday morning and I needed to have proposals ready.

All the while, though, my mind kept circling back around to Berger's wretched paradox. She'd claim—I could hear her say it—that the Atlantic Republic was being held hostage by its own technologies, that it was less stable and more vulnerable because it chose to run its transport network on imported oil and made itself dependent on complex systems reaching out past its borders. She'd point to that as one more example of the way that progress cost more than it was worth. Absurd as that generalization was, I couldn't think of a cogent argument to refute it, and that irritated me.

I actually ended up spending the better part of a couple of hours, when I could have been doing something useful, standing at my window staring out at the streetscape and trying to make sense of the whole business. When I finally noticed how much time I'd wasted, I grumbled something I won't write down, and decided to go out somewhere and chase the circling thoughts out of my head. I thought of Sam Capoferro's card; a jazz club sounded like a good choice, and with the help of the hotel concierge, I was sitting on a streetcar fifteen minutes later as it rattled its way down toward the waterfront district.

The Harbor Club was in a big square brick building with tall windows that spilled lamplight onto the sidewalks. The guy at

153

the door was big and tough enough to double as the bouncer, but he took a good look at the card I handed him, nodded, and waved me past the desk where other patrons were paying the cover charge. The band was tuning up, and people were standing in groups on the dance floor talking and flirting, waiting for things to get started. Me, I got settled on one side of a little two-person table, waited for a waitress, asked about a menu—they had food service, I'd seen coming in, and not just bar snacks—and, on a whim, ordered the same sort of Lakeland-style martini Melanie Berger got the previous night, just gin, vermouth, and an olive.

I honestly had no idea how it would taste. Every martini I'd ever had back home had stuff thrown in to flavor it—crème de cacao, crème de menthe, grenadine syrup, maple syrup, clam juice, carrot juice, butterscotch ice cream, sriracha-flavored mayonnaise, or what have you—and I'd always thought that's what a martini was: gin or vodka, and anything up to half a dozen sticky things to beat up your taste buds. The drink the waitress set on my table a few minutes later was a different creature entirely. I looked at it and sniffed it, and then took a sip.

It was delicious. I blinked, set the glass down for a moment, considered the taste, and then picked it up again and took another sip. It was just as good the second time. I sat back, let the alcohol smooth down the rough edges of my nerves, ordered dinner and waited for the band to start.

Meal and music arrived within thirty seconds of each other, and both were just as satisfactory as the drink. The food was tasty in that unobtrusive way that doesn't call attention to itself, but the band was something else again. I'd guessed, the first time I'd heard him on the piano, that Sam Capoferro could play a hell of a jazz number, and he was as good as I'd thought, playing stride piano like a reincarnated Fats Waller. The other players ranged from common or garden variety competent up to really good, and their notes danced and spun on top of Capoferro's driving rhythms. The playlist was mostly familiar jazz standards, with a couple of pieces I didn't recognize—if they were new, though, they'd been composed by someone who knew all the nuances of classic jazz, and was more interested in crafting a good tune than in trying to be original.

By the time the first set was over, the bad mood I'd had earlier had packed its bags and caught a train to somewhere else. I was on my second martini by then, which didn't hurt. The band finished up the last notes of "The Joint is Jumpin'" and the crowd clapped and roared. Half the people on the dance floor headed for tables and the other half clumped up to talk and flirt; a busboy came by and scooped up my empty plate; and maybe five minutes later, I saw a half-familiar face moving through the crowd, pretty clearly looking for somewhere to sit.

I don't think he saw me, but he passed close enough that I could call out, "Mr. Vanich."

He turned, quick as a cat, and spotted me then. I hadn't been mistaken—it was the quiet man with the improbably forgettable face and voice whom I'd met my first day in Toledo. "Good evening, Mr. Carr."

"You look like you need a seat." I motioned to the one facing mine.

"Here by yourself?" When I nodded: "Then please, and thank you." He settled onto the chair; the waitress came over, took his drink order, headed off into the crowd.

We chatted for a little while about little things, what I'd seen in Toledo and so on, and then I decided to take a calculated risk. "If you don't mind my asking, what do you do in government?"

"I work for the State Department." He sipped his drink. "Office of Research and Assessment, tracking foreign technology—thus I tend to come along when somebody from State or the President's staff meets a foreign dignitary, since I know what technologies they're used to using and can translate, so to speak."

I gave him a surprised look. "If I'd placed a bet, I'd have lost it. I had you pegged as an intelligence operative."

155

He laughed. "Good, Mr. Carr. Very good. You're not the only one who's come to that conclusion, but—" He shrugged. "I look far too much like a spy to make a competent one."

I nodded after a moment. "Foreign technology assessment. That's got to be an interesting gig—tracking the capabilities that other countries have that yours doesn't."

"True." He sipped his drink—something brown called an Old Fashioned. "But that's only part of my job. The other part, which is far and away the larger one, is tracking the vulnerabilities they have that we don't."

And there I was, face to face with Berger's wretched paradox again. I must have looked completely blank for a moment, because Vanich went on. "Almost always nowadays, Mr. Carr, when a country adopts the latest technology, the costs outweigh the benefits—but the costs aren't necessarily obvious. In many cases they're not public knowledge at all. I wonder if you're familiar with the actual economics of the nuclear industry, for example."

He had me there, and I knew it. "Yeah," I admitted. "Nukes never pay for themselves and they never even manage to break even; we learned that the hard way back in the 'forties. The only countries that have them are the ones that can afford to prop them up with big subsidies, and they do it purely so they can have a few bombs tucked away for emergencies."

"Exactly," Vanich said. "There's a term we use for that sort of thing in my office: 'subsidy dumpsters.'" I laughed, and he smiled and went on. "There are quite a few subsidy dumpsters in today's technology, and they have an astonishing range of costs. Then you have the technologies that have other costs—do you happen to know the real story about the 2020 US election, by any chance?"

That was another hard one to argue. "Yeah," I said again. "That's the one where hackers got into the electronic voting machines?"

"And made them report a landslide presidential victory for Bozo the Clown. Yes, that was the one. The costs there were less financial and more a matter of prestige and legitimacy—though the states did have to scrap their expensive new voting machines and go back to paper ballots that couldn't be hacked. One of my main jobs, when dealing with other nation's technologies, is figuring out what the costs are, where they're likely to show up, and how heavily they're likely to strain political, economic, and military institutions."

I covered my confusion with another swallow of martini. "Okay," I said. "But I'm not sure I'd agree with your claim that all new technologies cost more than they're worth—"

"Almost all," he noted with a bland smile.

"Okay, almost all. That still seems kind of extreme."

"Not at all, Mr. Carr. You're familiar with the law of diminishing returns, I imagine."

"Of course."

"That applies to technology as much as it does to anything else."

"Granted, it applies to individual technologies—" I started, and then saw his look. It was the classic Lakeland you-don't-get-it look I'd seen so many times before.

"Not just to individual technologies," he said. "To technology as a whole, just as it applies to every other human activity as a whole." He indicated my drink. "One martini is a very good thing. Three or four? Still good, but with certain drawbacks. Ten? You're kissing lampposts and walking on your knees. Twenty? You're in the hospital, or worse. We agree on that—but to claim that technology is exempt from the law of diminishing returns just because you're going from one technology to another, it's as though you insisted that when you've already had four martinis, you can have four Manhattans, and then four scotch and sodas, and then four Old Fashioneds, and then four gin and tonics, and you'll be just fine."

157

"On the other hand," I said, "a steak dinner and a few martinis is better than just the martinis by themselves."

"True," said Vanich. "But you can't get a steak dinner by piling up martinis, or even by piling up drinks. In the same way, you can't get a healthy economy or a stable ecosystem by piling up technologies. You actually have to shell out some of your funds for the steak."

I literally couldn't think of anything to say in response. A moment later, the band spared me the necessity of coming up with a response, launching into a good lively performance of "All That Meat and No Potatoes." The waitress came around, and I ordered a third martini and tried, with some success, to lose myself in the music and the drink. When that set was over, I tried to change the subject, and asked him about his take on the satellite situation.

"Just as bad as the media is saying," he said. "At this point it's a matter of months before everything in orbit is shut down more or less permanently." I raised an eyebrow at that word, and he smiled and said, "I have inside information, so to speak. My wife's a professor of astronomy at Toledo University, and she's done a lot of research on the subject."

The penny dropped. "Dr. Marjorie Vanich," I said. "I read something about her in the paper the other day."

"She's quoted there quite a bit these days," he said. "She really is better informed about all this than I am. Would you like to talk to her? I'm sure she can find some time for that."

We compared notebooks and I penciled in something for Tuesday morning before the band started playing its third and final set. By the time that was over, I'd remembered that I was planned to go to the Atheist Assembly the next morning, said my goodbyes, paid my bill, and headed out onto the street to catch a cab back to the hotel.

While I waited, Vanich's words circled in my head: Technology, as a whole, subject to the law of diminishing returns. That couldn't possibly be true.

158

Could it?

The question annoyed me, but I couldn't shake it off, even when I waved down a cab and headed back to the hotel.

I felt a little worse for wear the next morning, but not too bad, and so when the alarm on the wind-up clock next to the bed went off at eight-thirty I mumbled something unprintable and got up and got to work making myself presentable. My electric razor did its usual halfhearted job on my stubble, and I shook my head and wondered what men used in the Lakeland Republic to keep their chins smooth when they didn't let the barber take care of it. Probably some antique technology that works better than ours, I thought sourly.

To say I was in a rotten mood was an understatement, but it was my own doing. I'd decided on the cab ride back from the Harbor Club that I needed to call Melanie Berger and apologize. That's not something I enjoy at all, and I also knew perfectly well that it might be wasted effort, but there it was. Partly, the professional in me wasn't willing to lose a useful contact in the Lakeland government just because the two of us had both been too tired to be tactful; partly I felt embarrassed that I'd handled the whole thing so clumsily, and partly there was the chemistry I'd sensed between the two of us. There may have been more than that, too, but that was enough.

So I'd decided to call her early in the afternoon, after I got back from Assembly and had lunch. I was brooding over that while I shaved and showered and got dressed, and I was still brooding over it at nine-fifteen as I got my tie settled. Just then the phone rang, and wouldn't you know, it was none other than Melanie Berger.

"Peter? I hope I'm not calling too early."

"Not a bit," I said. "I was just getting ready to go to Assembly. What's up?"

She paused for a moment, in exactly the way I would have, and said, "I wanted to apologize for the way things went Friday night."

159

"I was going to call you later today and say the same thing," I told her. A moment of silence passed, and then we both started talking at the same time; we both stopped, and then she laughed, and so did I.

"Okay," I said, still laughing. "I'll gladly accept your apology if you'll accept mine. Deal?"

"Deal," said Melanie. "The thing is, I'd like to make it up to you. Are you free this evening?"

"Sure." That sounded promising. "What do you have in mind?"

"You mentioned that you'd wanted to see the Toledo Opera production of *Parsifal*. Jaya and Ramaraj Patel have season tickets, and I heard from them last night—they both came down with the same flu you got, and they're not going anywhere tonight—so I thought I'd find out if I could interest you in a night at the opera."

"I'd be delighted," I said, "on one condition."

"Oh?"

"That you let me take you out to dinner first."

"You're on," she said. We got the details sorted out and said goodbye, and I got out of the room and down to the street just in time to catch the streetcar to the Capitol Atheist Assembly.

The meeting was pleasant. Everyone I met greeted me as though I was already an old friend. The reading was a rousing bit of Bertrand Russell, and the talk was about telling the difference between reason and the habits of thought that people confuse with reason, which was edgier than anything I'd heard in the Philadelphia Assembly for a good long time. Afterwards we sat around in the social hall over coffee and cookies, and talked.

The tensions between Texas and the Confederacy got a good share of the talk—no surprise, that, given how many members of the Assembly were in politics at one level or another—and I listened closely when Senator Chenkin sketched out the situation to a couple of friends who hadn't been following it closely.

160

"Both countries would go broke without the income from their petroleum industries," she said, "and they've both had production declines for the last dozen years or so, so neither side is in any position to back down. This could get really bad."

"How bad?" one of her friends asked her. She didn't answer, just shook her head, but I could see the answer in her eyes, and it wasn't anything I wanted to think about.

So I filed that away and caught the streetcar back to the hotel not long thereafter. Once I was there I talked to the concierge about what you wear to an opera in the Lakeland Republic—I'd wondered whether they'd gone back to opera capes and top hats, and was relieved to find out that ordinary evening wear would do—and then went out to see if the barber I'd visited my first day in Toledo had Sunday hours. Fortunately he did, and he was just finishing up a shave and trim on another customer when I got there. When it was my turn, he greeted me effusively and said, "You got an evening with somebody special planned, I bet," and laughed when I asked him how he'd guessed. "Of course you do. Any guy comes in here midway through a weekend day for a shave and trim, dollars'll get you doughnuts that's what's on the schedule. Don't you worry, I'll get your face smoother than a baby's butt."

He did, too. I left there looking ready for an evening out. A pleasant lunch in the hotel café, a talk with the concierge about restaurants, and a couple of leisurely hours reading the Sunday paper and getting caught up on the news: that filled the rest of the time before I caught a cab over to Melanie Berger's, picked her up, and headed for a top-end restaurant not quite two blocks from the Toledo opera house.

We had a great time. The food was really good and the wine was better, and both of us had the common sense to keep the conversation well away from progress or anything related to it. Of course we talked about politics—get two people who work in any line of business together, even for a social evening, and they're going to talk shop—but that wasn't the only subject of conversation by a long shot. One of the others was the performance we were about to take in. The Lakeland National Opera had a homegrown bass, a young guy named Michael Bickerstaff, who would be singing the part of Gurnemanz. He'd done a stellar job the year before in his first major role as Sarastro in *The Magic Flute*, but of course Wagner's much harder on singers than Mozart ever dreamed of being.

"They say he's really good," Melanie said. "Good enough that a couple of European opera companies are interested in him, and some people here are talking about what kind of a Wotan he'd make."

That impressed me. "Are they planning on doing the Ring cycle here?"

"Jaya tells me there's been some tentative discussions with the Minneapolis Opera about a joint production," she said. "They've got some really solid singers—tonight's Kundry is one of theirs."

Dinner wound down pleasantly, and in due time we headed for the opera house. Like most of Toledo, it was new construction but old-fashioned design, with a spacious lobby and comfortable seats. Ours were about halfway toward the left wall on the first balcony. We got settled, and of course then had to stand up a couple of times while latecomers made their apologies and edged past to their own seats. Our conversation wound up, the lights went down, the conductor got up on his podium and the first bars of the Prelude sounded in the dim light.

When the curtains slid open, I admit I braced myself. In Wagner's operas, there's only room for one monumental ego, and it's his, but you get directors who don't realize that and try to make a production original by pulling some visual stunt or other. I've seen Wagnerian operas where all the singers were in Old West outfits, or superhero costumes, or bulbous yellow things that made them look like a flock of rubber duckies—I never did find out what those were supposed to be about. Apparently the Lakeland National Opera

162

had managed to escape that bad habit. The set was abstract to the point of starkness, with fabric veils and shafts of light providing most of the decor; you could tell the designer had taken a close and thoughtful look at Bayreuth productions from the middle of the last century. What's more, the costumes looked more or less the way you'd expect a bunch of Grail Knights to look, which was a pleasant surprise.

Then Gurnemanz got up from under the abstract tree where he'd supposedly been sleeping, and broke into his first line— *He, ho, Waldhüter ihr!*—and I knew right away that we were in for a treat.

Most of the singers were, in the strict sense of the word, second-rate: one notch below first-rate, which is still definitely good enough to enjoy. The soprano who sang Kundry, Maria Vargas Castillo, was better than that; she didn't have the absolute purity of tone you need for Wagner's most demanding soprano roles, but the role she was singing actually goes better with a little roughness in the voice.

Then there was Michael Bickerstaff. He wasn't just first-rate, he was world-class, a big barrel-chested young man with one of the best bass voices I'd heard in years. The role of Gurnemanz, the old Grail Knight, is the backbone of *Parsifal*; a good Gurnemanz can make a mediocre production enjoyable, while an unimpressive one drags like a lead weight on a performance that might otherwise be worth taking in. Bickerstaff was stunningly good—he more or less picked up the show and carried it on his shoulders. The production benefited accordingly, and I sat back and enjoyed the result.

The first act flowed past, and the second; Parsifal vanquished the self-castrated sorcerer Klingsor and recovered the Holy Spear; the third act got well under way, and Parsifal, Gurnemanz, and Kundry were on stage, surrounded by a tolerably good suggestion of a field of flowers created by artful spotlights. The passage that's called *der Karfreitagszauber*, the Good Friday Enchantment, got under way, Bickerstaff sang

Du siehst, das ist nicht so—"You see it is not so"—and that's when it hit me.

You know how sometimes you can brood over some problem for hours and get nowhere with it, and then when you go do something else for a while and you're not thinking about it at all, the answer basically downloads itself into your brain? That's what happened. I'd spent most of the day thinking of just about anything but the paradox Melanie Berger had dropped on me two nights before, and right then I realized that it wasn't a paradox at all. I managed to drag my attention back to the performance before Bickerstaff was more than a few words further on, and kept the realization I'd just had at arm's length for the rest of the evening, but it wasn't going anywhere and I knew it.

Here's what I figured out. As you might expect, it begins with opera.

These days, nobody listens to twentieth-century opera. That's not accidental; it's either completely derivative or it's impossible to sit through. Once I went to see a revival of one of Philip Glass's pieces, I forget which one, and what I mostly remember was the audience gamely trying to pretend that they were appreciating something that was about as enjoyable as listening to a chorus of dental drills. The standard joke in opera circles these days is that opera companies put on twentieth century works when they're tired of the inconvenience of performing in front of an audience.

One of my Philadelphia friends, who's a much more serious opera buff than I'll ever be, explains it like this. Any art form has a certain amount of notional space to it, and each work done in that space fills up part of it. Before you've filled up the space, innovation works more often than not, but after the space is full, innovation just generates noise. That's why the history of every art gets sorted out into a period of exploration, when you succeed by trying new things, and a period of performance, when you succeed by doing old things very, very well. If you

164

keep on trying to innovate when the notional space is full, the results are either going to be derivative or they're going to be noise, and either way they're not going to be any good, because the good options have already been taken.

You know that an art is getting close to the edges of its notional space when innovation involves a lot of risk. Wagner was right up against the edges of opera's notional space, which is why his late operas are so exhilarating—you can watch him tiptoeing right up to the edge of noise and balancing there—but they don't have the easy grace of operas written a generation or two before his time. You see the same thing in jazz, starting in the second half of the twentieth century: people like Thelonious Monk and Dave Brubeck were self-consciously testing the boundaries, figuring out just how far they could go without falling over the edge into noise. Another generation further on, and most of what you get is the kind of jazz that nobody bothers to play any more, because it's just pretentious doodling.

What's more, my friend said, every culture eventually gets to that place with all its arts taken together. Western civilization got there around 1900. Whether you're talking painting, sculpture, music, dance, architecture, you name it—after that, there are things that are original, and there are things that are good, but you won't find very many things that are both at the same time. The only exceptions are things like jazz that draw inspiration from different cultures, and even then you run out of notional space very fast—opera was breaking new territory for more than three centuries, jazz ran out of room and became performance after about seventy-five.

The thing that struck me then is that it's not just true of art. You won't find many people coming up with brand new alphabets any more, because that notional space got filled in a long time ago. Nobody's inventing new can openers or bathtubs, and nearly all of what passes for innovation these days in cars, say, is just gimmickry aimed at getting the clueless to shell out money. I knew all that, without ever really thinking about it, but it never occurred to me that technological progress followed the same trajectory. It had its period of exploration and then crossed over into its period of performance, but nobody noticed, and so everyone just kept on buying the latest innovations, even though most of those were noise, and had fewer benefits and worse downsides than the things they replaced.

I'd missed that completely. I'd been wandering around the Lakeland Republic, noticing that the way they did things had better outcomes, lower costs, and fewer downsides than the way people do things everywhere else, and I still didn't get it. It was as though I'd been listening to an opera by Mozart or Verdi and thinking that the poor people in the audience must be feeling horribly deprived because they weren't getting Philip Glass. *Du siehst*, sang Gurnemanz, *das ist nicht so.*

Writing it all out like that, it sounds all clear and straightforward. It wasn't. There was the first sudden realization while Bickerstaff was singing, and then other details—many more than I've written out—came dropping into my mind over the next couple of hours. All the while I was mostly paying attention to other things, such as a really solid performance of an opera I love, and the attractive woman I was seeing it with, and certain other things I'll mention in a moment, and these things were tumbling around in the back of my head. It wasn't until I was in the cab headed back to my hotel early the next morning that I finally sat back and let the whole thing come together into a coherent argument. Long before that happened, though, I'd stumbled straight through the door into a different world.

But again, there was an opera to take in. After the final minutes of *Parsifal*, when it always feels to me as though the opera house has shaken off gravity and gone soaring into the sky; after the applause—we were all on our feet, and when Michael Bickerstaff bowed I'm surprised the roar didn't cause structural damage to the building; after the house lights came

166

up at last, and people started filing out, Melanie said, "Season tickets get us into the reception, and there's someone there I'd like you to meet."

So we filed out and went down a side corridor; Melanie showed our passes to an usher out in front of an unmarked double door, and in we went. The room on the other side was big and airy, with a mural of scenes from famous operas on one wall, and a bank of tables along the other with champagne and finger food. It wasn't too crowded, and I gathered that the person Melanie wanted me to meet wasn't there yet, so we got a couple of glasses and sipped bubbly for a few minutes while more people filed in. Finally, when the room was getting good and packed, Melanie led me through the crowd.

"Janice," she said, "this is Peter Carr, from Philadelphia— one of Ellen Montrose's people." With an impish smile: "And a limited partner of yours. Peter, Janice Mikkelson."

Mikkelson was maybe sixty, with short straight hair the color of steel wool and a pantsuit with the kind of understated elegance you only notice at a second glance; given the tailoring and the fabric, I guessed that it cost as much as any of the fancy dresses in the room. She gave me an assessing look as we shook hands, and I said, "To the extent of one share of Mikkelson LLC."

She laughed. "Not exactly a vote of confidence, but I'm pleased to meet you anyway." I got introduced to her wife Sharon, a gorgeous Asian woman maybe fifteen years her junior in a stunning gown and a fair-sized galaxy of diamonds, and we stood chatting for a while about the performance. Mikkelson turned to me, then, and said, "Any chance you have time in your schedule to talk? I'm interested in the possibility of doing business in the Atlantic Republic."

"I can do that," I said. "Also, if you don't mind, I'd be interested in getting your perspective on things here in Lakeland." She nodded, we both checked our notebooks, and scheduled something for Tuesday afternoon. "Come up to my place,"

Mikkelson said. "Some drinks, some conversation, some business—I think it'll be productive."

We chatted a little more, and then moved on in the usual way. Not much later Melanie and I were on our way down the long ramp to the lobby and then out to the street, where cabs lined up waiting for easy fares. We took one to her place, a brick row house a dozen blocks from the Capitol, and I walked her to her door. I had a pretty good idea by then of how the evening was going to end, and so it wasn't any kind of surprise when she gave me the kind of raised-eyebrow smile that means exactly one thing. I went to pay the cab fare, came back to her, took her hand and followed her inside.

CHAPTER 10

A phone rang in the darkness. For a moment I had no
idea where I was, but then the bed shifted, footsteps
whispered across the floor, and Melanie's voice said,
"Hello." I blinked, and tried to guess what time it was. It felt as
though we hadn't been sleeping for long.

"Okay," she said then, in a completely different tone.
I finished waking up in a hurry. You don't hear someone speak
like that unless something's gone very, very wrong. "Okay,"
she said again. "I'll be in as soon as I can. 'Bye." The handset
clicked into its cradle, and Melanie said, "Peter?"

"What's up?"

"Trouble. Texas and the Confederacy are at war."

I sat up and said something unprintable.

"Pretty much," she agreed, and turned on a light. She was
as naked as I was, of course, but the look on her face wasn't
particularly alluring.

"Any details?" I asked.

"Just a few. Texan ships attacked three Confederate drilling platforms around one o'clock; no word on damage yet.
The Confederate navy came out, and there's fighting going on
in the Gulf right now."

"That's bad."

169

"There's worse. The Confederate Army's crossed into Texas territory between Shreveport and Texarkana. Our people down there think there's division-strength units involved."

I gave her a blank stare for a long moment. "Okay," I said, getting out of bed. "You're going in right away, of course."

"Yes. Not the way I'd have chosen to end a really pleasant evening."

I took her in my arms and kissed her. "No argument there," I said when the kiss was done. "Give me a call when you get some free time."

"I'll do that," she said, with a smile. Then: "If you can stand it, stay close to your phone. I may be able to arrange something for you."

I promised I would. She headed for the shower, and I pulled my clothes on, called a cab, and let myself out. She was right, it was a hell of a way to end a really pleasant evening, but if you're in politics you get used to that kind of thing. I knew that, and so did Melanie; if things worked out, we'd find some time to spend together before I took the train back to Philadelphia, and one way or another—

I stopped the thought in its tracks. Later, I told myself. Later, when a couple of really hard decisions are over and done with.

The sky was still pitch black when I left the apartment building and stood on the curb waiting for the cab. The clop-clop of horse's hooves announced its arrival a couple of blocks in advance. Moments later I was inside, watching the city of Toledo in its sleep. Here and there a light shone in a window, or a lone figure hurried down the street. It seemed hard to believe that not much more than a thousand miles away, robot tanks, assault drones, and long files of young men with guns were streaming through the pine woods of northeast Texas.

The cab got me to the hotel promptly enough, and I paid the cabby, said good morning to the tired-eyed desk clerk, and headed up to my room. I didn't really expect to get more sleep, but decided to give it a try, and blinked awake four hours later

170

with the pale gray light of morning coming in through the window. The clock said quarter past eight; I hurried through a shower, got myself shaved and dressed, weighed the odds that Melanie might call if I took the time to run to Kaufer's News to get the morning *Blade*, and decided to call the concierge instead. Not five minutes later a bellhop knocked on the door with a copy. "We got a stack of 'em down at the desk," he told me. "Half the guests are gonna want one as soon as they wake up." I thanked him and gave him a good-sized tip, and he grinned and made off.

The paper didn't have much more information on the current state of affairs than I'd gotten from Melanie, but the reporters had done their background research; the inside of the front section had big articles sketching out the history of the quarrel, running through both sides' military assets, quoting a couple of experts from Toledo University on the potential outcomes of the war, that sort of thing. Tucked away toward the end was a terse little article about two more satellites being taken out by debris. I was maybe halfway through that last article when the phone rang.

"Peter? It's Melanie. Can you get to the Capitol by nine-thirty?"

"Sure," I said. "What's up?"

"There's a courtesy briefing for the North American diplomatic community—the ambassadors will be meeting with Meeker; this is for attachés and staff. I've arranged to get you in as a special envoy from Ellen Montrose's staff."

"No kidding. Thank you, Melanie."

"Sure thing." She gave me the details, we said our goodbyes and away I went.

The city was wide awake as I walked the four blocks to the Capitol. Newspapers and conversations in low voices were everywhere. The streetcars, horsedrawn cabs, and occasional cars still rolled down the streets; lamps shone in windows, contending with the gray light; nothing had changed since

171

the morning before, and everything had. I remembered stories some of my older relatives used to tell about the first days of the Second Civil War—carefully sanitized stories coming over the mass media, wild rumors carried by blogs and social media and emails, and everywhere the sense that something had changed or shifted or broken once and for all, and the world would never be the same afterwards.

Somehow, the morning around me felt like that. I told myself not to be silly. There had been other wars since Partition—the three-way scramble between Texas, the Confederacy, and the Missouri Republic in '37, the Confederate-Brazilian invasion of the Lakeland Republic in '49, and the ongoing civil war in California—but this felt different.

"Extra!" shouted a paperboy on the sidewalk in front of the Capitol, where people were streaming by. "Richmond's declared war." He was selling copies nearly as fast as he could hand them out, but I managed to get one before his canvas bag was empty. I wasn't the only purchaser to turn toward the Capitol's big front entrance, either. We filed in the doors, and then some of us turned right toward the Senate end of the building, went down the first big staircase we found, and ended up in front of a big door flanked by two guards in uniform and a man in a wool suit. I recognized him after a moment: Stuart Macallan, the Lakeland Republic's assistant secretary of state for North American affairs.

"Mr. Carr," he said, shaking my hand. "Good to see you again. Yes, you've been cleared—favor to the incoming administration in Philadelphia." He winked, and I laughed and went on to the coatroom, where I shed hat and coat before going further.

The room inside was a big comfortable space with a podium up front and rows of tables and chairs facing it, the kind of place where important press conferences and public hearings get held. All the usual impedimenta of a high-end briefing were there—pitchers of ice water on each table, and so on—and something I hadn't expected: a notebook and pen in front of each place. Of course I understood the moment I saw them: lacking veepads, how else were the attendees going to take notes? Even so, that reminded me how many details of life in the Lakeland Republic I still hadn't seen.

I sat down and opened the paper. The Confederate Congress had voted to declare war, as the boy said; the Texan legislature was expected to return the favor shortly. In the meantime, the naval battle in the Gulf was ongoing, with people along the coast reporting distant explosions and smoke plumes visible on the horizon. Nobody was sure yet what was happening on the land front; the entire region from Shreveport and Texarkana west to the suburbs of Dallas was closed to journalists, and the entire highway system was off limits to anybody but government and military, but long lines of army-green trucks were streaming east across Texas toward the war zone, and a reporter who'd gotten as far north as Henderson before being turned back by military police reported that she could hear artillery rolling in the northern distance like summer thunder.

Someone sat down at the chair next to mine, and I did the polite thing and turned to greet him. "Hank Barker," he said as we shook hands, "trade attaché with the Missouri Republic embassy." I introduced myself, and he brightened. "You're Ellen Montrose's envoy here, aren't you? Once this is over, if you've got a minute to talk, that'd be real welcome."

"Sure," I said. It wasn't until then that I noticed that he was dressed the way I was, in typical Lakeland business wear. Most of the other people filing into the room wore bioplastic, though we weren't the only ones in wool. "Got tired of bioplastic, I see," I commented.

He nodded. "Yep. You see this sort of thing more and more often these days, out our way. 'Course a lot of the wool and leather Lakeland uses comes from our side of the Mississippi, so it stands to reason."

173

I glanced at him, wondered whether any other Lakeland Republic customs had found a foothold across the Mississippi. The Missouri Republic's big, reaching from the river to the crest of the Rockies and from what used to be Kansas and the north-western two-thirds of Missouri to the border of West Canada, but a lot of it's desert these days; it's pretty much landlocked—its only ports are river towns on the Mississippi and Duluth on Lake Superior—and if they were paying off World Bank loans and coping with the same economic pressures we were in the Atlantic Republic, they'd have to be in a world of hurt. Before I could figure out how to ask the question that was on my mind, though, the last of the attendees had taken their seats and a familiar figure rolled his wheelchair across the low stage to one side of the podium.

"I'd like to thank you all for coming," Tom Pappas said. "We're still waiting for more details from the war zone—"

"Like everyone else," said a voice with a Québecois accent close to the front of the room.

"I'm not arguing," Pappas said, with a broad grin. "But we've got a basic idea what's going on, and we can also fill you in on our government's response."

An aide, a young woman in Lakeland army uniform, came up onto the stage, went to the back wall and pulled on a cord. Down came a big, brightly colored map of the eastern half of the Republic of Texas and parts of the Confederacy adjacent to it. Pappas thanked her, took a long pointer from behind the podium, and wheeled over to the map.

"The three drilling platforms the Texans attacked last night are here." The pointer tapped a patch of blue water in the Gulf. "Those are the ones Bullard claimed were using horizontal drilling to poach Texan oil. Based on what information we've gotten at this point, all three platforms were destroyed. Confederate naval forces counterattacked less than an hour later, and both sides suffered significant losses—they've both got decent antiship missiles, and you know how that goes."

A murmur spread through the room. "The thing is, the Confederates didn't just fire on the Texan ships," Pappas went on. "They used long range missiles to target Texan offshore oil assets. We're not sure how many were targeted and how badly they were hit, but it doesn't look good—and the other nations with interests in the Gulf aren't going to be happy at all if this goes on and neither side is able to plug the wells below the damaged platforms.

"Right now, as far as we can tell, there's still a naval engagement going on, and both sides are bringing in naval assets from outside the area. Texas has a short term advantage there. The Confederates have a lot of their ships on the Atlantic coast, and it's going to take a while to get them around the south Florida shoals and bring them into action, but once those arrive, the Texan navy's going to be in deep—trouble."

That got a laugh. "Okay," he said, and moved the pointer up to tap on the area between Shreveport and Texarkana. "That's a sideshow. Here's the thing that matters. Our best estimate at this point is that the Confederacy's thrown three divisions into the ground assault: one armored division, two infantry. More are being brought up as fast as the transport grid will carry them. The Texans are throwing everything they've got on hand into slowing them down. It's anyone's guess whether they can get enough of their army into play before the Confederates reach Dallas; my best guess is that they will. Meanwhile Texan drones and land based missiles have been hitting military targets as far east as the Mississippi, and the Confederacy's doing the same thing—we've had reports of missile strikes as far west as Waco.

"And this is where it gets ugly. Both sides have allies overseas. The Confederates have already asked Brazil to intervene; no word from Brasilia yet, but given their track record in the past, it's probably a safe bet that Richmond will get Brazilian munitions and advisers, maybe more. Texas has a mutual-aid pact with China, and after the business in Peru two years ago, the Chinese have got to be itching for an opportunity to take Brazil down a peg or two; a proxy war would be one way to do that. So we could be facing a long and ugly war.

"That's the military situation. Stuart, you want to fill them in on our response?"

Stuart Macallan climbed up onto the stage. "Sure. Point number one is that we're staying out of it. We've declared ourselves neutral, and President Meeker is working with the other North American governments right now to draft a joint declaration of neutrality and an appeal to the combatants to accept an immediate ceasefire and settle this at the negotiating table, using the mechanisms set up in the Treaty of Richmond.

"Point number two is that we've ordered a defensive mobilization all along our southern border, just in case. Those of you who know anything about our military know that this isn't a threat to anybody, unless they decide to invade. If you're not familiar with our system, Colonel Pappas here can fill you in on the details after we finish.

"Point number three is that we're going to look for every possible way to expedite trade agreements with the other North American republics. Half our exports go via the Mississippi, and I know some of our neighbors are in the same boat—so to speak. We're prepared to help the other North American republics keep their economies intact, to the extent that we can, and we'd welcome any help you can give us along the same lines.

"Finally, there's the petroleum situation. For all practical purposes, the Gulf oil fields, onshore and offshore, have just dropped off the face of the Earth, and they're going to stay that way until this whole business gets resolved. That's a big enough fraction of world oil production to send markets into a tizzy, and I don't just mean oil markets. Latest from the Asian stock markets is that they're down between three and eight per cent across the board.

"The oil shortage won't particularly affect us, as you know, but it's going to be a problem for pretty much everyone else in

North America. We're going to look at agreements with each of your countries to try to cushion the economic hit, but whatever you're paying for fuel these days—our best estimate is that it's going to double, maybe triple, maybe more, if you can get it. The way so much oil production is locked up in long term contracts, some of you probably won't be able to get it at all."

Hank Barker, sitting next to me, shook his head. Under his breath: "We are so screwed."

The briefing finally wound up a little before one o'clock, and Stuart Macallan invited all of us to lunch in one of the formal dining rooms downstairs. I gathered that the ambassadors were having lunch with Meeker in the president's private dining room one floor up, but the meal we got was nothing to complain about: sandwiches on croissants, French onion soup, pear slices, Brie, and choice of beverages. You could tell something about each of the diplomats by watching who chose which of the latter—the ones who downed strong coffee to deal with too little sleep, the ones who tipped back a local beer to be social, and the ones who got something stronger than beer to keep from having to think about just how bad this mess could get.

I sat with Hank Barker and a couple of other people from the trade end of things: Jonathan Two Hawks, also from Missouri, Vera McTavish from East Canada, and one of the handful of familiar faces in the room, Lashonda Marvell from the Free City of Chicago—I'd been involved in rough-draft negotiations on a trade-in-services agreement with Chicago six years back, and she'd been on the other side of those talks. Two Hawks and McTavish were coffee drinkers, Marvell and I ordered beer, and Barker got bourbon straight, downed it, and then ordered another.

They were all interested in access to the New York canal system, of course. It had never really occurred to me how big a resource that was. People in the Atlantic Republic government treat it as a relic, but with the Mississippi closed to ship traffic by a shooting war, it had suddenly become the one way around the potential bottleneck of the Saint Lawrence Seaway. While I wasn't an official envoy, they all knew perfectly well that Montrose's landslide election win meant that the current embassy staff might not have the same clout in Philadelphia they once did, and they wanted to make nice with the new team.

I was perfectly willing to play that game, for that matter. Transit fees on international shipments via our waterways would bring in a chunk of hard currency at a time when we could really use that, and if the whole business was handled right, it would leave other nations owing the Atlantic Republic favors that could be called in later on. So, between bites of sandwich, I sketched out the kind of terms we'd want—I modeled them shamelessly on the draft agreement I'd worked out with the Lakeland Republic, of course—and they tossed back questions and counteroffers. It was a good lively discussion, the fun part of trade negotiations, and I think we really made some progress toward a set of agreements that would be win-win for everybody.

The official Atlantic Republic delegation sat pretty much by themselves over on the other side of the room, and gave me flat unreadable looks now and then. They knew perfectly well what I was doing, and what the people from the other delegations were doing. They were all Barfield's people, a lot of them would be out of a job in January, and since I wasn't here in any official capacity, I hadn't bothered them and they'd returned the favor. Still, that was before this morning. Once the lunch broke up and people started heading out, I shook hands with everyone at my table, made sure they had my contact info back in Philadelphia, and headed over to the handful of Atlantic people still sitting at theirs.

One of them was a guy I knew from back when I was in business, and I went up to him and shook his hand. "Hi, Frank."

"Hi, Peter," he said. "Hell of a situation."

"I won't argue."

He eyed my clothes, and said, "Gone native, I see."

I laughed. "When in Rome. I got tired of people looking at me like a two-headed dog."

"Whatever floats your boat," he said. "What can I do for you?"

"What's official policy on sending a message to the President-elect via diplomatic links?"

He gave me a bleak look. "'All reasonable accommodation,'" he quoted. "You guys pounded our butts fair and square, and it's your baby now." With a sudden edged smile: "Frankly, now that this new thing's blown up, I'm glad I'll be out the door in two months."

"I bet," I said. We talked about the details, and the upshot was that the two of us took a taxi to the Atlantic embassy six blocks away on Lakeland's Embassy Row. From the outside, it was a nice stone building of typical Lakeland design, like the other embassies, and the Atlantic flag, navy-white-navy with a gold anchor in the middle and a gold star in the upper left, whipped back and forth in a raw wind. Go through the door and everything's brushed aluminum and black plastic, with the kind of abstract art on the walls that looks like an overenthusiastic dog gobbled an artist's paint tubes and then threw up. I'd spent most of my adult life in settings like that, and gotten used to thinking of them as modern, cutting-edge, and so on. For the first time it really sank in just how incredibly ugly it all was.

Still, I followed Frank to the communications center down in the basement, got handed over to the comm manager and shown to a desk with a veescreen terminal. For the first time since I'd crossed the border, I had the once-familiar sensation of an image field projected into my visual cortex, and was surprised by how intrusive it felt. Still, I had work to do. I typed out something to Meg Amberger, the Montrose transition team's trade-policy person, letting her know about the potential shipping agreements with Missouri, East Canada, and Chicago, and asked her to tell the boss that the negotiations with Lakeland had gone well—I figured she could use the good news. I added four words that I knew Meg wouldn't understand, but would pass on anyway, and then hit the SEND button. A moment later that was on its way; I thanked the manager and left the comm center.

Frank was waiting for me outside the door. "Normally I'd invite you to come around and check your veemail here, but we're down to essential traffic only."

It took me a moment to realize what he was saying. "Satellite trouble?"

"Yeah. One more thing on top of everything else."

I eyed him, considered the options. "Can I buy you a drink?"

He paused, then nodded. "Sure."

He knew exactly what I was asking, of course. We went outside again, and he waved down a taxi and gave the driver an address I recognized, over on the other end of downtown. All the bars and restaurants close to Embassy Row are wired for sound by somebody or other. If you're embassy staff or intelligence, you know where your people have mikes, so you can take contacts there when you want something recorded, and you usually know where at least some of the other countries have mikes, so you can feed them true or false information as the situation requires. If you want to talk off the record, though, you go somewhere well away from Embassy Row, and never the same place twice, so it's tougher for anybody else's spooks to listen in.

So we rolled through the streets of Toledo behind the amiable clop-clop-clop of the horse, Frank looking glum and uncomfortable in his bioplastic suit, me being glad that old-fashioned wool suiting keeps out the chill. Neither of us said much of anything until we got out of the taxi. We were in front of the Harbor Club, the place where I'd listened to Sam Capoferro and his Frogtown Five and talked to Fred Vanich. It was open and surprisingly busy for three in the afternoon, but we had no trouble getting a table over to one side, across from the piano Sam had played. A spry old lady with silver hair and dark brown skin sat there now, playing Chopin with an ease that showed she'd had her fingers on a keyboard since she was six or so.

The waiter came over as soon as we were settled. I ordered a martini, and Frank gave me a sidelong look and ordered a double shot of vodka, straight. The bartender didn't waste any time, either.

"So," I said, once the drinks arrived. "Satellite trouble, and everything else."

"You know we lease satellite services from a Chinese firm, right?" Fred took a slug of his drink "We're supposed to have four high-speed channels. Right now we've got one, and it's high speed only if you give that phrase a really broad definition. Rumor has it that at least two embassies have no realtime comm links home at all, though nobody's admitting it, and it won't take too many more fender benders in orbit before our provider calls force majeure and we're shut out completely. Everybody's trying to figure out some way to get satellite service back, but it's going to be a while."

"A long while," I said. "How did embassies phone home before there were satellites?"

It seemed like an obvious question, but Frank looked at me as though I'd sprouted a spare head. "I have no idea," he said. "Who cares? Anyway, our provider's trying to see if there's a way to get new satellites into a higher orbit or something, but that may be years out. But that's just one more mess on top of the others. You know the Philly stock market's down hard."

"Along with everyone else's," I said.

"Worse." He gestured with his drink, which was getting toward half empty. "We had a lot more foreign investment than anybody realized—it was all through shell corporations, you know the drill—and when telecom stocks started dragging the market down, you had the usual flight to safety. Treasury stepped in, of course, and propped things up with hard currency loans, but they've only got so much of that on

181

hand and the World Bank isn't handing over any more. So even before this damn war broke out, we were looking at a major economic crisis—and now this. I honestly don't know how we're going to make it."

"We've had economic crises before," I said.

"Yeah, but it's different this time. Treasury is running in circles like a bunch of robot tanks with a garbled program, everybody else is trying to get as much money out as they can without making too much noise, and when the hard currency runs short the bottom's going to drop right out. I hope your boss has something up her sleeve, or we're going to be in for it."

I motioned for him to go on, and he said, "And now the war. This stays off the record." I nodded, and he went on. "Our NIS people here talked with their opposite numbers back home." NIS was National Intelligence Service, our spook shop in Philadelphia. "They've got sources down south. Word is that along with the drilling platforms, at least eighteen Confederate production platforms got blown to scrap, and fourteen of them were running stripper well farms."

"Meaning?"

"Meaning that there's not enough output to pay for replacing the platforms once the fighting's over. A lot of the Gulf oil industry works legacy fields, right? If the situation's similar on the Texas side, and that's the current best guess, a big fraction of Gulf oil production is g, o, n, e, gone, for good. That means another price spike, and maybe worse." He gave me an uneasy look; I gestured for him to continue, and he said, "Actual shortages. As in 'No, we don't have any at all' shortages. How do you deal with something like that?"

"There've been oil shortages before," I reminded him. "How did people deal with those?"

"I don't have the least idea," he said. "That was then, this is now. But our people back in Philly are just aghast. They're trying to game possible responses and coming up blank. I don't know if there's any option that will work at all." He finished his drink, waved down a waiter and ordered a refill.

I nodded and said something to keep him talking, and for the next two hours or so got an increasingly detailed account of just how screwed the Atlantic Republic was going to be without viable satellite services, foreign investment, or a reliable source of petroleum—we used less of that latter than most of the other North American republics, and a lot less than anybody thought of using back before the Second Civil War, but it was still something we couldn't give up without landing in a world of hurt. All the while, though, I was trying to fit my head around the way he'd blown off my questions.

The penny didn't drop until I got him onto a taxi—he was pretty wobbly by then, so I paid his fare and told the driver where to take him—and stood there on the sidewalk watching the back of the thing pull away. Two weeks ago, I realized, I'd have done exactly the same thing. That was then, this is now, it's different this time, that's history, we need to be thinking ahead of the times, not behind them: how many times had I mouthed those same catchphrases?

I'd meant to flag down another cab, but turned and started walking instead, taking the distant pale shape of the unfinished Capitol dome as my guide. Around me, Toledo went about its business as though this was just another day. The sky had cleared off, the wind was brisk but not too raw, and people were out on the sidewalks, shopping or heading for swing shift jobs or just taking in some fresh air. The crisis that had the Atlantic Republic tottering was just another piece of news to them. It was interesting news; a paperboy came trotting along the street shouting "Extra! Latest news on the war down south!" and found plenty of customers. Still, they didn't have to care. It wasn't something that was going to throw them out of work and shred the fabric of their daily lives. And the reason was—

The reason was that they had stopped saying "It's different this time," and started treating the past as a resource rather than an irrelevance.

I kept walking. Everything I saw around me—the horse-drawn cabs, the streetcars, the comfortable and attractive brick buildings, the clothing everybody wore—had been quarried out of the past and refitted for use in the present, because each one of them worked better than the alternatives. The insight that had come crashing into my thoughts in the middle of *Parsifal* returned: for us, for people in the North American republics and everywhere else in the industrial world, the period of exploration was over, the period of performance had arrived, and we had plenty of data about what worked and what didn't, if only we chose to use it.

A streetcar went by, packed with workers on their way home from the day shift; the conductor's bell went ding-di-ding ding, the way conductors' bells went on those same streets a hundred and fifty years before. I knew perfectly well why nobody in Philadelphia thought about putting streetcars back on the streets of the Atlantic Republic's cities, to do a job they did better, and for much less money, than the shiny high-tech modern equivalents. I'd been in the middle of the group think that made progress look like the only option even when progress was half a century into negative returns. Everyone I knew was well aware that "newer" had stopped meaning "better" a long time ago, that every upgrade meant more problems and fewer benefits, that the latest must-have technologies did less and cost more than the last round, but nobody seemed to be able to draw the obvious conclusion.

I shook my head and kept walking, while those ideas circled in my head.

It must have been most of an hour later when I realized I'd overshot my hotel by a good dozen blocks. The Capitol dome was behind me, and I'd strayed into a neighborhood of narrow row houses with little shops at some of the street corners. It was pretty obviously working class territory, but the houses looked clean and well maintained, and little flower boxes here and there promised bright colors come spring. One of the houses had a FOR SALE sign on it; I'd expected FOR RENT, and then it sank in that in the Lakeland Republic working class people could still afford to buy their own homes. I thought of the working class neighborhoods in Philly, full of dilapidated rental properties, which look like war zones and which you don't walk into if you don't want to be mugged or worse; the contrast stung.

I took my bearings from the Capitol dome and started walking. By the time I got there, it must have been past five o'clock, and people were trickling out of the Capitol, heading toward the street and the line of cabs that waited there for fares. I recognized one of them at a glance; I'm glad to say she saw me and turned up the sidewalk to meet me.

"Hello, Melanie," I said.

That got a tired smile. "Hello, Peter. Hell of a day."

"I won't argue." I considered the options. "Up for dinner?"

"About that."

I gestured to one of the cabs; she smiled again, and the cabby bounded down from his seat and opened the door for us.

We settled on a Greek restaurant close by, a place I'd been for lunch already. I passed that onto the driver as soon as we got into the cab, and slumped back against the leather seat as the driver climbed up onto the seat up front, snapped the reins, and got the horses moving. Neither Melanie nor I said anything. The lights of Toledo rolled by, and I wondered how many people behind the windows we passed were worrying about the war down south the way I was.

It was maybe five minutes, if that, when the cab rolled to a stop, and the cabby swung down from his seat and popped open the door. I climbed down, paid him, reached out a hand for Melanie; she took it gratefully, got down onto the sidewalk. "Thank you," she said, when the cabbie was driving off. "For a few minutes of silence, especially."

185

"We don't have to talk over dinner," I said as we headed toward the door.

"Don't worry about it. You won't be screaming at me in an east Texas accent for an hour straight."

I gave her a questioning look, but by then we were inside and the greeter was headed our way. Once we were comfortably settled in a booth over to one side, and the waitress had handed us menus and taken our drinks order to the bar, I said, "Seriously?"

"Seriously. The Texan ambassador wanted to see President Meeker right now, and no, she didn't care that he was in a cabinet meeting and that she was going to be the first to see him afterwards. It's one of the few times I've ever wished that diplomatic courtesies included the option of slapping someone hard enough to send teeth flying."

I choked, then pasted on a respectable expression while the waitress came back with our martinis and took our order. "I take it Texas doesn't put professionals in its embassies."

"Only the important ones, and we're not one of those. Velma Streiber's a Houston society matron who has good friends in the Bulford administration and wanted a fancy title." She shook her head.

"I hope you didn't have to deal with the Confederate ambassador too," I said.

"I did, but that was easy. John Bayard MacElroy is your basic Confederate gentleman. He might shoot you dead in cold blood and feed your bullet-riddled corpse to his hound dogs, but he'll be the very soul of politeness while he does it."

I choked again. Then, still laughing, I shook my head and picked up my martini. She gave me a startled look. "That doesn't look much like what you were drinking Friday night."

"It isn't," I admitted. "I decided to try a Lakeland style martini Saturday, and liked it."

That got me a long, considering look, and then a nod. "But that was my day—that and dealing with just about every other embassy in Toledo by phone or in person, scheduling meetings with Meeker, setting up briefings like the one you went to, attending a couple of briefings myself. Oh, and helping out two delegations—I won't say which ones—that lost their satellite links with home and have no idea how to get by without hardware in orbit."

That interested me. "I heard about that. How do your embassies phone home?"

"Shortwave radio, of course—the way everybody did before satellites took over. I had to explain that to both delegations." With a sly smile: "When the Atlantic Embassy loses its satellite links, have them give me a call. I can recommend a good radio firm that won't even put bugs in the hardware."

I gave her a dubious look, and she laughed. "I hope the briefing you got was worthwhile, by the way."

"Even more so than I'd expected. Turns out you're not the only people interested in freight transit through the New York canal system."

"Now surprise me." She sipped her drink. "Missouri, East Canada, and who?"

"Chicago."

"Oh, of course. That's good to know; I'll talk to Hank Barker with the Missouri delegation and see if we can coordinate shipping with them. We do a lot of trade with Missouri these days; the wool your suit is made of almost certainly came from their sheep, and possibly from their fabric mills."

"Barker mentioned that," I said. "Wool and leather."

Two bowls of avgolemono soup came, and neither of us said anything until the waitress was gone. "I'm going to risk mentioning a potentially uncomfortable subject," Melanie said. "The Missouri Republic is the one neighbor we've got that's shown any interest at all in learning from our experience. They haven't gone nearly as far as we have—you still see bioplastic clothing there, and they've still got a metanet, though it's pretty ramshackle these days—but the World Bank doesn't like them much any more." She shook her head, laughed. "I've been told that people from the World Bank threatened them with trade sanctions two years ago, after they refused a loan, and President Applegate told them, 'Didn't hurt Lakeland much, did it?' That shut them up."

I laughed, because I'd met Hannah Applegate at a reception in Philadelphia, and it took no effort at all to imagine her saying those words in her lazy Western drawl. Then the implications sank in. "They turned down a World Bank loan?"

"Of course. You know as well as I do that the only reason the World Bank makes those is to force countries to stay plugged into the global economy, so they can get the hard currency they need to make payments on the loan. The Missouri government knows that, too, and they're sick of it. We're Missouri's number one trading partner these days, we've both got the necessary arrangements in place to handle trade and investment in each other's currencies, and a fair amount of private investment from our side heads over there these days, so they decided it was time to take the risk and tell the World Bank to get lost."

"Good timing on their part," I said, thinking of the war.

"And on ours." In response to my questioning look: "They produce things we need and buy things we produce. The last thing we want is to see them bled dry."

"The way my country will be," I said. She glanced at me, said nothing, and concentrated for a while on her bowl of soup.

The waitress showed up conveniently a moment later, served us our entrees, made a little friendly conversation—Melanie was a regular, I gathered—and then headed off to another table. "As I said," Melanie said then, "it's a potentially uncomfortable subject."

"Given that your country is set up to weather this latest mess in fairly good shape, and mine might just end up as a failed state, yes."

Her face tensed, and after a moment she nodded. "If that happens, and you can make it to our border, have the border guards contact Meeker's office. It shouldn't be too hard to expedite your entry. I hope it doesn't come to that, but..." She let the sentence trickle off.

"Thank you. I hope it doesn't either." Then: "To the extent that you can tell me, how bad do your analysts expect it to get?"

She considered that. "I can tell you a few things. It's nothing you won't hear from your own intelligence people once you get back home—the NIS, isn't it?"

I nodded. "What do you call your spook shop here in Lakeland?"

"We've got three of them: the Office of Political Intelligence in the State Department, the Office of Economic Intelligence in Commerce, and the Office of Military Intelligence in Defense. Keeping it broken up like that helps prevent groupthink."

I motioned with my fork, granting the point, and she went on. "What OPI says is that Texas and the Confederacy were both in deep trouble even before this whole thing blew up in their faces. They both depend heavily on oil revenue to balance their budgets, they've both had declining production for years now, and you know as well as I do how badly they've been clobbered by these latest rounds of volatility in the oil markets. That's ultimately what's behind this war—neither country can afford to compromise because they both need every drop of oil they can possibly get—but this is going to take a lot of wells out of production until the fighting's over."

"Or permanently," I said. In response to her questioning look: "I was told off the record that a lot of both sides' offshore fields are stripper wells, and so a lot of the destroyed platforms won't produce enough oil in the future to be worth the cost of rebuilding."

She nodded. "That's OEI's bailiwick and I haven't talked to them yet, so thanks for the heads up. Even without that,

189

though, both countries are going to be hit hard even if the war ends in a few days—and it doesn't look like it's going to end in a few days."

I nodded. "Military intelligence?"

"Got it."

I didn't ask for details; she'd told me as much as she was cleared to pass on, and there are lines you don't cross in our business. Pretty clearly she'd attended a classified military briefing and gotten the latest information about the war, and I could think of at least a dozen signs that would warn the Lakeland government that neither Texas nor the Confederacy was going to back down any time soon. In a couple of days I'd be back in Philadelphia, and I could ask people I knew in Ellen Montrose's transition team for a summary.

"And if it drags on?" I asked.

She gave me an unhappy look. "Best case scenario is both countries end up economic basket cases, with per capita GDPs lower than the midrange for sub-Saharan Africa, but they both manage to hold together and begin to recover in about a decade. Worst case scenario is that one or both go failed-state on us. Either way we're looking at a big refugee problem, and a long-term economic headache if the Mississippi stays closed. We can deal with it, no question—it's just going to take some work. It's the people down south, in both countries, I feel sorry for"

We both concentrated on our meals for a minute or two.

"And the thing is," she burst out then, "this whole business is so unnecessary. If both countries weren't stuck on a treadmill trying to—" She stopped cold, catching herself.

"Trying to progress," I finished the sentence.

Another unhappy look. "I really don't think we should go there," she said.

"I think we should," I replied "I've been doing a lot of thinking about the things you said Friday evening, and you were right."

She was so surprised she dropped her fork. After a moment: "I'm sorry. I'm not sure I believe I just heard you say that."

"You were right," I repeated. "I spent all Saturday trying to find holes in your logic, and I couldn't find any." I shrugged. "I have no idea where to go with that yet, but there it is." Which was not quite true, but there were things I wasn't going to say in a restaurant that close to Embassy Row.

She considered me for a long moment, pretty obviously shaken good and hard, and I said, "Come on. I can't be the only person from outside who's told you that."

"It happens," she said then. "Once in a blue moon, maybe. No, that's not fair—working class people get it in a heartbeat, more often than not. They look at the way factory workers and store clerks live here, compared to how they live outside, they ask a few questions about why we do what we do, and they have no trouble at all figuring out the rest for themselves."

I thought about the family of immigrants I'd seen on the train from Pittsburgh, and the conversation I'd had with the father of the family. "But people who are well off, well educated, part of the system."

"The minority that still thinks that it gets some benefit out of progress," she said.

That stung, but I knew she was right. "Yes."

"Once in a blue moon."

Neither of us said anything for a while. Our plates got empty and our drinks got refilled; a couple of dishes of baklava came out for dessert, and when we started talking again it was about uncontroversial things, the Toledo Opera's future plans, funny stories about trade negotiations, that sort of thing. I guessed that she was still trying to process what I'd said, which was reasonable; so was I.

Finally the meal ended. She was looking really tired by that point—no surprises there—so we settled pretty much right away that nobody was going to end up in anybody else's bed that night. I gave her a kiss, helped her into her coat, and got

191

her onto a taxi. My hotel wasn't too many blocks away, so I waited until the taxi had turned the corner and set off on foot.

The sky was still clear and a rising wind swept down the streets, hissing in the bare branches of streetside trees. Overhead the stars glittered, and now and then something bright shot across some portion of the sky and burnt out, one more fragment of business as usual falling out of the place we'd stuck it and thought it would stay forever.

In less than forty-eight hours I'd be back in the Atlantic Republic: on my way home to Philadelphia, where three decades of one-party rule by the Dem-Reps had just gone out the window in a landslide and taken the status quo with it. The new administration would have to scramble to find its feet in a world gone topsy-turvy, where there were too many hard questions and nothing like enough straightforward answers. For that matter. I was going to have to face hard questions of my own, and I was far from sure I had any straightforward answers, either.

Another bit of dead satellite traced a streak of light across the sky, dissolved in a flurry of sparks. I kept on walking.

CHAPTER 11

The next morning I was up early, and walked to Kaufer's News while the sky was still that vague gray color that won't tell you yet whether it's clear or overcast. The *Blade* had done the smart thing and printed extra copies of the morning paper—the stack in the bin was almost as tall as I was—and I watched three other people buy copies as I walked up the street to the newsstand. The Lakeland Republic flag snapped in a brisk wind from the flagpole out in front of the Capitol, and lights already burned in the windows. The Republic's government had a long day ahead of it, and so did I.

Back in the hotel, I settled down in a chair and spent a few minutes checking the news. Most of the front section was about the war down south, of course; both sides' naval forces were still duking it out with long-range missiles, and the Confederate advance toward Dallas-Fort Worth had begun to slow as Texan forces reached the war zone and flung themselves into the struggle. The presidents of Missouri, New England, East and West Canada, and Quebec had joined Meeker in calling for an immediate ceasefire and a negotiated settlement of the dispute over the Gulf oil fields; back home, outgoing President Barfield and president-elect Montrose would be holding a joint press conference later that day to announce something of the same sort. That last story made my eyebrows go up. The Dem-Reps had been sore losers in a big way since their landslide defeat a few weeks back. If Barlow had loosened up enough to appear on a stage with his replacement, things might have shifted, and not in a bad way.

There was more—another attempt at a ceasefire in the Californian civil war, another report by an international panel on the worsening phosphate shortage, another recap of the satellite situation that ran through a roster of collisions, and estimated that the world had less than three months left before all satellite services in the midrange orbits were out of commission—but I folded the paper after a glance at each of those and tossed it on the desk. I had a little over a day left to spend in the Lakeland Republic before catching the train back home, and most of that was already spoken for. Between talking to Marjorie Vanich at the university and Janice Mikkelson in her mansion, I had decisions to make that would affect the lives of a lot of people I'd never meet.

You learn to get used to that if you're in politics, but if you get too used to it you land in trouble really fast. Half the reason the Dem-Reps got clobbered in our elections a few weeks back is that they'd gotten into the habit of thinking that the only people who mattered politically were the people who had the money and connections to show up at fundraisers and get their interests represented by lobbyists—and much more than half the reason why Montrose's New Alliance swept the legislative races and put her into the presidency with the strongest mandate in a generation was that she'd had the sense to look past the lobbyists and fundraising dinners, and reach out to everyone whose interests had been ignored for the last thirty years. I'd played a part in that strategy, and the choices ahead of me might also play a certain part in determining whether Montrose's victory would turn out to be a long-term gamechanger or a flash in the pan.

So I sat there in my room for a few more minutes, then called Professor Vanich to confirm our appointment and headed out to the street. A few minutes later I was tucked into the cab of a two-wheel taxi, heading northwest from the Capitol district through one mostly residential neighborhood after another. I'd gotten used to Lakeland habits by then, and so it didn't surprise me that the houses looked sturdy and old-fashioned, with flower beds out front that would be blazing with color come spring; that trees were everywhere; that there were corner shops all over and little retail districts at intervals, close enough that people could walk to do most of their everyday shopping; that the schools didn't look like prisons, the libraries didn't look like prisons—in fact, I passed something I'm pretty sure was the county jail and even that didn't look like a prison.

The houses got bigger as we went further from the Maumee River. None of the trees looked more than thirty years old—I recalled from some half-forgotten history vid that there was a major battle west of Toledo during the Second Civil War—and all the houses looked better than a century older than that, even though I knew they were all recent construction. I looked at them and mulled over everything else I'd seen over the last two weeks.

Finally the buildings of the university came into sight, and I had to remind myself that they were just as new as the houses. They were all built of white stone, with the sort of university Gothic look you see in the few places where colleges and universities managed to dodge the architectural fads of the late twentieth century and the bombs and missiles of the early twenty-first, and the trees and lawns and brick walkways reminded me of universities I'd seen in history vids. Back home, if you visit one of the universities that hasn't scrapped teaching altogether and turned into a sports team franchise pure and simple, you're going to find a ten- to twenty-story glass and steel structure where a couple of thousand students at a time file into big auditoriums to watch prerecorded lectures. One look at the buildings suggested that that wasn't the way things were done here.

The cab let me off at a midsized white building with a sign that said RITTER PLANETARIUM. It took me a couple of tries to find the right door, but finally I got into the office and classroom part of the building, followed the directions I'd gotten from Fred Vanich, and eventually found my way to Dr. Marjorie Vanich's office, a pleasant little space with shelves practically creaking under the weight of big hardback books.

"Yes, Fred told me about your conversation," she said when we'd finished saying the usual polite things. She had thick glasses and a mop of mostly gray hair, and typical Lakeland clothing, a hempcloth blouse and a brown woolen jacket and skirt that had probably seen years of wear. "He mentioned you were interested in the satellite situation—I'd be happy to discuss that, since it's been a major research project of mine for close to twenty years now."

"I'm definitely interested in that," I said, "but also in the university system here generally—and I've got one simple practical question." In response to her raised eyebrows: "How on earth do you calculate satellite orbits without computers?"

That got a sudden smile, and it wasn't the usual Lakeland you-don't-get-it smile, either. "That's something we're really proud of," Dr. Vanich said. "I can demonstrate that once I've fielded your questions about Toledo University and our universities here in Lakeland generally."

It didn't take many questions on my part to get her talking enthusiastically about the university system, and she didn't mind at all that I pulled out my notebook and started jotting down details. The short version was that the Lakeland Republic, like everyone else, had its higher education system flattened by the Second Civil War, but they'd gone about rebuilding it in a completely different way.

"One of the big problems of higher education back before the war," she explained, "was that the universities tried to turn themselves into trade schools for every possible profession. Want to be a police officer? Get a criminal justice degree.

Want to be a practical nurse? Get a nursing degree. Want to be a garbage collector? Get a waste stream management degree—and yes, there were institutions offering that last one before things finally fell apart.

"So when the fighting was over and the Republic needed people to do every kind of skilled and unskilled job you care to name, an assortment of former university administrators got together and drew up a grandiose plan to build hundreds of new universities, and train tens of thousands of new professors, so that after a decade or two they could start turning out graduates in all the necessary job categories. The provisional legislature told them that the country couldn't afford to wait for a decade or two, they insisted that there wasn't an alternative—and then the Restos came up with a better alternative."

"The apprenticeship programs," I said.

That got me the look you'd expect a teacher to give a bright student. "Exactly, Mr. Carr. The Restos knew that most teachers, lawyers, physicians, engineers, and the like were educated by apprenticeship in the nineteenth century, so they brought out a plan to do the same thing, and of course it was adopted. The university people kept insisting that their plan was better, but before long it became clear to everyone else that apprenticeship really was the best way to go for most of those things—and that's when a group of professors who'd taught at prewar colleges went to the legislature with a proposal of their own.

"Their proposal took the same tack the Restos' did. Back in the nineteenth century, you see, universities weren't saddled with the kind of huge overpaid administrative staff they got in the second half of the twentieth, and they didn't try to teach everything under the sun. They were mostly run by faculty senates and taught the scholarly disciplines, along with advanced degrees for specialists in medicine and law. So the professors drew up a proposal to relaunch higher education in the Lakeland Republic on that basis, they got the Restos on

197

board with it, and the result was the higher education system we've got now."

I nodded. "That makes sense. How much does it cost for an average bachelor's degree?"

"In terms of cost to the student? Not a cent." At my surprise, she smiled. "Entrance is by competitive examination, and if you qualify for admission and keep your grades above a C minus, tuition is free. We treat higher education as a public utility; it's not that much of a tax burden because none of the universities admit that many students—the last thing any country needs is a couple of million people with degrees they'll never be able to use."

"Don't you think there's something to be gained by general education?"

"Of course! We also run public education classes, mostly nights and weekends, that are open to anyone. I teach astronomy classes here two nights a week, and run weekend trips to the university's observatory in Defiance County—it's tier one, so there are no streetlights and very few other sources of light pollution at all, and we've got a new eighty-inch Newtonian reflector that gives just stunning views of the sky. You've never seen what wonder looks like until you watch a class full of ten-year-olds get their first look at the rings of Saturn."

"I bet," I said.

"Now, as far as the satellite situation goes, probably the best place to start is with this." She opened a desk drawer, pulled out something that looked like a complicated ruler with a long strip down the middle that slid. "I don't imagine you've seen one of these before, but the rockets that put human bootprints on the moon were designed using them. It's called a slide rule—think of it as a pocket calculator with no buttons. This one has scales for spherical trigonometry, since that's the branch of math we use for orbital calculations."

Two books came down from a bookshelf and joined the slide rule on the desk. "This one's got trigonometric tables, and this one's something we worked up here at U of Toledo, a set of orbital tables that factor in Earth's gravity and diameter. With these three things and the places and times from two clear observations of an orbiting object, you can work out its orbital parameters in about twenty minutes."

"Without a computer," I said, shaking my head.

"Without a computer. The mechanics of orbiting objects were worked out back in the seventeenth century, and the equations we use to calculate orbital parameters were invented by Gauss in 1801. For the last thirty years, we've been refining our methods so that we can track any satellite or satellite fragment and predict its position as far into the future as we want. It's been a great program, but it'll be shut down at the end of this school year."

I gave her a startled look. "Why are you doing that?"

"Because the space age is over."

For a moment the silence was deep enough that I could just faintly hear the sounds of traffic on the far side of the windows. "Manned space flight was never really more than a stunt," Dr. Vanich said then, "and the notion of putting colonies on other worlds went away once scientists found out that Earth is the only habitable body in the solar system with a magnetic field strong enough to keep off the radiation from the Sun. A trip from here to Mars and back amounts to a death sentence from radiation poisoning, you know."

"I'd heard that," I admitted.

"That left satellites, which do pay for themselves. The problem there, of course, was that nobody took the time to think about what was going to happen if we just kept on launching volleys of satellites every year into the same finite set of orbits. Even after the Kessler syndrome in low earth orbit kicked off in '29, too many people and too many governments insisted that there was no alternative to an ever increasing load of satellites in the remaining orbits—and here we are." She glanced at me. "I cowrote a paper for *Nature* in '51, suggesting that it was past time for an international agreement to ration access to orbital space. You might find it educational to look up the dismissive responses I got. They were all variations on the theme of 'they'll think of something.' I never did find out who 'they' were, but somehow 'they' never did."

I pondered that. "The paper this morning said that the mid-range orbits won't be free of debris again for some appalling length of time," I said.

"We did a series of estimates based on different initial assumptions. The average worked out to just over twelve hundred years, with a standard deviation of three hundred eighty years. The low earth orbits will be usable again in two to four hundred years, we've calculated."

"And the high geosynchronous orbits?"

She shook her head. "Probably not within the lifetime of our species."

I stared at her for a good long moment.

"That didn't have to happen," Dr. Vanich said. "As a species, we could have paid more attention to the future and less to immediate gratification—but we didn't. Now certain possibilities are gone forever, and we'll just have to live with that." She shook her head. "I've cowritten another paper on that theme. It's been submitted to *Nature*, too, but I haven't yet heard whether they're going to publish it or not."

I sat there trying to process it all.

"On the off chance we're wrong," she said, "we've made sure that there are plenty of copies of our book of tables in circulation. Still, it's a bit sad to have put so many years into something that is probably never going to be used again."

We talked a little more about the satellite situation, and then I excused myself and left. I had another appointment to keep, and lunch to get before I kept it; Janice Mikkelson had said something about drinks, and I didn't want to try to deal with that on an empty stomach. Still, there was more to it than that. Even though I'd been tracking the satellite situation for years now, it had never really quite sunk in that we weren't just talking about a temporary thing.

Sure, I'd heard all the grand plans to use ground-based lasers and the like to knock debris out of the near-earth orbits; everybody has. Those sound really great until you tot up exactly how much electricity those would need to draw to make any kind of difference, and ask where that's going to come from, when most of the world's industrial countries can't reliably keep the lights on in their capital cities when the temperature spikes. I'd heard the same line Dr. Vanich had mentioned more times than I could count—"they'll think of something"—and of course she was right; whoever "they" were, "they" hadn't gotten around to thinking of anything that mattered.

I laughed, then. Fortunately I was crossing part of the campus that was mostly empty and nobody heard me, because it wasn't a pleasant laugh. It was the kind of bitter laugh that comes out when you realize the joke's been on you all along. When Melanie said that progress had turned into the enemy of prosperity, I'd realized, she was understating the case considerably. If people hadn't let short term interest blind them to hard realities, we wouldn't be looking at the end of the space age, but we'd all just assumed that progress would fix everything and gone walking straight ahead into a preventable disaster.

One more preventable disaster, I thought. On top of all the others.

I was on the edge of campus by then, and the district of restaurants and shops you always find around a university was right in front of me. It didn't take too long to find a place for lunch, and I took my time because my appointment with Janice Mikkelson wasn't until two o'clock. A meatball sandwich and a green salad made a decent meal; I read through the campus paper—it was full of pieces on little intramural sports teams, but there apparently wasn't an intercollegiate team of any kind—and then did a little window shopping at the places along the street.

I was familiar enough with the Lakeland Republic by then that the grocery store full of fresh produce and bulk grains and beans, the butcher shop wrapping meat up in white paper parcels, and the drugstore with a soda fountain down one side and a compounding pharmacy of its own in back, didn't surprise me at all. The record store on the corner was a bit of a shock, though, because it sold actual records: big black disks in paper sleeves meant to be played on the kind of old-fashioned record player my grandmother still had for her old opera records. I guessed that the disks weren't actually vinyl, Lakeland resource taxes being what they were, but they looked like it. No doubt one of the Lakeland Republic's mad scientists had gone digging through old journal articles, the way Emily Franken had found her maser, and figured out how to make something close enough out of industrial hemp or some other locally produced feedstock.

By the time I got over my surprise it was time to catch a cab for Janice Mikkelson's place. I flagged one down; the cabbie gave me a startled look when I told him the address, but he didn't argue, and a minute later we were on our way, first through your typical student neighborhood, then through big comfortable houses, and finally into what was obviously one of the wealthier districts in the greater Toledo area. Finally the taxi turned off a winding road onto a circular driveway, and brought me up to the door of a genuine mansion.

The place was the sort of big half-timbered pile that makes you think of ivy-covered English aristocrats and nineteenth-century New York robber baron industrialists. I gave it a slightly glazed look, then paid the cabby and went to the door, and I kid you not, it opened right as I got there. The doorman asked my name and business in the sort of utterly polite tone that sounds ever so slightly snotty, which amused me, and then handed me over to some other category of flunkey in formal wear, who took me up one of the grandest grand staircases I've ever seen, down a corridor lined with the kind of old-fashioned oil paintings that actually looked like something, and into a big windowed room with a grand piano near one wall, an assortment of tastefully overpriced furniture, and Janice Mikkelson.

We shook hands, she asked about my preferred drink, and then sent the flunkey off to get a couple of martinis while we walked over to the windows. Down below was a formal garden, with a crew of gardeners doing whatever it is that gardeners do in late November; further off were trees, lots of them, and roofs at intervals, most of them large but none as large as the one over my head just then.

"Quite a place," I said.

She chuckled. "Thank you. I try to set an example."

I gave her a startled look, but just then the flunkey came back in with the martinis. Mikkelson thanked him, which was another surprise, and then we took our drinks and waited while he vanished.

"I'd like to talk business first, if you don't mind," she said then. I'm not in the habit of arguing with the very rich, and so I agreed and we spent half an hour discussing the prospects of selling Mikkelson locomotives, rolling stock, and streetcar systems to the Atlantic Republic.

"I've got one requirement," she said, emphasizing the number with a sharp gesture. "If other transport modes get a subsidy, rail and streetcars get an equal subsidy, or they get treated as a public utility. If rail and streetcars don't get subsidized, neither does anything else. Are you at all familiar with the way they handled funding for different transport modes back in the old Union?"

"Not to speak of," I admitted.

"Roads, highways and airports got huge subsidies from federal, state, and local governments, and so did car and airplane manufacturers. Rail? Pennies on the hundred-dollar bill, and then the politicians yelled that rail was a waste of public funds and should get its subsidies cut even further. I won't enter a market that's run on those terms—it's like gambling in a crooked casino. Equal subsidies for all modes, no subsidies for any, or a straightforward public-utility model like we use here for streetcars, I'm fine with any of those."

"I'm surprised you don't lobby for more subsidies than other modes," I said.

"Not a good business plan," she said at once. "Look at the way the nuclear industry's tanking—everyone knows at this point that nuclear power never turns a profit, and the only thing that ever made it look economically viable was huge government subsidies."

"Someone I know calls nukes subsidy dumpsters."

That got a quick smile. "Nice. I'm not willing to risk my products going the same route. If what I'm producing can't compete on a level playing field, no matter what gimmicks I use to try to hide that, eventually that's going to bite me in the butt. So I ask for a level playing field, and my systems can match anybody else's on that basis."

"Do you do a lot of export on those terms?"

"A fair amount. Missouri's gone to a no-subsidies system across the board, and they're buying my locomotives and rolling stock as funds permit; they aren't flush with cash, so it's a few at a time. Quebec treats urban transit as a public utility, which works for me—I've sold three streetcar systems there since the borders opened, and my people and theirs are negotiating two more. East Canada? The car manufacturers still have too much clout to allow parity for rail, so no dice. The Confederacy's still sore about the way the '49 war went, so they buy from Brazil." She shrugged. "Their loss. Our products are better."

"I don't happen to know about the subsidy regime back home," I said.

"Don't worry about it. You've got some highway and airport subsidies and a lot of public funding for roads, but no domestic auto or aircraft industries and no subsidies for buying those from overseas. If Montrose's people are willing to negotiate, we can work something out—and from what I hear, your urban transit is a disaster area, so her administration could get even more popular than it is by getting streetcar systems up and running in half a dozen of your big cities."

All in all, it wasn't exactly hard for me to figure out why she was the richest person in the Lakeland Republic; we talked over the possibilities, I agreed to discuss the matter with Ellen Montrose when I got back home, and the conversation strayed elsewhere.

When we got to the third martini each, I asked, "You said you try to set an example. I'm still trying to parse that."

That got me an assessing look: "I was the first of our homegrown millionaires here in the Lakeland Republic—there's a good dozen of us now, and there'll be more in due time, but I was first through that particular gate." She gestured around at the mansion. "Quite a place, as you said. During the Second Civil War, my brother and I—we were the only two of our family who survived the bombing of Toledo in 2025—we lived in the basement of a wrecked house in a suburb thirty miles south of here. We ate a lot of rat, and were glad to get it. I decided then and there that if I survived, I was going to live in the fanciest house in the state of Ohio, and all I'd have to do is snap my fingers and somebody would bring me a roast turkey, just like that." She laughed reminiscently. "I got so sick of roast turkey."

I laughed too, but I knew that she meant it. "Did your brother survive the war?"

"Fortunately, yes—he's younger than I am, and wasn't old enough to be drafted by either side until after the war was over. He's a professor of political science at Milwaukee these days—he came out of the whole business wanting to know why it is that nations do dumb things. Me, I just wanted to get rich." She sipped her martini. "And fortunately I learned an important lesson on how to do that and survive. Do you mind hearing an ugly story?"

205

"Not at all," I said, wondering what she had in mind.

"This was right after the war, when I was working any job I could get, trying to put aside enough cash to start my first business. I got hired as day labor to do salvage on what was left of a gated community, west of here a ways. It was one of the really high-end places, where the very rich planned to hole up when things came crashing down; it had its own private security force, airstrip, power plant, farms, the whole nine yards.

"Now here's the thing. There were sixty big houses for the families that lived there, and every single one of them was full of what's left when you leave dead people lying around for four years. As far as we could tell, right after the old federal government lost control of the Midwest, the security guards turned off the alarm systems one night and went from house to house. They shot everyone but the domestic staff, took all the gold and goodies they could carry, and headed off somewhere else. That wasn't the only place that happened, either."

"I heard some really ugly stories from the Hamptons back in the day," I said.

"I bet you did. The thing that really made an impression on me at the time, though, is that they didn't shoot the domestic staff. All the skeletons were up in the family quarters. That told me that it wasn't just about the money. There was a grudge involved—and if you know how the rich used to treat everyone else in the old Union, you know why." She sipped more booze. "Rich people only exist because the rest of society tolerates us, you know. Have you ever considered why they do that?"

I shook my head, and she went on. "Part of it's because we give them a place to anchor their unused dreams. People here daydream about the rich the way that people back before the war obsessed about Hollywood stars or people in Britain follow the doings of their royal family. They'll put up with the most astonishing things from the people they idolize, the people they allow to get rich and stay rich, so long as the rich keep their side of the deal. I could get by with a quarter of the

206

staff I have here; I could get by without the four-star dinners with a big tip for everyone right down to the dishwashers, the big donations to every charitable cause in sight, the private railroad car with its own chef, for God's sake—but that's my side of the bargain."

"It gives everyone else something to dream about," I guessed.

"Yes, and it also pays one hell of a lot of wages and salaries."

I took that in.

"They tolerate me because I live out their dreams for them," Mikkelson said. "They can afford to tolerate me because I don't let myself become too expensive a luxury, and they want to tolerate me because their sister's best friend got a hundred-buck tip the last time I had dinner at the restaurant where she waits tables, and their cousin's husband works in the garden down there for a good wage and a big bonus come Christmas, and a guy they know from high school just got promoted off the shop floor at the Mikkelson factory and is getting trained as a mechanical engineer on my nickel."

"As I recall," I said, "You get some pretty fair tax benefits from that last one."

"Of course." She smiled. "And I lobbied like you wouldn't believe to get that into the tax code. Partly because I don't mind being paid to do the right thing, and partly because I knew it would keep my work force happy. Half the reason Mikkelson products are better quality than anybody else's is that all my people know that if the company wins, they win. There's a stock ownership plan, bonuses based on the annual profit, plenty of opportunity to move from the shop floor to better-paying jobs. All of it gets me a break on taxes, but it also means that I and all my limited partners do better in the long run, and so do my employees and the union."

I gave her a puzzled look. "I didn't know you still had unions here."

"Couldn't get by without them. Of course we have binding arbitration on contracts—if my people and the union can't reach an agreement, the Department of Labor sends in an arbitration team and they decide what the new contract will be—but the union does a lot of the day-to-day management of the work force. When I need to sort something out with my factory employees, I can pick up a phone and call the local president here in Toledo, say, and settle it in ten minutes or less. They're not pushovers—the union presidents and shop stewards can be tossed out of office by the workers by a two-thirds vote on no notice—but they work with me. They know their jobs depend on the company making a profit, and the union funds have a big stake in Mikkelson stock and seats on the board, so it's in our interest to work together."

She turned toward the windows. "That was what nobody seemed to be able to figure out in the old United States," she said. "You can cooperate and compromise, share the gains, and keep things going for the long term, or you can try to grab everything for yourself and shove the poor and the weak to the wall, and watch it all come crashing down. In world politics, the United States tried to grab everything; in domestic politics, the executive branch tried to grab everything; in the economy, the rich tried to grab everything—and down it came." She glanced back at me over her shoulder. "I wonder if anyone thinks about that in Philadelphia."

It was a hell of a good question, and I didn't have an answer for it.

208

CHAPTER 12

A taxi brought back to my hotel from Janice Mikkelson's mansion—one of her servants called it for me—and I spent most of the ride staring out the window and thinking about what she'd said about the prewar rich. I'd heard plenty of stories along the same lines, of course, everybody has, but for some reason my mind kept circling back to the way that they'd dug their own graves and then jumped into them. Why didn't it occur to them that voting themselves one billion-dollar bonus after another, while driving their own employees and the rest of the country into poverty, was going to blow up in their faces sooner or later?

I was thinking that, staring out at the darkening sky, when a little pale streak brought me back to reality. The dozens of governments and corporations that kept launching satellites even after 2029, when the Kessler syndrome in low earth orbit should have given them a wake-up call, had gone waltzing just as cluelessly straight into a preventable disaster of their own. I thought of the mess we'd gotten into back home by going long on nuclear power plants in the 2040s, long after it should have been clear to everyone that nuclear power was—what was Fred Vanich's phrase again?—a subsidy dumpster, one more technological white elephant that never paid for itself, and only looked profitable because most of the costs were shoved

209

out of sight one way or another. I thought of the war going on a thousand miles south of me just then, and wondered sourly why a species that was so smart at coming up with clever technologies was so dumb about so much else.

The taxi stopped outside the hotel, and I went in, climbed the stairs to my room, and made a phone call. Yes, the call was to Melanie Berger; yes, we spent the evening together; no, I'm not going to go into any of the details. We didn't talk about progress or technology or the future of the Lakeland Republic, for whatever that's worth.

Another taxi brought me back to the Capitol Hotel about seven-thirty the next morning. I tried without noticeable success to coax my electric shaver into giving me a decent shave, then showered and got everything but the day's clothing packed. I'd considered more than once putting on ordinary bioplastic businesswear for the trip back, knowing that people back home would look at me as though I had two spare heads if I got off the train in Pittsburgh dressed in my Lakeland clothes, but that resolution lasted just about long enough for me to reach into the closet and grab a business suit. The slick clammy texture of the thing made my skin crawl. So I dressed in hempcloth and wool instead, checked my appearance, put on my trench coat and porkpie hat, and headed out the door to my final appointment with the President of the Lakeland Republic.

The weather had turned cold and damp overnight, and stray raindrops spattered down as I walked the familiar six blocks to the Capitol. Another round of scaffolding had gone up on the unfinished dome, and stonemasons were already clambering around up there, laying another course of marble blocks beneath the shelter of brown tarps I guessed probably weren't made of plastic. Down at street level, people were already picking up the latest papers at Kaufer's News. I bought the *Blade*, glanced at the headlines on the front page: the fighting in the Gulf and in northeastern Texas seemed to be grinding toward a stalemate; the other North American republics had appealed to the Brazilians and Chinese to stay out of the fighting and try to talk their respective client states into accepting a ceasefire; one of the big Indian telecom multinationals had gone bankrupt—the first corporate casualty of the satellite crisis, though I knew it wouldn't be the last by a long shot—and stock markets everywhere but Toledo were doing another sickening downward lurch in response.

I stuffed the paper into one of the big outside pockets of my trench coat, crossed the street, and went up the long walk to the main entrance of the Capitol. It was five to nine, still too early for kids on field trips or photo ops in the Rotunda, so the only people I saw were members of the legislative staff hurrying this way and that, getting ready for what would probably be another hectic day, and a couple of white-haired politicians, one light-skinned, one dark-skinned, talking intently as they ambled toward the Senate end of the building. Me, I headed straight across the rotunda to the door in back and went in.

It still startled me that you could just walk into the offices of the President of the Lakeland Republic. No doubt the uniformed guards in the Rotunda weren't the only guards in the place, but they were the only ones I saw. I went down the corridor into the front office, said hi to Gabriel Menendez, waited while he called back, shed my coat and hat in the cloakroom, and then through another corridor and the round room with the spiral staircase to Meeker's office.

"Mr. Carr," said the President, as we shook hands. "It's good to see you again." He gestured toward the side of the room. "Please have a seat."

The same people who'd been present for my first meeting with Meeker were waiting: no surprises there, though I hadn't expected them to be sitting in precisely the same chairs. I shook hands all around. "Mr. President, Mr. Macallan, Ms. Patel, Mr. Vanich—" With the faintest of smiles, just for her: "Ms. Berger."

211

We got settled. "Before we get to business," the President said, "I have a bit of good news to pass on: to you, of course, but also through you to Ms. Montrose. Our State Department heard backchannel last night, via an embassy I won't name, that the Confederate and Texan governments are both potentially willing to talk about a ceasefire. No word yet about when or where, much less what terms either side's likely to demand, but at least they haven't rejected negotiations out of hand."

"That's good to hear," I said.

"We certainly have hopes," Meeker went on. "That's all we have so far, though." A gesture dismissed the issue. "I hope you've found your stay here—shall we say, instructive."

"That's one way of putting it," I replied. "I don't mean any criticism at all when I say that in some ways, it's been two very long weeks."

Meeker nodded. "Melanie mentioned that you've found yourself reconsidering some of your ideas about technology and the like."

I considered him. "Again, that's one way of putting it—and that brings me to one last item I'd like to mention before I leave for home."

"Of course," said Meeker, smiling. Fred Vanich and Melanie glanced at each other, and I wondered if they'd made another bet.

"I suspect you're aware," I said then, "that I had more reasons for coming here than the ones we discussed earlier."

Meeker turned to look at Stuart Macallan, who said, "Mr. Carr, I hope you won't mind if I state the obvious. None of us could think of any reason why Ellen Montrose would have sent one of her key advisers here right after the election, when almost any competent staffer could have handled the preliminary work on the three agreements we worked out. We've had plenty of other unofficial envoys come here since the borders opened, of course, and most of them had some agenda other than the one they told us about. We assumed you had one too."

212

"With that in mind," said Meeker, "I'd be most interested in hearing what your other reasons for coming here might be, to the extent that you can talk about them."

"Fair enough," I said, meeting his gaze. "You know that Ellen won the election promising across-the-board changes in our national economic policy. She means it, too—we've already got the first round of legislation drafted, and everybody's going to hit the ground running the day after inauguration. I'm sure you know the basic thrust of it."

"What's been made public, yes," said Meeker. "She hasn't mentioned defaulting on the foreign debt Barfield and his predecessors ran up, but that's almost certainly going to have to be part of it. Even before this business down south got going, there was no way she could keep her election promises without renegotiating the debt, and that means at least a technical default."

I gave him a bland look and said, "I don't know anything about that." He chuckled, and I went on. "The new administration's going to have its hands full getting the economy a little less dysfunctional, and now there's what the satellite crisis is doing to stock markets and the telecom industry, not to mention the Confederate-Texas war, to add to the fun and games. Beyond that, though, there's another set of plans relating to economic regulations, the tax code, and a range of other policies. Those haven't been made public yet, but when they are, you're going to find some of them just a little familiar."

"Indeed?" Meeker said, his eyebrows rising. "Please go on."

"The short form is that she wants to redirect government support for business away from the high-tech sectors of the economy and into manufacturing and agriculture, and change the tax code and other public policy incentives so that they reward employment rather than automation."

Jaya Patel waited a moment to make sure Meeker wasn't about to speak, then said, "I'm sure I don't have to tell you how sensible that sounds from our standpoint."

"No. When she outlined them to me, though, I told her to her face that she was stark staring nuts."

That got slightly glazed looks from the others. "I'd be interested in knowing how she took that," the President said.

"She expects that sort of thing," I told him. "You've heard about her reputation for blunt talk, right? She hires staff who will talk to her the way she talks to them. Half the reason Barfield's administration ran into so much trouble is that he only hires people who tell him what he wants to hear."

He nodded, gestured for me to go on.

"I told her that there was no way the Atlantic Republic could go back to a twentieth-century economy, that nobody would put up with it, and even if we could and they did, it just meant that we'd be eaten alive by less backward nations that kept up with the latest technology. She pointed out that the more we invested in the latest technology the further behind we got, and I dismissed that as the product of outside factors. We had a fine donnybrook—the kind where everybody else on the floor gathers outside the door to listen—and I finally insisted that it simply wouldn't work. She just smiled and said that it was already working."

"So she knew what we've done," said Melanie.

I nodded. "She told me that policies like the ones she had in mind were working on this side of the border. I simply wouldn't believe it, and so we made a deal. If she won the election, she'd come up with some plausible reason to send me over here for two weeks right afterwards and see for myself. After that, if I could give her a good reason why her proposals wouldn't work, she'd reconsider them."

Meeker paused, and then asked, "And what will you tell her when you get back?"

The words came more easily than I'd expected. "Something that I couldn't have imagined proposing a week ago. I'm going to advise her to go considerably further than she'd planned, and begin moving the Atlantic Republic in the same directions that you've gone here."

When I was a kid, my grandmother used to talk about deep silence by saying it was quiet enough that you could hear a pin drop. That's what came to mind just then; I'd have had to drop it onto Meeker's desk—the floor was carpeted—but if I'd done it, nobody in the room could have missed hearing it. Everyone but Melanie was staring at me; she was smiling.

"Well," Meeker said, recovering before any of the others. "If I may say so, Mr. Carr, that's quite a compliment."

"Thank you," I replied. "I'm not sure whether it's a compliment to the Lakeland Republic, though, or a criticism of everyone else. It shouldn't have been so hard to figure out that if you've gone down a blind alley, the only way you can go forward starts by backing up."

Fred Vanich glanced at his boss, and then at me. "It's a little more complex than that, Mr. Carr," he said. "Progress, development, going forward. Those are powerful metaphors, and it's not always easy to think clearly when they're being waved around by those who have blind faith in them—especially if rich people stand to get much richer by convincing others that here and now, going forward means buying whatever technology they happen to be selling."

I gestured, conceding the point. "Have you decided how you'll propose going about the transition?" Jaya Patel asked.

"No," I admitted. "I've only had a couple of days to think about it, and quite a few other things to do in that time. When we get the first couple of rounds of legislation passed, cope with the end of satellite services, and figure out how we're going to deal with the blowback from the war down south—ask me then and I can probably tell you."

"If there's anything our government can do for yours in the process," Meeker said, "I trust you'll let us know." With a sudden amused smile: "For reasons that are not entirely altruistic, of course."

"I know Janice Mikkelson would love to sell us some streetcars," I observed.

That got a general laugh. "Yes," Meeker said then, "but there's also the point you made when we first talked, about not wanting a war zone or a failed state on your country's border. If I may be frank, if the Atlantic Republic had kept going the way the Dem-Reps were leading it, it's an open question whether you could have avoided serious trouble for long. The changes Montrose has announced will help, but it's going to take quite a bit more to achieve the kind of economic and political stability we've managed here. If we can help you make that happen, that's an investment we'll consider." He smiled again. "'You' in this case meaning the Atlantic Republic and Ellen Montrose primarily. I don't claim to know what role you personally will be playing in all this."

"That's another issue," I said. "My position in the new administration was one of the things hinging on my deal with Ellen. Of course there's the confirmation vote on our side and the usual formalities on yours, but part of our deal was that if I ended up agreeing with Ellen, I was committing to four years as our ambassador to the Lakeland Republic." I drew in a breath. "So I expect to be back here early in the new year, if everything goes according to plan."

Meeker considered that and nodded. "That's welcome news, Mr. Carr."

"Thank you, Mr. President." We shook hands. Past the President's shoulder I could see Melanie's face. She was smiling as our eyes met.

There wasn't much more to be said after that, and so we all mouthed the usual things and I headed back to my hotel. The rain had settled in good and hard by then, so I didn't dawdle. Back in the room, I got my coat and hat hung up to dry a little, and then turned the radio on to the jazz station, settled into the chair, and read the morning news. I had one more appointment before I caught the train at 2:26 that afternoon, and not a thing to do until then; I knew that I was going to be up to my eyeballs in meetings, briefings, and two weeks of unanswered text mails the minute I got back home; and just at the moment, the thought of taking some time at the Lakeland Republic's less frantic pace and trying to make sense of the world had a definite appeal.

I'd already read the headlines, so there weren't too many surprises in store, though a United Nations panel was warning about an impending zinc shortage and meteorologists were predicting that the monsoon rains would fail in south Asia for the third year in a row. Two more satellites in the midrange orbits had been taken out by debris; a second jokulhlaup down in Antarctica had chucked another thousand square miles or so of ice sheet into the Indian Ocean; stock markets everywhere outside the Lakeland Republic had had another really bad day; the ceasefire negotiations in the California civil war had gotten off to a rocky start, and more details had gotten through about the opening rounds of the Texas-Confederate war—both sides' offshore oil fields had taken even more of a hit than the original reports suggested.

That was only about half of the first section, though, and it was the other half, and the rest of the paper, that held my attention. That was the stuff that wasn't about shortages and crises. It was about what people do when they're not being held hostage by shortages and crises. I read birth announcements, marriage announcements, obituaries; a new streetcar line out to one of Toledo's eastern neighborhoods was in the planning stages, with public meetings scheduled to sort out the route over the winter and tracklaying planned to start next May; a high school student was honored for volunteering more than a thousand hours reading the daily newspaper over one of the Toledo radio stations, for blind people and shut-ins; the big local shipyard had just bought another piece of property and would be hiring another three hundred people to meet the demand for three-masted schooners for shipping on the Great Lakes.

Then there were the help-wanted ads, pages and pages of them, looking for shipwrights, file clerks, millworkers, secretaries, mechanics, all the jobs that got automated or off-shored out of existence back home and were keeping people busy and self-supporting here. There were two full pages of apprenticeship ads—if I'd wanted to become a carpenter, a pharmacist, a plumber, a doctor, an electrician, a millwright, a teacher, a sailor, or a lawyer, just for starters, I would have had no trouble in the world figuring out where to apply.

All the while, though, the thoughts that had circled through my head on the trip back from Janice Mikkelson's mansion hung in the air around me, and not even Louis Armstrong's trumpet solos on the radio could chase them away. People knew long before I was born that the things we were doing were going to end really, really badly, and yet everyone just kept on marching ahead, making the same dumb decisions over and over again, convinced that if they just did the same thing one more time it would undo the bad results they'd gotten every other time they'd done it. If you discover that you're in a hole, the saying is, the first thing to do is stop digging—but that's exactly what nobody was willing to do, because they'd convinced themselves that digging the hole deeper was the only way to get out of it.

That was the thing that twisted like a knife. The climate mess that was dumping icebergs off Antarctica and had already turned half of Manhattan into a rusting ruin that flooded deeper with every high tide, the Kessler syndrome that was busy putting an end to the space age, the cascading shortages that were taking a bigger bite out of the world's economies every single year: none of those had happened by accident. They weren't the result of fate, or destiny, or any of that clap-trap. We'd *progressed* straight into each of them.

Of course progress also churned out plenty of good things back in the day—that's why the jobs in the help-wanted ads weren't limited to "peasant." Somehow, though, most people outside the Lakeland Republic never got around to noticing when the costs of progress started to outweigh the benefits.

218

Everybody kept talking about how progress was supposed to make people's lives easier and better even when it started making people's lives harder and worse, and when some part of that became too hard to ignore, everybody insisted that the only option was to go in for yet another round of progress.

And somehow, I thought, I'm going to have to explain all this to the people back home.

So I was in a pretty sour mood, all things considered, by the time the radio stopped playing jazz and the eleven o'clock news came on instead. I turned it off, got my coat and hat back on, grabbed my suitcase, and headed down to the lobby to check out. After two weeks in the Lakeland Republic, I wasn't too surprised when the clerk wrote something with a pen in a notebook full of sheets of paper, took my key, and wished me a good trip home in less time than it would have taken a hotel clerk elsewhere to get the computer to do whatever it is hotel computers do. Then I was out on the sidewalk under the canopy in front of the hotel door. The rain was still pelting down, but I flagged down a cab to go the train station.

Not quite half an hour later I got out in front of the station, paid my fare, got my suitcase, and headed in. The big vaulted space with benches on one side and ticket counters on the other was pretty well stocked with people going about their lives. I headed over to a window to one side of the ticket counters, stashed my suitcase with the clerk there—I'd asked Melanie about that and so knew what to do—and then headed for one of the restaurants on the side closest to the street. The place was starting to fill up with the lunch trade, but a glance back at the big clock on the wall above the platform doors showed me that I was still early. I went in anyway, asked the greeter for a table for two, got seated at a little table over by the windows looking at the street, shed my coat and hat, and ordered a chicory coffee to kill the time.

I'm not sure how much time passed, and how many cabs stopped to disgorge their passengers on the curb out front, before one of them finally let out the person I was waiting for. It was Melanie, of course, bundled up in a raincoat and broad-brimmed hat the way she'd been when we'd first met. She got most of the way to the station entrance before she spotted me there in the window; she waved, so did I, and then she hurried inside out of the rain and came around to the restaurant entrance. A few moments later she was settling into the chair across the table from me.

The waitress came over pretty much the moment Melanie sat down, so we got menus and talked about little things that don't matter for a bit, until the waitress came back and took the menus and our order. I waited until she was gone, and then said, "I admit I'm really curious about Meeker's reaction."

"I bet," she said, with a sly smile.

That was what I expected her to say, and she knew that I expected it, so I smiled too. Everybody in my line of work makes jokes about horizontal diplomacy; of course it's discouraged, and of course it happens, and if you're in politics and get into that kind of situation you know exactly where the lines are, and edge up to them now and then just to firm up the boundaries. When you get a relationship between two people in politics, you make extra sure that both know where the boundaries are so they don't get in the way of the relationship, and one of the things that I liked about Melanie was that she was as professional about it all as I was.

"I'll say this much," she said after a moment. "You took him by surprise, which isn't easy to do—but it was a pleasant surprise. If there's any help you need from our side to help push things along, let us know and we'll see what we can do."

"Please thank him for me," I said. "I don't have much more of a clue about how to push this thing than I did this morning, though."

She nodded. "May I offer a suggestion?"

"Of course."

"Focus on cutting subsidies. It costs a lot to prop up the illusion of progress, and if you actually make every technology cover all its own costs, things sort themselves out quickly."

"Granted," I said, "but you know as well as I do that the tech sector and the other resource hogs are going to scream if anybody tries to push them away from the feed trough."

"True. The one advantage of this wretched war is that Ellen Montrose may have a little less trouble making that happen."

I nodded, conceding. "The war and the economy," I said. "Our stock market had another ghastly day yesterday, and I don't think the impact of losing the Gulf oil fields has really hit yet."

The waitress came back with lunch, made a little conversation, and headed off to the next table. "One thing that might help," I said then, "is if more people from our side of the border come here and see what you've done here. I know I was completely clueless about what was going on here, even after reading a pretty fair stack of briefing documents. I'd like to see more people see for themselves, if that can be done without putting too much of a burden on you."

"We can handle it," said Melanie.

"I also meant you personally," I said with a smile.

"I survived the Honorable Velma Streiber," she said, with a smile of her own. "After that I think I can handle just about anything."

I laughed, and so did she. We busied ourselves with our plates for a few minutes.

"I wonder," she said then. "If you really want people from your side of the border to see what we're doing on ours, one way to do it would be to have President Montrose make an official visit. We'd be happy to host something like that."

I considered her. "That's a possibility." Then: "Have you had other heads of state visit?"

"A few." She gestured with her fork, dismissing the idea. "Once diplomatic relations got reestablished after the Treaty of Richmond, we let it be known that we'd be happy to welcome any head of state that wanted to pay a visit, and reciprocate. The President of Chicago's been here, of course—show me a country in North America he hasn't visited—and we've exchanged state visits with Quebec and Missouri, but everyone else has backed away uneasily from the suggestion." The fork jabbed down into her chef's salad. "We're still North America's pariah nation, you know."

"Even though your way of doing things works," I said.

"No." She glanced up at me. "*Because* our way of doing things works."

We ate in silence for another few minutes. Of course her words made me think yet again of the same frustrating question I'd been brooding over earlier. It must have showed in my face, because she said, "Penny for your thoughts."

"Just wondering why everyone else keeps making the same mistakes over and over again, trying to fix their problems by doing more of what made the problem in the first place."

"Progress?"

"Yes."

"I have a suggestion." When I gestured for her to go on: "I think it's because all your talented people get put to work building new gadgets, instead of solving the problems that gadgets can't fix. That means you have too many gadgets and a serious shortage of solutions."

I stared at her for a moment. "And since your people aren't working on gadgets—"

"We've found some solutions. Yes." Then: "There was nothing wrong with seeing how far progress could go and still get useful results. The problem was simply that people forgot to stop once they passed that point. We've got all the gadgets we need; you've got more than you need—and maybe it's time to stop putting all our talents and our efforts into more gadgets and get to work on some of the other things that go into being human."

I nodded after another, longer moment, but I knew already that I had my answer.

We talked about other things after that, mostly personal; I promised to write—the Atlantic Republic still has a postal system, though it's nothing like as good as the one the Lakeland Republic has—and so did she; I paid the bill, we kissed, and then she went back to the Capitol and I got my suitcase from the baggage room and headed for the doors to the platforms.

"Train Twenty-two to Pittsburgh via Sandusky, Canton, and Steubenville," someone called out. "Now boarding at Platform Six. Train Twenty-two."

I showed my ticket, and a couple of minutes later I was on Platform Six. A conductor took another look at my ticket and sent me three cars up, to a car that was going all the way to the end of the line. I climbed aboard, got my suitcase stowed, and settled into a window seat on the right hand side.

What was going to happen when I got back home, I knew, was a complete crapshoot. Among Ellen's top advisers, I'd been the most outspoken critic of her plans, and so it was pretty much a given that once I threw my support to the plan, it would go ahead. Just how far the legislature would be willing to cut government subsidies for technology and stop penalizing employers for hiring workers was another question, and just how much of the broader Lakeland Republic program would be adopted was an even bigger one. The more clear it became that what they were doing worked, and what we were doing didn't, the easier it would be to push that ahead, but there would be plenty of resistance among those who still thought that it made some kind of sense to keep doing the same thing while expecting different results.

Maybe I could make it work, and maybe I couldn't. Maybe my term as ambassador to the Lakeland Republic would be successful, and maybe I'd flop. For that matter, though I had high hopes for the relationship Melanie and I had gotten going, there was no way to know in advance if that would work out in the long run or turn out to be a flash in the pan. The future hides in a cloud, and you just don't know what's going to pop out of it.

The conductor came through, calling out his "All aboard!" as a last handful of passengers got on. Doors clattered shut. No, I thought, there's no way to tell in advance what's behind the cloud that hides the future, but maybe—just maybe—I can make a difference.

The car jolted once, and then began to move.

Printed in the USA
CPSIA information can be obtained
at www.ICGtesting.com
JSHW032128251024
72426JS00007B/59

9 781915 952158